Joy King

So Pretty...In Pink

Publisher's Note

This book is a work of fiction. Names, characters, places and incidents are products of the author's imagination or are used fictitiously. Any resemblance to actual events or locales or persons, living or dead, is entirely coincidental.

Copyright © 2004 by So Pretty In Pink LLC
www.soprettyinpink.com

Manufactured in the United Stated of America
For information regarding special discounts for bulk purchases, please contact So Pretty In Pink LLC at 1.877.569.5464 or orderbook@soprettyinpink.com

ISBN: 0-9755-8110-4

Second Printing

10 9 8 7 6 5 4 2 3 2 1

Book Design by Theron Sisco
www.Iwantitloud.com
Book Edited by Lynn K. Hobson

Acknowledgements

This book is dedicated to Edward and Logan who are my motivation for everything positive I do in life. I want to thank my Mother who has always been my biggest cheerleader. Robin; you are more than a sister you are my heart. Ella; my beautiful niece, you're my little Princess. Theron Sisco; you blessed me with my book cover and website, you are my angel. Lynn Hobson; "Lynnie I Love You." Ohio Daddy; no man can hold a candle to you. Maryland Daddy; unfortunately tragedy brought us together, but I feel so blessed to have you back in my life, I pray for your full recovery every night. Ron Outcalt; you held it down for me through the storm and will always hold a special place in my heart. Terrence Brown; you are my best friend. Darren Coleman; if you ask you shall receive; I asked for you to come in my life and you came. You've inspired me to be a better writer and I will forever love you for that. My NYC ladies crew; Lissa Resnitzky, Marsha Irving, Eunice Liriano, Tasha Marbury, Sophia White and Medina! My NC ladies; Adama Parker Robinson and Trixie Matthews. Adiam Berhane; you came into my life when I needed you the most; you have a beautiful heart. Johnny aka Joanna; thank you for the Judith Leiber bag, we both know the meaning behind that gift; you're a sweetheart. I want to give a special shout out to my boy in DC Keith Lemons. Charmelle Coffield; I always knew you were a star, now the world will know. My brothers; Omar, Frank, Tim and Reggie. J.O.; thank you for making me a better woman. Special thanks to Shemella Jones and Colin Thorne; the best book vendors in New York City, B. Lawson Thornton, and most of all to the beautiful ladies; our struggles inspired this book, I'm truly every woman!!!

Joy King

<u>*So Pretty In Pink*</u>

When you close your eyes what do you see?

When you look inside what do you believe?

I've asked myself time and time again, until I realized the answers are within; now I can be So Pretty In Pink.

So Pretty In Pink is what it means to me, to say that I am free.

So Pretty In Pink is what I have to be to love me for me.

That's why I can be So Pretty In Pink...

So Pretty In Pink

Introduction
(The Power of Pink)

All girls are born beautiful and pink. Pink personifies everything that is pure, fascinating, and mysterious about the female species. Every female has the color pink and its power inside of them. It may not shine through all the time but every woman, from birth, has pink within. The pink is the connection to the inner child that lives inside forever no matter what your age. So Pretty...In Pink is about Tyler Blake finding the Power of Pink inside of her and her struggle to find, nurture and protect the little girl inside of her.

This book is for every woman and teenager that has asked themselves *'Why me?'* or *'Where did I go wrong?'* or most importantly, *'How can I make it right?'*

In writing 'So Pretty In Pink' my goal was to teach, inspire and encourage. By sharing my unique experiences and mistakes I hoped to share this message. You need not get discouraged or agonize over small stumbling blocks because all goals will come to fruition if you just believe in yourself and reach deep down inside and find that inner strength. I truly believe that although we have family, friends, and love ones that we care about, in all actuality all we really need can be found within ourselves to achieve true happiness and everything else is just sprinkles.

It's like we need water and food to live but then you want dessert. That's how life is. You have your main course but then you want a little bit extra, and whatever those extra things are, it isn't a necessity but a desire. So you order the extra things in life to try to fulfill yourself but really all you need is inside of you. If more people, not just women, know that you have what you need inside yourself to overcome all the obstacles that have come your way in life, I believe our lives would be a lot less complicated.

In my life, there have been many times that I felt so overwhelmed and so burdened that I would stay in my bed and just cry. I would wonder why are these things happening to me and how am I going to get through this. I would just feel so morbid inside. Somehow I would find the inner strength to make it through and I'm not an exceptional human being who only has that quality. We all have that quality to survive. Someone once told me that if God takes you to it, He will take you through it.

In this book I want you all to experience that innate instinct to survive; to fight when you have to; to overcome any battle to win the war; to do whatever necessary to protect yourself and the ones that you love; to not give up no matter how overwhelmed you feel and no matter how much the cards seem to be stacked against you; and that you can win. Winning doesn't mean that with every challenge you are always going to come out on top that very first or second or even third try, but winning is when you fall down and you get back up every single time. You always have to get back up--always. If anybody tells you differently then you don't need that person in your life because true winners surround themselves with other people who believe they are winners. Anyone who doesn't believe you are a winner is someone who doesn't believe in you. But first and foremost you have to believe in yourself. That is more important than any degree. That is more important than any companion. That is more important than any self-help book.

You have to know that at the end of the day it is all about you and you alone. The stronger you are, the better you will be for everyone else in your life and that means your children, your parents, your siblings; or companion, whether that is your boyfriend, fiancé, husband or wife. It took so much for me to endure to really and truly trust myself. Now that I do, I feel there is nothing that I can't accomplish and nothing that I can't achieve if I focus and put my mind to it and believe in me. I've fought many demons internal and external and experienced a great deal of pain and heartache in my still young life. The constant questioning of myself and what my future holds. I had to go down many dark paths to finally realize that at the end of the day when I walk through that door no matter how imperfect my life may seem, I always feel "So Pretty... in Pink."

Chapter One: Baby Girl
(Born Pink)

When I was born August 3, 1980 in Atlanta Georgia my Mother said that I had a head full of jet black curly hair and was sweet and juicy. In her eyes I was perfect. She adorned me with a beautiful pink bow in my hair of course. I'm sure that all parents think that their newborn is the most beautiful baby in the world and Mother was no different. When I was three she said, "Darling when you grow up you're going to be famous; that's why I named you Tyler Blake because it's a movie star's name and you were born ready for your cover shot."

Mother would sit on the bed brushing my hair and lovingly tell me, "Tyler you are everything I dreamed you would be and more. You're my little Princess and one day a lucky man will make you his Queen." Mother figured that if I didn't become famous then surly some rich man would come and sweep me off my feet. Little did she know I would go through many changes in my life trying to find a man who would make me his Queen; through much of that, I didn't think life was so pink. But as women, we are all born pink. The real triumph is maintaining the pink inside of you no matter what obstacles come your way in life.

I spent hours studying Mother brush her long black wavy hair or applying makeup on her angelic face, wondering if I would grow up to be that beautiful. One morning Mother saw me admiring her through her vanity mirror, she smiled and said, "Observe and learn Tyler because when you blossom into a woman, you will meet a man who will promise you the stars, but you must also demand the moon. You're my little Princess and you can't accept any less." Mother instilled that in me from the day it seemed I was born. It started with the make believe world that we created which we adoringly named Barbie Land. I would create the most glamorous stories and lived them through my Barbie Dolls. They had the big houses, cars, and designer clothes. I would dress them in fabulous beaded gowns, adorn them with sparkling jewelry, and comb their hair in seductive styles. They lived jet set lives and Mother promised that one day, so would I.

That was somewhat hard for me to imagine when I scrutinized myself because I never felt beautiful like my dolls. They were slender. I was chubby. They had long flowing hair and I wore my hair in pony tails. They were tall and lean and I was short and dumpy. But they still inspired me. They, along with the encouragement of Mother gave me hope that one day I would transform into a dazzling diva like them and live the glamorous life. Mother was determined to guarantee that for me, my sister, and herself.

One evening Mother came home late for the third straight night in a row. My Father was waiting in his favorite chair with a glass of Johnny Walker in one hand and the remote control in the other. My sister Ella and I knew the moment Mother walked through the door because the loud screams woke us. We immediately jumped out of our twin beds and ran to the top of the stairs to see the argument unfold right before our eyes. Father rambled towards the front door and began yelling with a drunken slur, "I know you been with that man again. Don't lie to me woman."

Mother marched towards the kitchen ignoring Father as if she didn't even see him. The blatant disrespect pushed Father even further over the edge. He lunged at Mother with overwhelming speed. "Maria don't you walk away from me. I'm the man of this house and you better treat me with respect."

My heart sunk as I heard Father speak those words. I knew Mother didn't respect him and if anybody was the head of this household it was her. Father worked as a Plumber making little money, but we lived in a middle class suburban neighborhood with a house full of brand new furniture, a big color television and Mother even managed to get us a brand new car after Father's old hooptie constantly broke down. Ella and I never questioned where all the money came from because Mother would always say, "No matter what, only the best for my two girls."

Within a moment of Father lunging at Mother, he was on top of her with his hands around her neck, choking what seemed to be the life out of her. Ella and I remained frozen as Mother jolted her legs and reached for his arms trying to save her life. Father was in such rage which turned into an anger fueled sermon. "You think I don't know about that man you been seeing; you ain't nothin' but a whore. Sashaying out this house with your fancy new dresses and expensive perfume from money you got from that man. I'm gonna choke the devil right out of you, do you hear me!"

I felt like I was watching a bad movie and I desperately wanted to change the channel. But this was real life. My Father was murdering my Mother right before my eyes. As I sat there with my hands around the staircase I heard Ella whisper, "You stay here Tyler, I'm going to save Mother." She ran downstairs and picked up the glass vase Mother purchased from a local antique store. Before I could scream and warn Father to move, the glass shattered and blood was spilling from his head as he lay on the hardwood floor looking dazed and confused.

Mother gasped for air as Ella held her gazing as if her life had just flashed before her eyes. That night as she packed up all of our clothes and whatever belongings could fit in the car, Father begged in vain for Mother to stay. He cried out, "Maria, Maria please don't leave me baby. I'm sorry I'll never put my hands on you again. I love you Maria. You're my life." His cries fell on deaf ears.

When Mother made her mind up about something she didn't look back. Although Father was wrong for trying to kill Mother, I still loved him and hated to leave. As we drove off, Mother looked at me and Ella and said, "If a man hits you once he will hit you for the rest of your life unless you decide to end his or he decides to end yours. I want to live, and I want your Father to live so we will never come back to this house again."

From the backseat I waved bye to Father and watched him chase the car still sobbing and begging for Mother to come back. That night we stayed at a hotel and I cried myself to sleep. I couldn't believe that Daddy was gone and I would never see him again.

The next morning I heard Mother on the phone talking sweet to somebody and before she hung up she said that she loved them too. For a brief hopeful moment I imagined maybe she decided to give Daddy another chance, but that hope was quickly shattered. Mother sat us on the bed and gaped at us with her angelic face and endearing eyes, "Ella and Tyler today you are going to meet your new Daddy."

"But I already have a Daddy Mommy," I said trying to restrain the tears that were swelling up in my eyes."

"No baby, that isn't your Daddy anymore. Your Father tried to kill me last night. He is now dead to us."

"He didn't mean to hurt you Mommy, he just wanted you to stay home with him like you use to."

Mother began stroking my hair, picked me up and sat me on her lap. "Tyler I need for you to be a big girl for Mommy. I know you love your Father, but your new Daddy is going to take good care of us. Remember how I told you that one day we would live in a big house with fancy cars and beautiful clothes?" I nodded my head acknowledging that I did remember that life that she promised me. "Well honey, all that is about to come true; Mommy has found her Prince Charming and he has promised me the moon and the stars. All I ask is that you and Ella be the little dolls I raised you to be and treat your new Daddy with the utmost respect. Will you do that for Mommy?" Ella and I looked at each other and we reluctantly agreed to do as Mother said. What choice did we have, she always got her way.

Mother pulled out a bag from some fancy department store and laid out two pink laced dresses and matching socks and shoes for me and Ella. She combed our hair in a long pony tail and braided it going down our back. With a couple of well placed pink barrettes we looked like the most perfect little girls. After Mother got us dressed she made us swear we would sit still and not get as much as a wrinkle in our dresses. I had never seen Mother so giddy and nervous at the same time. After 45 minutes she stepped out of the bathroom looking like she was the winner of a beauty pageant. Mother was so beautiful, so pretty and such a lady.

She was always so pretty in pink. I don't mean that Mother wore pink all the time, but she always exuded pink. She was soft, classy and ladylike but yet Mother was also strong and determined.

When I heard a knock at the door, my heart began pounding. I couldn't believe I was about to meet my new Daddy. Ella and I held hands tightly as Mother opened the door and the man grabbed her around her small waist and gave her an open mouth kiss. I never saw Mother kiss my Dad like that. She would only let him kiss her on the cheek or give her a peck on the mouth.

She was allowing this man to tongue her down like he was Billy Dee Williams or something. When the man finally released her from his embrace, Mother had a school girl grin on her face and with great joy beamed, "Michael these are your two daughters Ella and Tyler." She then turned back to us and said, "Come on my little angels. Give your Daddy a hug." Ella and I walked towards the man and looked up at him. He smiled at us with perfect white teeth and knelt down to give us a hug. I was drawn to the strong but pleasant smell of his cologne. I held him a little tighter because his smell was hypnotizing me. I could feel his muscular arms trying to break free from the restraint of his expensive suit.

He peered at us and asked in a charming voice, "What can I get for my little Princesses? Would you like to go to the toy store and get some new dolls?"

"That would be perfect," Mother answered for us. My new Daddy picked up our luggage and we headed out the door. He was driving a big luxury car that had leather inside and it smelled like he just got it off the car lot. He put everything in his trunk and Mother told us to get in. I wondered what she was going to do with her car but thought it better not to ask. We went straight from the hotel to *Toys R Us* just like our new Daddy promised. When we walked in the store all the ladies ran to assist him. Daddy oozed charm and sophistication.

The teenaged looking sales lady approached him with non discrete flirtation, "Good afternoon Sir. What can I help you with today?"

"I'm looking for the most beautiful dolls you have for my two little Princesses'."

"Isn't that nice, they sure are pretty," she stated, while briefly glancing at us and then back to Daddy.

"Why yes they are. They take after their gorgeous Mother. Maria come over here so this nice woman can see where my little Princesses get their looks from." Mother gladly strutted next to Daddy and he put his arm around her and kissed her on the cheek. I could tell the sales lady was not pleased by the way Daddy was fawning over Mother. The sales lady gave a gracious but fake smile as she acknowledged Mother and reluctantly led us to the selection of beautiful dolls. Mother had a wide smile spread across her face. It didn't bother her the least that the young sales lady was blatantly flirting with her man. She seemed almost turned on that this woman wanted Daddy, but he was with her.

After shopping all day and eating at a fancy restaurant we finally arrived to our new home in Cates Ridge. It was the biggest house I had ever seen. Mother was grinning from ear to ear as we walked up the driveway. There were two luxury cars parked outside. One was a small red sports car with a big bow on top. Daddy walked up to Mother and handed her a pair of car keys. "This is my welcome home present to you," he said and then playfully patted her butt.

"Oh Michael, I can't believe you did this for me."

"Maria you are my Queen. I'm going to give you the world." Mother gushed with joy as he spoke those words. She finally found her prince charming that swept her off of her feet. As she sat in the driver's seat of her new sports car, I heard someone calling out to our Dad.

"Hey Dad, what's going on out here?" I heard a male voice ask.

"What's up Evan, you remember Maria. These are her daughters and my little Princesses' Ella and Tyler. Say hello to your new sisters."

"Hello," the teenage boy said in a soft voice. He reached out to shake our hands and I immediately felt uncomfortable by his touch.

We all went in the house and Mother took me and Ella to our new room. "Isn't our house beautiful," Mother gushed as though she could no longer contain her excitement. "You girls are welcome to have your own room, but I thought for now you would like to share." She was right, I needed to feel safe in my new surroundings and although Ella was only five years older than me, she always seemed like a second mother. I needed to be near her in our new home. Plus the room was humongous. It was decorated in all pink *Hello Kitty*, with two canopy beds, one on each side of the room. We had our own big color television with a room full of dolls and toys. It was as if this bedroom had been waiting for us all our lives.

It was easy to adjust to our new home. Daddy showered us with presents and love and Mother never seemed happier. The only thing I didn't like was my step brother Evan. He seemed sinister to me, but he was leaving in a couple of days to visit his mother for the summer and I was relieved. I always felt uneasy in his presence and couldn't wait to have him out the house.

In the middle of the night I woke up to use the bathroom. Mother told me not to drink anymore *Kool Aid* before bed but of course I didn't listen. When I walked out of the bathroom, Evan startled me when I noticed him standing in the hallway eating an oatmeal cookie Mother baked earlier that day. He inspected me with his dark eyes and offered me a piece. I shook my head 'no' as I was walking past him, and was totally taking off guard when he grabbed my arm and pulled me in his room. He had one hand across my mouth and used the other to shut the door. I couldn't comprehend what was going on but I knew from the sheer force of how Evan was holding me, he was up to no good. He quietly whispered in my ear, "Tyler I don't want to hurt you. When I take my hands from over your mouth please don't scream or you'll be sorry. Do you understand?"

I nodded my head as to agree with his request. As soon as he released his hand I let out a slight scream before he back slapped me across the face and put his hand back over my mouth.

"I told you not to scream you little bratty bitch," Evan huffed. He was now breathing hard and my heartbeat was racing. Evan lifted me up with one hand still across my mouth and carried me over to his bed. My legs were kicking, but at six years old I was no match for this sixteen year old teenaged boy. After laying me on his bed, with one hand he began taking off his blue boxer shorts. I finally realized what Evan planned to do to me. This was like the movies that came on television and Mother warned me to stay away from men like that. I felt like I was going to throw up with the torrid thoughts of what my step brother was going to do to me. He finally emerged from his pants and I saw the hardness of his penis and began to thrust my legs with rapid speed. He moved my cotton nightgown out of his way and reached for my floral panties. As he pressed my head down hard on the pillow, part of me wanted to give up the fight and give into the inevitable, but I didn't want to be a victim. I didn't want to be like the other little girls I heard about who had been raped or molested. But at the same time my mind and body was frozen and I couldn't react. The worse sort of fear was coming over me and I felt sick and alone.

There was dead silence between us, but with the moonlight coming through his window I could see the depraved look in Evan's eyes. A surge of energy came over me and I instantly moved more abruptly, fighting for my innocence. He was too strong and athletic, but feeling his cold hands invading my body made me fight harder. The frustration of me fighting back took over Evan so he balled up his fist and gave me a solid punch to my right jaw. As my head tilted to the side from the impact of his punch, from the corner of my eye I could see the door slightly open and a shadow run away. My stomach dropped and a feeling of defeat came over me. Could someone have been watching this happen and just leave me to this fate? My body began to die as Evan finally ripped off my panties and was about to enter me when his bedroom door bust open. Mother, Father and Ella were standing in the doorway. Father turned on the light switch and was riled to see his son standing over me with one hand still over my mouth and his penis hanging out for all to see. Evan immediately jumped up full of shame being caught in such a despicable act.

Father lunged at Evan, punching the side of his face with such force it caused him to fall to the floor. He began stomping him and yelling, "You sick sonofabitch. This is what you like to do? Fuck little girls."

Mother called out, "Michael calm down, you're going to kill him."

"Any man that messes with a little girl deserves to die; and if it's a son of mine, I'm going to kill him myself because he's already dead to me." He continued to stomp Evan until he saw blood rolling down the side of his mouth and Evan no longer could beg for mercy.

Mother and Ella were now holding me close and examining the bruise that Evan had brandished across my face. Father stood discerning Evan with disgust. Father's voice was swimming with emotion as he said, "Boy you are dead to me. As far as I'm concerned I don't have a son. You were never born. You can stay here tonight, but first thing in the morning I'm going to put you on the plane and I don't ever want to see your face again." As Father wandered away, Evan still laid on the floor in the fetal position.

When I woke up in the morning Evan was gone. Later on that day some movers came and cleaned out his entire room. Any picture or item that had to do with Evan was removed. Father had erased his memory as though he never existed. No one was to ever speak his name and Father tried even harder to spoil me hoping I would forget the incident ever happened. But no matter how many gifts or trips to amusements parks I had, that dreadful night with Evan remained fixated in my mind.

Chapter Two: Blossoming Flower

(Discovering Pink)

During the summer of 1994 I began to emerge from my phase as a caterpillar and cocoon into a beautiful butterfly. I was now a slender but curvaceous teenager with full breasts a small waist and round butt. Lots of boys wanted to date me and I wanted to date too, but not one of the clowns in my school. The boys gossiped more than the girls. They would brag about who was going all the way or who was just giving head. Their conversations always turned vulgar and I was determined not to be a topic of any of it.

"Girl we got our asses kicked tonight by Druid Hills. Our team needs to step it up," my girlfriend Lisa said full of frustration.

"Who cares? I'm starving, so let's go get something to eat."

"You always eating and I don't know where all the weight goes wit yo little ass," Lisa said as she sucked her teeth.

"Whatever. Let's go."

"Can I come with you?" a soothing male voice said. I turned around to put the voice with the face, and was pleasantly surprised to see the gorgeous guy standing in front of me. Lisa immediately jumped beside me and stuck out her enormous chest giving the guy a lingering up and down look.

"Aren't you Chad Mills the star quarterback for Druid Hills?" Lisa asked sounding like she was about to eat him up.

"Yeah that's right. What's your friend's name?"

"Oh that's just Tyler." Lisa swung her hand as if dismissing me. "I'm Lisa. It's a pleasure to meet you," she stepped forward extending her hand. Chad did her one better by extending his hand directly at me.

"Hi Tyler I'm Chad. It's nice to meet you," he said as he took my hand and held it. I could feel myself blushing and felt uncomfortable. Lisa made it worse by standing beside me with her lips poked out.

"I've never seen you before. Are you new to North Atlanta?"

"Yeah this is actually my first year. I went to Sutton Middle School last year."

"Oh, so you're a Freshman?"

"Yeah," I answered shyly.

"You have to be the prettiest Freshman I've ever seen."

"Your sweet," I gushed, sounding like a love struck teenager.

"I would love to call you. Can I get your number?"

"Sure," I said gleaming. Chad was just the type of guy that I had been searching for. He was handsome, at least a Junior so he had to be somewhat mature, and he made me feel at ease. I definitely had stars in my eyes.

After our initial encounter Chad and I were inseparable. He would come over and we'd make out for hours. My parents were oblivious to what we were doing because they thought Chad was the greatest and had no problem leaving us alone. Besides they were trying to salvage what was left of their shaky marriage. For the last couple of years it had been deteriorating. It totally hit rock bottom when Ella left for college. Mother was convinced Father was having an affair and so she began her own fling. One evening she was supposed to be at a

Country Club meeting preparing an upcoming dinner honoring the women socialites of Atlanta. Worried that she never showed up her friend Beatrice called the house looking for her. Father played it off as though something came up at the last minute and she couldn't make it. When Mother came home he asked her how her meeting went and she said great not knowing that Father already knew she never showed up.

"Maria don't fucking lie to me, Beatrice already called here looking for you after you didn't show up."

"I know I got there right after she hung up the phone with you. I got held up trying to make some last minute revisions and was late to the meeting." Mother always knew how to remain cool under any type of pressure. She spoke so matter of factly that you couldn't help but want to believe her.

"Okay, then you'll have no problem getting Beatrice on the phone to confirm your story."

"I'm not a child Michael, and I won't be calling Beatrice asking her such elementary questions." Once again, but now as a teenager I stood on top of the stairs watching the drama unfold.

"Maria, you better get Beatrice on the phone right now."

"Or what Michael, you're going to run out and go see your mistress? Tell her I said hello."

It was like deja vu when I heard Dad say, "Maria don't you walk away from me." After I heard the loud thump sound from Mother hitting the marble floor in the foyer, I ran downstairs to save her like Ella did so many years ago.

"Daddy stop," I screamed before Father was about to land a second punch. He gazed at me with the same shameful look that Evan had across his face when he got caught with his pants down.

"Tyler go back upstairs, this is between your Mother and me." Mother lay on the floor looking so helpless and scared.

"Michael please don't do this in front of Tyler, you promised that no matter how angry you got, you would never put your hands on me in front of the children." What was Mother saying? Had Dad hit her before and I just didn't know about it? Dad took a deep breath and Mother slowly began to stand up. I felt confused, I knew my parents had problems but never did I believe the relationship had become abusive. Dad walked downstairs to the entertainment room and Mother grabbed my hand and asked me to follow her upstairs. We went in my bedroom and sat on the bed as Mother held my hand like she used to when I was a little girl.

"Tyler I'm sorry you had to witness the altercation between your Father and me. I never expected him to hit me with you in the house."

With great curiosity and fear of hearing the answer I asked, "Has Dad hit you before?" Mother glanced at me with sorrowful eyes giving away the answer.

"But I thought you said if a man ever hits you, you must immediately leave him?"

"Baby look at everything your Father has provided for us. We are accustomed to a lifestyle that most people only dream of but very few reach. He has fulfilled our every fantasy." As Mother spoke I couldn't help but feel confused, torn and disgusted.

With great sarcasm I said, "So Mother its okay for a man to knock you around if he is rich and takes good care of you, but if he is poor like my real Dad was then it's not worth sticking around for all the punches."

"Tyler you watch your mouth. Your Father was worthless. He had no ambition and couldn't hold a decent job. If I stayed with him, we would be stuck in the land of the dead. Do you think you would be living in a million dollar house and wearing designer jeans? Hell No! Michael has provided us with a better life and if he loses his temper once in a while then so be it."

I couldn't believe the words that were coming out of Mother's mouth. She had sold her soul for money and material gain. Not only was Father having an affair but he was beating her ass and it was okay as long as the lifestyle continued. I was pissed and I wanted to aggravate her even more.

"So the man you're fucking now, are you going to leave Daddy for him the way that you left my first Dad, or are his pockets not deep enough?" Mother stood up and slapped the shit out of me, and I grabbed my face trying to subdue the sting from her hand.

"I know I haven't been the perfect Mother, but everything I've done has been for the love of you and Ella. All I ever wanted was to provide a good life and not have you all faced with the same struggles I did growing up. No matter what you may think of me, you respect me. You respect the bullshit I endured in life in order to escape the dreadful existence that would have been your life if you didn't have a Mother who was determined to find a better way. One day when you have your own kids and you want a better life for them, you then come have a conversation with me and let me know what you will and won't tolerate from a man." With that Mother turned her back and walked away but not before I saw the tears rolling down her cheeks. I had hurt her and I never wanted to do that. Mother was my hero and I loved her more than life itself.

_____

As the school year began to wind down, Chad and I had become closer than ever. He made me feel special. He would surprise me with flowers, romantic hand made cards and little gifts. He seemed like the ideal boyfriend--good family, intelligent, a star athlete, and handsome. What more could a girl ask for, but I wasn't in love. I was physically attracted to him but I wasn't passionate about him. Chad was safe because he was feeling me more than I was feeling him so there was no way he could break my heart. After seeing the drama in both of my

Mother's marriages I began thinking that love was way overrated but at the same time I yearned for a man to make me feel loved.

Although I was only fifteen that desire pushed me to take my relationship with Chad to the next level. My parents were out for dinner and I asked Chad to come over and keep me company. We were watching *9 ½ Weeks* and I began teasing him about how sexy Mickey Rourke was. "Chad look at how Mickey Rourke is fucking the shit out of Kim Basinger, I bet she has had at least three orgasms."

"What you know about an orgasm?" Chad asked full of curiosity and anger since he thought I was a virgin, which I was.

"I've never had one, but my girlfriends tell me that once a man makes you reach your climax, you'll be in love with him for the rest of your life."

"Is that what they tell you, well why you don't find out for yourself." Chad came closer to me on the couch and started kissing my neck. His lips always felt so warm on my skin and my nipples instantly became perky as his tongue made its way to my mouth.

He whispered in my ear, "Baby do you want me to make love to you?" His breath smelled fresh like *Trident* gum.

"Yeah, I want to feel you inside of me." Chad kissed my top lip and then the bottom before putting his tongue down my throat. He unbuttoned my red silk shirt and unclipped my bra exposing my voluptuous breasts. As his mouth swallowed my nipples, my pussy instantly became wet and I unzipped his jeans longing to see and feel his dick. As he got up to take off his clothes, I stood in front of him in the new laced thong I purchased from *Victoria's Secret* for this monumental occasion.

Chad looked at me with pure lust in his eyes and said, "I've been dying to be inside of you for so long. I promise you won't be disappointed." With that I laid across the couch waiting for him to finish undressing so we could make love.

I had never seen Chad stark-naked and I wasn't disappointed. All those sporting activities left his body perfectly chiseled. He lay on top of me and began kissing all over my body. He literally licked me from head to toe. I was filled with lust and desire and could barely contain myself. The anticipation of what might happen next was driving me crazy. Looking at his erect penis I knew all of him would fill me up. I kept saying, "Please put it in," and finally he did. Chad glided inside of me like silk. When he entered I felt pain, but it was the best sort of pain, and not nearly as bad as it could've been. Chad had been finger popping me for so long with damn near three fingers that my pussy was right and not too tight to handle his well endowed manhood.

I finally understood why when it felt right you could make love over and over again because that was all I wanted to do after my first time with Chad. It was like "Wow" this whole sex thing is incredible. You know they say your first sexual experience will dictate how you feel about sex for the rest of your life, so I recommend that all girls make there first time beautiful if possible.

For the next few months after making love to Chad every which way possible I became extremely bored. He never mentally excited me in the first place and I was becoming restless; partaking in drinking parties with my girlfriends was becoming increasingly more exciting to me. What exactly was a drinking party? Well when my parents were out on the town, me and my girlfriends would raid their bar and mix all sorts of liquor together and see who could drink the most and the fastest. Sometimes we would each have a bottle of champagne and see who could gulp down their bottle first. Talk about getting fucked up! That was what I preferred to do over seeing my boyfriend. I knew we had a problem when I preferred a bottle over some good loving. But, I still tried to hang in there thinking maybe I was just in a bad funk.

One weekend when Chad's parents went out of town we were at his house laying in front of the fireplace after making love. It was sensational and I put my tongue into his right ear and nibbled on his earlobe trying to get him aroused for a second lovemaking session. But 'oh' boring Chad wanted to talk. He babbled on about going off to college the next year and how much he would miss me. As I lay on his chest, he lifted my chin up so we were looking in each other's eyes, "Tyler if you promise not to be intimate with anyone else while I'm at college, when you graduate I want us to get married." I was thinking to myself I couldn't wait for two weeks let alone countless months without sex.

"Chad, don't you think you're jumping the gun a little bit? You don't know what will happen when you go off to college next year. You might meet some pretty little cheerleader and fall in love."

"Tyler no one is prettier than you. You're my dream girl and I want to spend the rest of my life with you." His words were cutting me deep in my stomach. Yes, I wanted a man to love me and take care of me, but I also knew what marriages actually meant watching the destruction of both of my Mother's. Plus I wasn't in love with Chad. The thought of him being the last man I would ever feel inside of me was more than I could take.

"Baby let's not talk about this now. School isn't even out yet, and we have the entire summer. Let's enjoy the time we have now and not worry what the future holds." I gave Chad a long kiss before he could say another word. This was one conversation I would delay until all options ran out.

After my evening with Chad I knew our relationship was on the road to nowhere. He was getting much too serious and I wanted a lot more excitement and something different. I tried to go strong with my so called first love, who I had given my virginity to, but I think that whole "Your First" is overrated. When I have flashbacks of my sexual experiences, 'my first' is not the one that comes to mind. I cared deeply for Chad in my own way, but our relationship was floating on a sinking ship.

Due to the extreme boredom of Chad's personality, I wanted a man who was the complete opposite; a man that would bring nonstop drama to my life and stimulate my mind and not in necessarily a positive way, but more so edgy. I basically wanted a bad boy. I was about to learn the hard way that you have to be careful what you ask for.

One night I went to a Clark Atlanta University function with Lisa. Lisa and I both looked a little older, especially with Lisa's size D breasts, make that a double D. We were at a talent show and I was standing outside the bathroom waiting for her to come out. I looked up and noticed this guy standing in front of me telling a ridiculous joke that made me laugh. From then on, I was intrigued. His name was Trey. He was another so called 'Pretty Boy.' He was wearing cream slacks with a cream cashmere sweater. Very clean cut--just the way I envisioned my boyfriend to be. He was handsome, flashy and confident with a great sense of humor. We chatted, exchanged phone numbers and he called me later on that night. Luckily I had my own line so when the phone rang it didn't wake anyone. "Hello," I said trying to sound half sleep although I was completely awake.

"What's up this is Trey. Are you sleeping?"

"Almost but I'll get up. What you doing?"

"Talking to you," he said with a slight snicker. We began an in depth conversation, and it was quickly obvious that Trey was cocky and overly sure of himself. I began to fuck with his ego trying to see just how inflated it was.

"You know Trey you talk a lot of shit, but by the time I walk out of your life you're going to be so in love with me that I'll cause you to lose your mind." He let out the biggest laugh as if I just told a Chris Tucker joke.

"Tyler baby, no woman will ever cause me to lose my mind and the only person that ever walks away in my relationships is me," he barked with pure confidence.

"Oh really?"

"Yes really."

"Why is that?" I asked like I really gave a fuck.

"Because every woman that I'm with, I first blow out their back and then I blow out their mind." I had to admit that his confidence was making me horny. He sounded so sure of himself and I wanted to know if he could deliver on the goods.

"Why don't you come over and try to blow out my back and mind," I suggested.

"You mean right now?" He asked with shock and excitement.

"Yeah right now." After we talked for a little while longer, thirty minutes later Trey pulled up in his black Ford Explorer. I already told him to park in the cul-de-sac so from the top of the stairs through the vast glass windows, I saw him running towards the driveway. When I opened the reddish Honduras Mahogany doors, Trey stood in awe of the European styled house. He gazed steadily at the marble foyer and cathedral ceilings and couldn't manage to get a word out. I grabbed his hand and lead him downstairs.

I turned on the night light and put in my slow jam CD. I was wearing a tiny pink teddy with no panties. We looked at one another letting our eyes do all the talking. We gravitated to each other with a lingering kiss. He led me towards the couch and laid me down kissing me and fingering me at the same time. He then took the finger that had been inside of me and licked it. He smiled and said, "You taste good." With that he put his head down and put his tongue deep inside. He lifted my ass up as his tongue went deeper and deeper. He licked my clitoral for what seemed like thirty minutes and by the time he finished, I wanted to pass out and go to sleep. Obviously Trey could tell that I felt I had just run a marathon and was exhausted although he had actually done all the work.

"Do you think I'm going to satisfy you and let you fall asleep? No baby girl it doesn't work like that. I've gotten this pussy nice and wet and now it's time for me to get mine." Trey took off his clothes and dove in like he was taking a dip in the pool. He was pounding me hard and fucking me rough. He flipped me over and pulled my hair back as he talked dirty in my ears. Chad had never fucked me like this before. But then again we always made love. Trey and I definitely weren't making love, but his intense energy and rough play was turning me on. He kept saying, "Yeah you like this big dick inside of you."

"Yeah, baby you feel good," I heard myself saying without as much as a thought. By the time we finished I was in complete awe of Trey. He had me open and he knew it. His confidence was definitely justified and I decided I wanted him. Little did I know that everything you want is not necessarily good for you.

After our night of passionate sex, I was totally caught up in Trey. I was running out of excuses for canceling dates with Chad and realized it was time to put our relationship to an end. On a warm spring night Chad came over and we were standing on the deck overlooking the pool. I looked him in his eyes and said, "We need to talk." By the way he kept fidgeting I could tell he felt uneasy not knowing where the conversation was going but he tried to remain cool.

"You seem so serious Tyler. What's going on?"

"Chad you know that I care deeply for you and I always will, but I'm no longer happy being in this relationship."

"What are you saying?" he asked sounding taken aback by my comment.

"The relationship is over Chad." His eyes instantly enlarged as if I had just given him a death sentence.

"Tyler what are you talking about? Did I do something wrong? We can fix this." Chad was blabbing on and on as if he couldn't help himself.

"Just stop Chad. It isn't you, it's me. I don't love you anymore." The words rolled off my tongue and I instantly regretted saying them. Chad sat down on a patio chair and put his head down. I had only seen him look this defeated after his football team lost the state championships.

"Why Tyler? I thought we were happy together."

"I haven't been happy for awhile."

"Why didn't you say something before now?"

"I didn't know how to tell you."

"Answer this one question, and I want you to tell me the truth."

"What is it?" I asked as my heart started pounded. I already knew what the question was and I didn't know if I had the heart to answer honestly. But maybe Chad deserved that. I had led him on for so long and I wanted him to be free to be happy with someone else.

As though it took every ounce of strength in his body Chad finally said, "Tyler are you seeing someone else?"

With great reluctance I nodded my head yes. Chad stood up, walked towards me, and I stepped back reasoning he was about to become violent as I had seen many times in the past with Mother and her dysfunctional relationships. But instead, Chad gently grabbed my face and kissed me goodbye. Just like that I dumped my boyfriend and broke his heart, but something inside of me was missing emotionally. I truly believe you get back what you put out there because I was about to take a dance with the devil and after the way I treated Chad, I more than deserved it. I traded in my All American Football Player for what I would soon realize was a troubled man. The journey I was about to embark on with him would transform me forever.

Chapter Three: Eyes Wide Open

(The World Isn't Always So Pink)

When I got involved with Trey, I had no idea that he would change my life forever. We embarked on an extremely turbulent relationship. He was different from me in so many ways, but we were alike in many others. Trey was from the streets and came from a broken home. He grew up with no type of guidance and basically went through life doing exactly what he wanted to do. He was in college, highly intelligent and had numerous admirable qualities, but on the inside, Trey was fighting caged demons. He seemed haunted and brought the pain of those issues into our relationship.

After I broke off my relationship with Chad I soon found out that Trey had a girlfriend who so happened to be the ex girlfriend of my ex boyfriend Chad. She was also a senior at my high school and a girl I always admired. Her name was Chandler and she was so beautiful and had a body to die for. Chandler was mocha chocolate with long black hair. She had a tiny waist with a bodacious butt. She was bootylicious way before Beyonce or J Lo. The fact that I was seeing her boyfriend astounded me; but I also wanted no part of any drama. As soon as I became aware of their relationship I told Trey, "Until you straighten out your relationship with Chandler we can not see one another." Of course he denied it but I knew he was lying.

I didn't quite believe that Trey was going to leave this gorgeous Senior for a measly Sophomore, but I certainly wasn't about to play second fiddle either. More importantly, I didn't want any trouble or develop a reputation for stealing other girl's boyfriends, especially since I had to fight that all through Junior high. I wasn't about to let those problems follow me to North Atlanta High School. Between classes I made a pit stop to the girls' bathroom. I was looking in the mirror trying to get something out of my eye when Chandler walked in looking gorgeous as ever in a skin tight red dress and confronted me about Trey.

"Tyler I need to speak to you about a nasty rumor that's been circulating around school." I acted as though I didn't have a clue as to what rumor that might be.

"What rumor is that Chandler?" She sucked her teeth and looked me up and down as if she knew I was full of shit.

"The rumor about you and my man Trey, you haven't heard anything about that?"

"Me and your man," I pointed as though it was news to me. "Actually I'm single Chandler, so whoever brought me into that rumor must have me confused with someone else."

"I don't think so, because see I only know of one Tyler Blake and that's yo ass." Chandler walked towards me with vengeance in her eyes.

"Listen you high-yellow heifer. I don't know what type of game you're trying to play, but you're playing it with the wrong bitch. Trey is my man and if you know what is good for you keep your young ass away from him."

My romantic denials fell on deaf ears and Chandler wasn't trying to hear none of it. After one last interrogation, she flashed her long red nails across my face and left the bathroom with these departing words. "I got my eyes on you bitch, so watch your back." On that note I decided to skip sixth period and take my ass home.

Later on that night while doing my pedicure the phone rang, "Hello."

"Can I speak to Tyler?" the female voice sounded familiar but I couldn't quite pinpoint it.

"This is she." I responded wishing I had never taken the call.

"This is Chandler."

"How did you get my number, and what do you want?"

"I called you so I'm asking all the questions, and don't even think about hanging up the phone," she blurted out as if she was reading my mind. "Listen Tyler, I'm not trying to cause you any problems, but I want to get to the bottom of this shit regarding Trey. I want to take a ride to his apartment and confront him about the rumors of him fucking with you."

"That's not necessary Chandler. There is nothing going on between me and Trey."

"Well I don't believe you."

"That sounds like a personal problem that I can't help you with. Now please leave me the fuck alone about this bullshit." I slammed the phone down and after Chandler called back for the fifth time I took the phone off the hook.

It was mind boggling to me that someone as beautiful as Chandler Thompson was sweating a Sophomore about her so called man. Although I loved spending time with Trey, this was becoming way too complicated. The last thing I wanted was a whole bunch of girlfriend drama. I've never liked drama and to this day I still don't. I run from unwanted drama.

After I could no longer duck Chandler in school, we had one last and final conversation. More like she talked and I listened. After cornering me at my locker she said bitterly, "I know you're fucking Trey, but now he is all yours. I refuse to share my man with some snotty Lolita who doesn't know how to keep her legs closed." With a devilish grin spread across her flawless face she added, "By the way I informed Trey how old you really are and that he is robbing the cradle; Tootles

Bitch." As she turned her back to walk away she tossed her long black hair in my face and sashayed down the hallway like she owned the place.

When I got home Trey called and wanted to come over so we could talk. I wasn't in the mood but agreed. The first question he asked as we sat on my bed was, "Why didn't you tell me how old you were?"

"Because you didn't ask," which he hadn't.

"I assumed that since you were at a college function you were at least legal."

"I will be in a few months, but if you don't want to wait I totally understand." Part of me would understand, but I still wanted to be with Trey now. Throughout this whole episode with Chandler we hadn't been intimate, and seeing him looking so sexy, I definitely wanted our relationship to continue.

"Well, what do you want to do?" he asked sounding the same way I felt.

"It's up to you." When he reached over and began kissing me and rubbing his hand on my breast, I knew it meant the waiting wasn't necessary. Luckily my parents weren't home because we immediately started catching up on lost time. From that day forward Trey and I were boyfriend and girlfriend.

In the beginning everything was new and exciting in our relationship. I had never been with a guy like Trey before. He came into my life at a point where school, my friends and my life in general was boring to me. He was like a head rush and it was very addictive. We were glued at the hip. Most days I would hang out with him at his college campus. Although I only had my learner's permit, my parents had gotten me a car and I would drive myself to and from school. Whenever possible, I skipped classes to be with Trey. Hanging with him was more interesting than anything they were teaching me at school. To this day I still wonder how I was able to make decent grades and graduate.

On a rare occasion when Mother had time for me, we went to The Dining Room at the *Ritz Carlton* for Sunday Brunch. Ever since I found out Father was physically abusive towards Mother our relationship was strained and we rarely talked about what was going on in each others' life. "So how's Chad doing?" Mother asked unaware that we had broken up a couple of months ago.

"Chad and I aren't together anymore."

"Oh you'll be back together, what you have a little spat?"

"No actually I have a new boyfriend." Mother looked at me suspiciously.

"New boyfriend? I haven't met him. Does he go to your school?"

"Actually he attends Clark University," I said all perky because I was proud to have a college boyfriend.

"He's in college," she paused. "Isn't that a little old for you?" I lied and said he was only a Freshman and just turned eighteen.

"Would you like to see a picture of him?" The other day Trey had given me a college flip calendar, and he posed for the month of April. I had it in my tote bag and was anxious to get Mother's reaction.

"Sure honey," she said nonchalantly. I reached in my tote bag, pulled out the calendar and flipped to Trey's picture. Mother's mouth dropped and I knew she wasn't pleased. Trey was wearing a cream linen suit that complimented his light reddish skin, with a gun tucked inside his pants. He looked hot and I was proud to tell Mother this pretty boy was my new boyfriend. She liked to have died.

"He is nothing but the devil and you need to stay away from him," she said with fear in her voice. Of course instead of being afraid, it added to my excitement and I wanted to be with Trey more than ever.

Just as I grabbed my jean jacket and purse to head out the door to meet Lisa at the mall, the phone rang. "Hello," I said in a rushed voice.

"Hi Tyler are you busy?" I was surprised to hear Chad's voice on the other end of the phone. We hadn't spoken in over a month.

"No, how have you been?"

"Great, just trying to get everything in order for college; I was actually calling to see if you would still go to the Senior Prom with me." He rushed the question out as if he knew I was on my way out the door. "I know we're not together anymore but I don't have anyone to go with."

"Oh Chad please, any girl would die to be your date for the prom."

"Yeah maybe, but they wouldn't be you. Tyler I'd really love if you come, as friends of course."

"I would love to go," although that wasn't exactly true, I felt that I should after the abrupt way I broke up with him.

"Wonderful. It's next Saturday and I'll pick you up around seven," Chad quickly hung up the phone, as if he thought I might change my mind. But I had no intentions on doing that. I was looking forward to getting all dolled up and buying a new dress.

Mother was thrilled to hear I was going to the prom with Chad. We went to Neiman Marcus to pick out a dress. As I tried on a beautiful white laced dress that hugged my curves in all the right places and dipped in the front giving me an enticing cleavage, Mother beamed, "That's the one. You look beautiful my little Princess." Mother hadn't called me that in so long and it brought chills to know she still felt that way.

"Darling I'm ecstatic you're getting back with Chad, he is a wonderful young man."

"Mother Chad and I aren't back together, I only agreed to go to the prom with him; nothing more, nothing less."

"I just assumed you were over your fixation with that Trey character and was now thinking about your future."

"Mother I'm only fifteen; I have plenty of time to think about my future."

"Time flies sooner than you think. If I'd planned ahead I would've never wasted all those years with your Father. Don't make the same mistake I did. Chad is a great catch. He is either going to be a professional football player or an attorney, so you know he will be a wonderful provider. He comes from an excellent family and he's a very handsome young man. Tyler you would be a fool not to stick it out with him. If you want to have meaningless dalliances with that Trey character so be it, but by no means take him or the relationship seriously."

As Mother paid for my dress I thought about what she said: *Maybe I should stick it out with Chad. He was a wonderful guy and my first love. Trey was fun but definitely complicated. Chad was going off to college in a couple of months; I could always see Trey on the side.*

When Chad picked me up Saturday night he looked gorgeous. Both of us had on white and we looked like the African American version of Ken and Barbie. It took us twenty minutes just to get out the door because Mother wouldn't stop taking pictures. After dinner we arrived at the *Peachtree Plaza Hotel* for the prom. The ballroom was decorated beautifully with orchids and roses everywhere. When we walked in Monica's *Before You Walk Out My Life* was playing and Chad took my hand and led me to the dance floor. As he put his hands around my waist and we swayed to the music, he pulled me closer as though he never wanted to let go. For a moment it seemed like old times.

The prom winded down and Chad asked me to come upstairs to his suite for a drink and to talk. When we got upstairs, he pulled out a bottle of champagne and poured me a glass and turned on the radio to 107.9. We chatted about what college he decided to attend and how happy he was to get a full scholarship. After getting caught up in the moment and gaining a slight buzz from the champagne when Chad kissed me, I kissed him back. But when he unzipped the back of my dress, I gently pushed him away and said, "This isn't right."

"What are you talking about, nothing could be more right. Tyler we belong together," he said as he continued to kiss my neck.

Pushing him back as his wandering tongue persisted I huffed, "That may be true, but not now, not like this. I need time Chad."

"Time for what?" he wolfed with anger creeping across his face.

"I need time to think things out."

"What fucking things Tyler?" he asked as he grabbed my arm and held it tightly.

"Chad you're hurting me, let go of my arm." I tried to break free, but his grasp was too tight. The look in Chad's eyes was scaring me. It was a look I could never erase from my mind; depraved and full of rage. This was the same look that I had seen in Evan's eyes almost ten years ago. I shook my head in disbelief because it wasn't possible for Chad to be that sort of monster.

"Chad please let me go, you're hurting my arm," I repeated. But Chad's eyes were blank. It was as if he zoned out and he couldn't hear my words. I swallowed hard right before deciding to make my getaway to the door. Looking around I didn't see anything within reach that I could pick up and hit Chad with; so right before I lifted myself off the bed, with all my strength I swung my left arm and hit Chad in his neck to knock him off balance. It worked and by natural reflex he let go of my arm and I made a dash towards the door. As I ran the door seemed so far, yet so close.

Right as my hand reached for the door knob I heard, "Tyler where the fuck do you think you're going?" My neck snapped back from Chad pulling my hair. The force was so strong I fell and landed on my back.

Within seconds Chad was on top of me ripping off the beautiful dress Mother bought for his prom. "No Chad please stop you don't want to do this, pleeeeeeeeeeease," I begged to no avail. Chad was looking right through me, he was possessed and there was no bringing him back. I screamed at the top of my lungs but my cries were overpowered by the music playing in the back. But just to make sure no one heard me, Chad put his hand over my mouth.

"No one can hear you Tyler. I have you all to myself. You used to willingly let me make love to you, but I guess now you want me to take it." As I lay in the middle of the hotel suite pinned to the floor, feeling Chad spread my legs apart and ripping off my panties, I couldn't believe this was happening to me again. But this time there was no Daddy coming to the rescue. My eyes filled with tears as Chad jammed his dick inside of me and pounded me over and over again releasing all the hatred he had inside. What seemed like a lifetime, Chad finally let out a loud moan as he came inside me. His heavy body felt like a car rolling over my foot. But my energy was drained to the point that I didn't have the strength to attempt to move him off. I could see the sweat trickling down the side of Chad's neck and after five more minutes of intense breathing he finally rolled off of me and stood up. As he zipped up his pants he gave me the glance over and shrieked, "Why did you make me do this Tyler? It didn't have to be this way, if only you would act right."

I couldn't believe my ears. Chad was blaming me for the rape he just committed. "You sick bastard. You just raped me and you have the nerve to stand there and blame me for your animalistic act!"

Chad walked towards me and knelt down to the floor I was still laying on, "Don't you ever say that again. I didn't rape you. This was a lover's quarrel that got out of hand."

"Is that the lie you're running with; because a ripped dress, torn panties and bruises on my arm and inner thighs all symbolize rape to me, you sonofabitch." My attitude had now shifted from fear and pain to relentless anger. I stood up looking at my destroyed dress and bruised body. "Chad you will not get away with this. I'm going to tell my parents and they will no doubt report you to the police."

"Yeah you do that Tyler, and I'll let everyone know what a whore you are."

"Whore," I shouted. "We didn't have consensual sex. You raped me."

"So you say, but I could always explain by telling the police you like it rough. What do you think people will say when they find out that you have a boyfriend but went to the prom with your ex? You need to think long and hard before you start throwing around accusations."

"These aren't accusations they are facts, and the fact of the matter is that you raped me, do you hear me?" My voice cracked as I got louder and louder.

"Well you go right ahead, but by the time you make it to court, everyone will know that sweet little Tyler is nothing but a freak. Fucking a grown ass man and fucking me too, no one will feel sorry for you. They will think you are nothing but a hot ass bitch that has no self control. Your boyfriend will be brought up on statutory rape charges and your family will be embarrassed and disgraced."

A wave of despair flooded through my body. The emotional roller coaster I was on now took another turn. I went from fear to anger and now shame. I put my head down replaying the words Chad just spoke to me. Everyone would think I was a whore. My parents would find out how old Trey really is, and he would know that I lied about hanging out with Lisa tonight and was actually with Chad. I felt helpless.

After his insistence, Chad dropped me off at home and luckily my parents were sleep. I went in the bathroom and turned on the light switch. The reflection in the mirror of the once beautiful face with the perfectly applied makeup had two raccoon eyes from the tears smearing my eyeliner and mascara. I took off all my clothes put them in a plastic bag and planned to toss them in the trash. I pulled back the floral shower curtain and turned the knob to hot. I stepped inside and let the burning water drench my hair and entire body. I was hoping all the evil that had just violated my body would be washed away. That was the best I could hope for. After going over my options I decided to keep this horrific night to myself. I convinced myself that I got what I deserved for even going to the prom with Chad. The shame I felt was too much to share with anyone let alone my parents or the police. This was a chapter of my life I would put behind me.

The following months after Chad raped me I fell into a deep depression. I did a good job hiding it from my family and friends, but every night when I was alone I would cry myself to sleep. With Ella away at college, Mother focusing on her social life and Father traveling more and more on his so called business trips the only person I felt I had was Trey. Besides going to school I spent all my time with him and we had now been together for over a year. But our relationship had begun taking on many different dimensions. The other side of Trey was showing its ugly face and it was far from the fun loving guy that I fell in love with. Trey was screwed up emotionally and I was already unstable so he started to screw me up even more too. It began with the occasional nasty comment about a new hairstyle or an outfit he didn't approve of. Then it became an all out daily assault that slowly chipped away my self esteem and left me feeling insecure.

Trey was excited about his new apartment and finally having no roommate. Between going to school during the day and promoting parties at night he was making decent money and was able to afford a one bedroom in a brand new luxury apartment complex. In Trey's bedroom I was unpacking a box full of tapes, CDs and video cassettes, and came across one tape that had 'Joy Time' written in black bold ink and it was dated about a month ago. I was curious to see what was on the tape and slid it in the VCR. When an image first flashed across the screen it was Trey sitting on the couch at his old apartment speaking into the camera. He walked over to the camera and took it from someone's hand and turned the camera on them. It was a pretty ebony complexioned girl who looked no more than twenty four. I heard Trey's voice in the background saying, "Come on Nikki do a striptease show for me." Music was playing in the back, and then another young lady stepped in the camera who looked about the same age and physical build as the other girl but just a tad bit lighter.

"That's right ladies move that ass to the music. Take it all off." The women were now completely naked and grinding to what sounded like reggae music. "Play with each others' tits, while daddy watches." The women were rubbing each other down and sucked each others' nipples like they were babies nursing. The whole scene was bizarre. I had never seen two women making out before. Right when I was about to push eject, Trey propped the camcorder in a prime position and was now butt naked frolicking with the ladies.

"Come here Stephanie," Trey said grabbing her gigantic ass. She was giggling as she made her way towards him. "I want you to deep throat it for me like you did last night," Trey demanded. This was all too much. The girl got on her hands and knees and swallowed Trey's manhood.

The other girl Nikki chimed, "Ya not gonna leave me out the mix." She grabbed Trey's hand and he willingly lay on the floor while Stephanie continued to suck him dry. Nikki sat on Trey's face and he ate her pussy like he was munching on a prime piece of steak. I couldn't bring myself to turn off the tape, I was entranced with it. I sat on Trey's bed in disgust not believing the threesome taking place in front of my eyes with my boyfriend playing the starring role. I put my hands on my forehead, shaking my head in disbelief, when Trey walked in.

His eyes popped out as he witnessed the sex tape he made only a month ago. He ran to the VCR and with clumsy force struggled to rip the tape out. Why I don't know, since the damage had already been done. "Tyler it's not what you think, this tape is from a couple of years ago."

"Trey I saw the date on the tape. You made it last month." Honestly I didn't even care. I knew Trey was cheating on me but I was at such a low point in my life that it didn't matter to me. Plus after Chad raped me I didn't even enjoy sex anymore. I preferred to be left alone. I only gave into Trey sexually because I felt obligated.

"Nah baby that's the right date but the wrong year," he countered.

"Save it Trey. No need to explain, the tape speaks for itself. It's actually a good thing. I've been having reservations about our relationship and this tape makes it clear that it's time for us to go our separate ways."

"What the fuck did you say?" Trey's demeanor changed in less than eight seconds. He went from denying and apologetic to hostile and aggressive. "I know you not trying to end this over some bullshit tape with some chicken-heads."

"Yeah some chicken-heads that had your dick in her mouth and the other had her pussy spread across your face. That's Funny," I chuckled. "Trey it's all good. Shit happens but this is the last time it will happen with me." I stepped off the bed preparing to leave and as soon as my feet touched the carpet, Trey punched me in the left eye causing me to fall back on the bed.

"Bitch you think you gonna leave me? Hell No! I told you don't nobody leave me." Trey stood over me yelling like a three year old having a temper tantrum. Spit was flaring from his mouth as he continued to rant and rave. He lifted his leg and put his Nike shoe to my throat, "You ain't never gonna leave me. You hear me?" He pressed his shoe deeper into my throat and I was beginning to lose my breath. Trey knelt down and grabbed me by my hair and dragged me to the mirror in his bathroom. My eye was now swollen and red from the punch Trey planted on my face.

"Take a long look at yourself. If you ever leave me I'll have this pretty little face so disfigured your own mama won't recognize you."

Trey's words stung. Was this my life? What had I done to deserve my miserable existence? That night Trey fucked me while forcing me to watch his porno tape over and over again. He said it was to teach me not to go through his shit. I say it was another way to further degrade me.

For the next few months I endured busted lips, black eyes, and constant beat downs. I had become so alienated from my family and friends it seemed like nobody cared. I spent most nights at Trey's apartment and because my parents were busy living their own separate lives they never made time to see how I was doing. I could've left for a month and no one would've noticed. Besides Trey, I only spent time with one other person and that was Patrick. I met him through Trey because they had a couple of classes together and we would sometimes sit and talk while I waited for Trey.

One night during a heated argument with Trey he punched me in the nose and blood was everywhere. I ran out of the apartment and drove off. While driving back and forth down Peachtree Street I called Patrick from my cell. He told me to come over so we could talk. When I got there he examined my nose and luckily it wasn't broken. He gave me some cold towels to stop the bleeding and had me tilt my head back. The questioning immediately kicked in.

"Why does a girl like you that has so much going for yourself stay with a man like Trey?" Patrick asked as he adjusted the towel around my nose.

"It's a long complicated story," I sighed.

"I'm in no rush," Patrick said with a warm smile. He had a way of making me feel at ease. I could easily talk to him for hours without even realizing the time was passing us by.

"When I first met Trey he was fun and exciting. Different from the other guys I dated. He was the quintessential bad boy and I was attracted to that. Never did I think he would turn out to be so demonic."

"So why stay?"

"The first time Trey hit me, he threatened to basically end my life if I ever tried to leave him. No one had ever placed that sort of fear in my heart. Part of me also feels unworthy of any type of real love."

Patrick turned my face to his and lovingly placed his hand on my shoulder. "How can you say that? You come from a good family and the world is yours for the taking."

"You mean I come from a rich family, because nothing about it is good. Living in a big house and having nice cars doesn't make a good family Patrick. No one even notices when I'm not around. My Father is too busy having an affair and my Mother is so wrapped up with her socialite friends and her casual flings that they could care less whether I'm coming or going. My life is empty."

"I'm sorry Tyler. I had no idea that your family life was causing you so much pain, but then again it should have been easy to figure out. If your parents were halfway paying attention to you they would see how volatile your relationship is with Trey. But Tyler I'm here to tell you that you do deserve more. You're a beautiful, smart and loving young woman with so much to give. You deserve more than Trey. I can't force you to leave him, but if you're only staying out of fear, I will make sure that he never puts his hands on you again."

I moved closer to Patrick and gave him a long lingering kiss. No one had ever made me feel so safe and secure. "Patrick I want to give myself to you. Please make love to me."

"Tyler you have more to give than just your body. I want all of you; your mind, your body and your soul. But that will take time. Right now you need to focus on ending things with Trey and focusing on healing yourself." Patrick was right. I had so many inner demons I needed to fight and the first one was Trey.

"Instead of making love, can we lie in the bed and you just hold me until I fall asleep?'

"I'll do more than that; I'll hold you until you wake up." Patrick reached for my hand and led me to his bedroom. He gave me a t-shirt to put on and we slid under the covers and Patrick held me all night as I fell into the deepest sleep which I hadn't had in many months.

I woke up early the next morning and Patrick was still sleep. I moved his arm from around me and quietly got out the bed. I threw on my clothes and wrote Patrick a letter telling him I would call him later and headed out the door. When I got in the car I had twenty missed calls and ten new voice messages all from Trey.

As I drove up the driveway I felt a great sense of relief to be home. When I opened the front door my parents were sitting on the stairs in their pajamas as though they were up all night.

"Tyler where have you been and what happened to your nose?" Mother said with the look of death on her face. My parents hadn't questioned my whereabouts in so long that I was thrown off.

"I spent the night at Lisa's house, and I accidentally banged my nose on her bathroom door."

"Don't lie to your Mother," Father said as if he was disappointed with where this conversation was going.

"I called Lisa last night, and she tried to cover for you but once I explained the severity of the situation, she admitted that she hadn't spoken to you." My mind started racing as to what was the severe situation Mother was speaking of.

"Did something happen to Ella?" That was the only person I could think of since Mother and Father were standing in front of my face.

"No, Ella is fine. The emergency is you." Mother's lip began to quiver as it did when she was either stressed or extremely nervous.

"Me. What about me?"

"Last night Trey kept calling here looking for you. He said you weren't answering your phone and thought maybe we knew where you were. After the third call he became irate and started cursing and screaming saying I was lying about knowing your whereabouts. I didn't know it, but he was calling from outside the house and before I could tell your Father about the conversation there was a knock at the door and when he opened Trey put a gun to his head. He told your Father to tell you that if you don't come back to him you're as good as dead. What the hell is going on Tyler?"

All the built up pain and fear emerged from inside me and I burst out crying. Father ran towards me and wrapped his arms around me. Mother stood there looking confused. "I'm so sorry," I wailed. "Trey beat me up last night and I stayed with my friend Patrick because I was afraid and didn't want to come home."

"Beat you up? Is that what happened to your nose?" Mother asked.

"Yes."

"Was that the first time he hit you?"

"No Daddy, he has hit me many many times." My body fell into his chest as I purged one of my painful secrets.

"My little Princess," Father kept saying over and over again as he rubbed my back.

"I knew that man was evil. How dare he do this to a daughter of mine? We called the police after Trey left and they came over and filled out an incident report. I want you to press charges for the busted nose he gave you."

"Mother I just want to forget any of this ever happened and forget Trey ever existed."

"Are you crazy? You have a maniac after you and you want to act like you're not in danger," Mother hissed.

"Tyler you have to be realistic about the situation. This isn't just going to go away. We need to take the necessary steps to protect you and that means going to the police." Father was right. Trey was crazy and there was no telling what he might do. Maybe if he knew the police were involved that would scare him enough to leave me alone. My parents drove me to the police station where I filed a criminal complaint and they issued a temporary restraining order against him. I finally felt that maybe Trey was completely out of my life.

Initially Trey continued to call with threats and even came to my house and school looking for me. But after he was arrested for violating the restraining order he seemed to have gotten the message and backed off. Patrick was there for me the whole time. Although we hadn't been intimate we were closer than any two people could be. He was truly my rock and I felt blessed to have him in my corner. The tragic events in my life had briefly united my parents and they seemed to rekindle their love. But after things cooled down Father was back to the mistress and Mother was back to her social life.

"Let's go check out that new Denzel Washington movie tonight," Patrick said with enthusiasm.

"That sounds good. I'll be at your crib in an hour." After hanging up with Patrick I jumped in the shower. I put on a new baby blue mini dress I picked up at this boutique in Lenox Square Mall. It was a warm summer night and I put the top down on my new BMW 325. It was a present for my seventeenth birthday that just passed. I blasted *Hypnotized* by the late great Biggie Smalls as I made my way to Patrick's house. While bopping to the music I noticed the same black jeep that seemed to have been behind me for the last ten minutes. My heart started jumping and instantly I thought of Trey. Right when I was dialing Patrick's number to relay my fear the jeep made a right turn at the light. I laughed at myself for being so paranoid. When I reached Patrick's crib I blew the horn and he came running outside. He jumped in the passenger seat gave me a kiss on the lips and we headed off to the movies.

"That movie was crazy; did you see how Denzel blasted that dude?" Patrick said all hyped.

"Forget that. Did you see how Denzel put it down with that chick? He has got to be the sexiest man in the world, next to you of course," I laughed before giving Patrick a kiss.

"Isn't this special, my friend and my girl all hugged up together." As we stood in front of the car, for the first time in over three months Trey was standing in front of me. My hands began shaking and Patrick pulled me closer detecting my fear.

"Trey I think its best that you leave; Now!" Patrick stood in front of me without the least bit of fear.

"Or what Patrick, Huh, what you gone do?" he continued with a smug look on his face. "You might think you got yourself a prime piece of pussy, but that's my bitch you're fucking. She will always be my bitch."

"Whatever man, you keep holding on to those memories because that's all you have left." With those words, Trey snapped and swung his fist and barely missed Patrick's jaw. I stepped back as Patrick and Trey went to blows.

"Trey please leave," I screamed hoping he'd realize he was fighting a losing battle. But they were in a full blown fight. People were gathering around wondering what the hell was going on. After Patrick landed two straight jabs, one in Trey's stomach the other under his chin the fight seemed over. Trey stood there bending over in pain looking defeated.

"Take that, you bitch ass motherfucker. You like pounding on women, but you can't pound on no man. Don't you ever bother Tyler again or I swear I'll kill you. Patrick grabbed my hand to walk away and Trey reached in the back of his pants and pulled out his gun.

All you heard was people screaming, "He has a gun, he has a gun!" Everyone was ducking behind cars and running for cover. Patrick squeezed my hand tightly as to tell me not to be afraid. But I was beyond afraid. Trey pointed the gun towards us as if at any moment he would pull the trigger.

I didn't want to die and I felt the need to plead for my life. "Trey don't do this. Killing me and Patrick won't change anything. I know you're better than this." The tears were rolling down my face as I prayed my words would make a difference. Trey stepped closer to us with the gun pointed steady in our direction. I was hoping that Patrick wouldn't try and be a hero and get a hold of the gun.

"All I ever wanted to do was love you Tyler. You're my life. Never in my wildest dreams did I believe I would have a girl like you. You can't blame me for doing whatever I had to do to keep you. But you've moved on and I can't let you be happy without me." My chest was thumping and I was becoming dizzy because I knew Trey was about to put a bullet in me and Patrick's head. I heard police sirens in the distance but they were too far to make a difference. All it took was a second for Trey to end our lives. He yanked the gun forward with intensity as if he was about to pull the trigger. I knelt over still holding Patrick's arm knowing we were about to die together.

"Tyler I'll love you forever. Remember this moment because my face will haunt you for the rest of your life." Everything after that seemed to move in slow motion. Patrick tried to use his body to cover me but I moved forward and looked directly at Trey, as if I wanted to look my death in the face. Trey's arm raised and the next thing I heard was what sounded like a large explosion. Everyone gasped in horror as Trey's brains splashed across the concrete.

I screamed, "Noooooooooooo," as Trey's body fell to the ground. I hated the way Trey had treated me, but never did I want him to die. But there he was, lying before me dead. As the police pulled up, running towards Trey's dead body I realized that could've been me.

Chapter Four: Letting Go

(Closing the Pink Door)

"*I* want to give a shout out to the class of 1998's North Atlanta High School graduates, Lisa Duncan and Tyler Blake," the DJ yelled over the mic. *All About the Benjamins* was blaring from the speakers and Lisa and I were grinding to the music at Club 112. I didn't know how Lisa got Chris to announce that over the mic, especially since you're supposed to be twenty-one to get in the club. But who cared. I was so psyched about being free from high school I wanted to party all night long. With eyes closed, I was running my fingers through my hair dancing in my own world, when I felt a pair of strong arms wrapped around my waist. The arms felt so good that I didn't even move them. I was in a zone and slowly grinded in their embrace. My eyes were still closed when the soft lips kissed my neck and their sensual scent intoxicated me. Whoever was holding me felt so right. The kiss on my earlobe made my nipples hard and the whisper in my ear ended the mystery.

"You just letting any old nigga run up on you."

"Nah only the one that I miss, like you Patrick." I turned around and faced him.

"How did you know it was me?" he said sounding surprised and happy that I wasn't letting just anybody grind on me.

"I didn't at first, but then your voice gave it away."

"Oh, so you didn't know who I was and allowed me to feel up on you like that?"

"Yeah, shit you had me in a zone. I was already vibing with the music and when you touched me it felt so right. Anyway how are you going to question me, I haven't seen you in over six months." After Trey killed himself I totally lost my mind. I couldn't sleep or eat and all I saw was his face. Patrick tried to console me but I didn't want any part of it. Being close to him kept reminding me of that fateful night. Eventually he dropped out of school and disappeared. We lost all contact. Over time I somewhat pulled it together mentally but when I tried to find Patrick I hit a dead end. I got leads, but nothing ever panned-out and now, here he was, standing in front of me. I stared at him for a good minute. With his tall, dark strong build, Patrick's presence was always felt, but even more so now with his new bling bling look. He had on a flashy *Rolex* watch with two huge diamond studs in his ears. He was always a stylish dresser, but now he was immaculate.

"Damn Patrick, you looking good. I guess wherever you've been they've been treating you right."

"Not as good as if I had you."

"Funny, because you seem to be doing just fine to me; not a card, a phone call, nothing."

"Tyler you know you're the one that pushed me away. I couldn't get you on the phone and when I came to your house; your Father said you didn't want to see me. I was devastated. There was nothing left for me here, so I bounced."

"I did come looking for you once I got my mind right, but you were no where to be found. Where have you been?"

"I live in Chicago now."

"What you do in Chicago?"

"A little bit of this, a little bit of that." I glanced over Patrick again, checking out his gear and he looked like nothing but money. Young black man, doing this and that, looking like a million bucks, sounded like a pharmaceutical dealer to me.

"So what brings you back to Atlanta?"

"I had some business to take care of, but now that I ran into you hopefully it will also be pleasure." Patrick smiled and I smiled back. I was happy to see him again and I didn't want him to leave. Patrick was supposed to be in and out of Atlanta, but after our encounter he got a suite at the Four Seasons Hotel so I stayed with him for the whole week. My best friend was finally back and I started feeling complete again.

"So baby girl what you wanna do today?" Patrick and I had gone to every fancy restaurant, seen every movie and shopped nonstop. I didn't know what was left, besides making love. The funny thing was that as close as Patrick and I were we had never made love. It didn't seem to bother him but he was a man and I'm sure he had needs.

"How about we go to the park and have a picnic?"

"A picnic, you're kidding right?"

"No, what's wrong with a picnic?"

"I have a better idea. Why don't you go to the dresser open the top drawer and look inside the box." I gave Patrick a quizzical look but followed his directions. When I opened the drawer a *Tiffany & Co.* box was in there with an envelope. I opened the box first and was shocked.

"Patrick you got this for me, I can't believe it. It's the most beautiful bracelet I've ever seen in my life." The tennis bracelet had over forty huge diamonds that were clear and flawless. It was stunning. I looked back at him still shaking my head in disbelief.

"Why don't you open the envelope?" I actually forgot about it. I was so caught up in the iced-out bracelet. I opened the envelope and saw the First Class ticket to Chicago dated for next Friday.

"Will you come, please?" Patrick was now standing next to me and held my hand as he asked me the question.

"How can I say no, after you just gave me this unbelievable gift?"

"I don't want you to come because of the bracelet; I want you to come for me." The sincerity in his voice moved me.

"Of course I'll come and not for the bracelet but for you."

The following weekend when I visited Patrick in Chicago I decided we would take it all the way. He booked a Premier Suite at the *Ritz Carlton*. When I realized it had convenient indoor access to the exclusive Michigan Avenue Shops I was ecstatic. I spent my day at the Carlton Club Spa, did a little shopping, and that evening I met Patrick at The Greenhouse for drinks. I wore a fitted white *Dolce & Gabbana* pantsuit, with my hair up with a few cascading curls framing my face. After a few drinks, admiring the view of the city and listening to the beautiful song *My Funny Valentine*, coming from the piano, I was ready to go to our suite and make passionate love.

By the time we reached the 30th floor we were basically undressed. Luckily Patrick had managed to take out the room key and when he opened the door we had a long lingering kiss until we reached the king size bed. He fingered my nipples and then his warm mouth kissed my breast. I moaned with ecstasy while caressing his manhood. He started going down on me and I screamed with pure pleasure. Then he stopped and marveled at my beauty before we made love. We made love for a long time before becoming exhausted and falling asleep in each other's arm. Patrick's strong muscular body next to mine made me feel so loved. The next morning when I opened my eyes Patrick had already ordered breakfast. I ate a couple of strawberries before going into the marble bathroom to take a shower. As soon as I walked in I saw that Patrick had already prepared a bath for me. He also had a glass of mimosa on the table next to the bathtub. He remembered it was my favorite drink in the morning. After I lounged in the Jacuzzi tub for awhile I went back and joined Patrick in bed and once again we made love.

Looking out at the Chicago skyline and the lakefront view, I was relieved that Patrick and I were compatible sexually because now we had a chance at a serious relationship. At the same time, because he knew so much about my past I was afraid it would cause problems in the future. You should never ever date a guy that was your best friend and knows all of your secrets because Patrick never believed in us. I guess he shouldn't have because I wasn't in love with him and he knew it. He was older and ready to settle down and have a family. Although I was young and having fun, I never wanted to be locked down and have a baby with someone in the pharmaceutical business. What type of life is that? I had bigger goals and ambitions in life. Patrick was someone that was intriguing to me at the moment. I loved driving around in his brand new red 500 SL in front of my friends. He was the first guy that was giving me a thousand here and two thousand there just to go shopping and that was big to me. I felt like I was balling. Here I was a teenager and this guy was treating me like a Princess. All my friends were envious of me and I loved it.

"Oh fuck, if I throw up one more time I'm going to die," I screamed out loud on my way to the bathroom. I had been extremely nauseated for the past week and a red flag was waving steady. I purchased a *Clear Blue Easy* pregnancy test and of course I was pregnant.

"I can't believe this shit," I kept saying walking back and forth in my room. I simply wasn't about to have Patrick's baby. I flipped through the yellow pages and made an appointment to have an abortion. I knew Patrick would be devastated because he was twenty six and had no children. He wanted a baby more than anything in this world, but it wasn't going to be with me.

Tomorrow was my appointment and I still didn't have anyone to come with me. I decided to bite the bullet and call Lisa. If I had my way no one would know about the abortion, but I had to have someone to drive me home after the procedure.

"Hello," I heard Lisa say under the sound of loud ass music.

"Girl, turn that shit down."

"What is it?" Lisa asked sounding aggravated over my music request.

"I need you to come with me to the Doctor's office tomorrow."

"Doctor's office, for what?"

"I'm having an abortion and I need someone to drive me home after the procedure," I said matter of factly.

"Abortion! Girl your mama is going to kill you." Lisa could be so damn dramatic and that's why I didn't want to even tell her silly ass, but my options were limited.

"If all goes well, there is no need for her to find out about it dumbass."

"Don't be getting smart wit me, I'm doing yo yellow ass a favor."

"Whatever Lisa, I'll pick you up at nine o'clock in the morning."

"Hold up. Why can't Patrick go with you?" I wanted to reach through the phone and smack Lisa because she knew damn well why I couldn't tell Patrick. I complained to her on several occasions about the constant hint dropping Patrick would do to let me know he wanted me to have his child. She knew if Patrick ever found out that I killed his baby he would never forgive me.

"Lisa you know if Patrick knew I was pregnant he would lock me up for the whole nine months to guarantee his baby was born. You are my only option, so please stop with the third degree and just be there for me."

"Alright girl, I'll see you in the morning," and Lisa hung up the phone.

A couple of days after my abortion I went to Chicago to see Patrick. We were lying in the bed asleep when a sharp pain woke me up. "Oh, goodness," I sighed.

"What's wrong baby?" Patrick asked still half asleep. The pain was becoming more intense and my arms were wrapped around my stomach trying to minimize the impact.

"Oh shit, I'm bleeding," I screamed as I looked down and saw the blood on my thighs. "Baby please take me to the Emergency Room." When we got to the hospital, the nurse escorted me back to the room and I waited for the Doctor to come in. I told Patrick to wait for me in the front because I didn't want him to hear the conversation I was about to have with the Doctor. He reluctantly agreed but seemed suspicious or maybe he was just concerned and my guilt was making me paranoid. Before the Doctor examined me, he asked me a series of questions--one being was I pregnant or had an abortion recently.

"I actually had an abortion a few days ago." The Doctor examined me while continuing his line of questioning. Then he paused and looked at me.

"Ms. Blake, unfortunately you had a botched abortion."

"What does that mean?" I asked nervously. Ignoring my question the Doctor proceeded.

"Was your procedure done in the Chicago area?"

"No, I'm from Atlanta." I was now shaking and wanted the Doctor to explain what the hell a botched abortion was.

"Whoever performed your abortion did not completely remove the fetus."

"Excuse me," I said horrified.

"Your abortion is what we would consider incomplete. Whatever Doctor performed this procedure was incompetent."

"I actually don't know exactly who the Doctor was. I didn't go to my normal family physician because I was afraid my parents would find out. I basically flipped through the yellow pages and picked who could perform the surgery the quickest and the cheapest." The Doctor was shaking his head in what looked like a combination of disappointment and disgust.

"Ms. Blake an abortion is a very serious procedure and shouldn't be taken lightly. Not often, but women have died during this sort of operation. When making a decision like this you have to do what is the safest, not what is the cheapest or quickest." I felt ashamed as the Doctor lectured me.

"You need surgery immediately to make sure the entire fetus is removed or you can develop a life threatening infection." Tears were pouring out my eyes and I didn't know how I was going to explain this to Patrick.

"Will I be able to get pregnant again and have a baby?"

"Yes, if we perform this surgery immediately there should be no permanent damage." I breathed a sigh of relief, thinking that all hope wasn't lost.

"Doctor can I see my boyfriend before you take me to have surgery?"

"Sure, but only briefly. I'll have the nurse call him in." I nervously rubbed my hands wondering what I was going to say to Patrick. When he walked through the door, Patrick looked so afraid for me.

"Tyler what is going on, the nurse said there about to take you in for emergency surgery."

"Baby I didn't know I was pregnant and had a miscarriage. They don't think the entire fetus came out and they need to perform surgery before I get an infection." The lie just started flowing, so I rolled with it. It sounded a lot better than the truth. Patrick's eyes swelled with tears as he wrapped his arms around me.

"Tyler I'm so sorry. Everything will be okay. I'll be here waiting for you." Guilt had taken over my body. Patrick was so caring and understanding, unaware of all my lies. But it was for the best. Patrick would be devastated if he knew the truth. The nurse came in and told me they were ready for me. Patrick kissed me on the forehead and with a tear rolling down his cheek, he waved goodbye as they took me out the room.

When I woke up the next morning, Patrick was right there sitting in the chair in a deep sleep. The Doctor came in and told me the surgery went fine and would be signing off so I could check out the hospital. He gave me a prescription for an antibiotic; I gave him my thanks and was anxious to get the hell outta there.

After picking up my prescription and stopping to get a bite to eat Patrick and I headed home. It had been basically complete silence between us and I knew Patrick was in deep pain. He finally reached over and took my hand and said, "Tyler I'm so sorry this happened. I know how much we both wanted a baby, but don't blame yourself it's not your fault. We can always try again after your body heals."

"I know," I said quietly.

When we got home I immediately went upstairs to take a long hot shower. While I washed away my sins in the hot water I heard my cell phone ringing. After a couple of rings I heard it stop and thought whoever called must have hung up.

"Hello," Patrick said as he answered the phone.

"Hi, is that you Patrick?"

"Yeah, who else would it be?"

"Nobody, I'm just surprised you answered Tyler's phone."

"She's in the shower and when the phone rang I saw your name show up."

"Oh, and you wanted to speak to me," Lisa said being flirtatious.

"Actually I thought maybe you were calling to check up on her."

"Why, is she okay?"

"Actually she's a little upset. Last night she had a miscarriage. She didn't even know she was pregnant."

"You mean an abortion?" Lisa said, trying to sound like she misunderstood him, but knowing exactly what she was doing.

"Nah, I said miscarriage. Tyler wouldn't have no abortion."

"Oh, I thought you were talking about the abortion I took her to have a few days ago."

"Excuse me, what the fuck are you talking about?"

"I'm sorry Patrick, I must have misunderstood you. I took Tyler to have an abortion a few days ago and when you said she was upset I thought maybe it was because she felt guilty after discussing it with you."

"I guess I'm the one that misunderstood," Patrick said knowing full well that the concerned speech Lisa just gave was bullshit. But regardless, if what she was saying was true then Tyler had a lot of explaining to do.

"I'll tell Tyler you called Lisa," and Patrick threw down the phone. When I got out the shower Patrick was standing in front of the window looking at the view of the city.

"Baby let's stay in the bed all day and watch movies, how does that sound?" Ignoring my question, I walked towards Patrick thinking maybe he was in deep thought and didn't hear me. As I came closer he turned around and looked at me. His eyes were red and his face expression was ice cold.

"Lisa called while you were in the shower. I saw her name pop up when the phone rang and thought you wouldn't mind if I answered."

"That's fine, what did she want?"

"Nothing really; I thought maybe you called her earlier about the miscarriage and she was checking up on you."

"Oh." I was biting on my bottom lip so hard I thought it was going to start bleeding. My gut told me that whatever Patrick was about to say wasn't good and it showed all over my face.

Patrick continued to stare me down. "When I told Lisa you were upset she assumed I was talking about the abortion you had a few days ago. She thought you were feeling guilty. What do..." I cut Patrick off before he could continue.

"It's not what you think. I didn't mean to deceive you Patrick, but I wasn't ready to have a baby."

"So you went and had a fucking abortion behind my back, then you gave me this song and dance about a miscarriage. You lying bitch! Why the fuck did you really have to have surgery?" I was overwhelmed at this point and couldn't seem to speak. "Answer me Tyler, what the fuck was the surgery for?" Patrick had now completely lost his cool and was screaming at the top of his lungs. I finally managed to speak up.

"The place I had the abortion didn't remove the entire fetus. If they didn't perform the surgery I could've developed a life threatening infection." Patrick eyes were full of hate and disgust. "Sweetheart, the surgery went fine though and we can have another baby. I promise." Patrick put his hand around my throat and held me like I was an enemy.

"You killed my seed, do you think I want to have a baby with you. You are an evil, sick woman. I can't believe I ever fell in love with you. Now I know why Trey killed himself because you are nothing but poison." Patrick tossed me down on the bed like I meant nothing to him. He turned back and looked at me. "When I get back, I want you out my house. Don't ever contact me again." Patrick went to his drawer and tossed an envelope at me. "Use this to do whatever you need to do to get the hell out of my life." After Patrick stormed out and I heard the door slam downstairs I looked inside the envelope. It was full of hundred dollar bills. I burst into tears and fell on the bed and buried my head in the pillows. Patrick hated me and now I felt like I had no one.

I waited in the living room for the taxi to pick me up. I didn't want to deliberate on the conversation Patrick and I had, so instead focused on the drawer chest in the foyer. The body was in a rich cordovan finish, while the legs and trim were executed with silver leaf detail. His exquisite taste amazed me and once again I realized why we were best friends. I heard the taxi honking the horn; I walked to the door and looked around the beautiful duplex one last time before I said, "Goodbye."

To this day I wish I never crossed that line with Patrick and decided never to get involved with a man that started out as my best friend. Knowing the type of person I am, my friendships would outlast a romantic relationship any day. I learned a valuable lesson regarding Patrick and if I had the opportunity to go back, I would change so many things. Unfortunately time doesn't stand still for anyone.

"Mom I'll be ready to leave for the airport in about thirty minutes."

"Okay honey, I have to run to the store right quick, I'll be back in fifteen minutes."

"Okay don't be late. I don't want to miss my flight." After my relationship ended with Patrick, I started thinking about what I was going to do with my life, getting myself together and what type of career did I want. I wanted to get out of town and do something bigger and better and leave all my demons behind. I decided to transfer from Spellman to NYU. Ella was now attending Grad school at FIT so the location was perfect. She said I could stay with her until I found off campus housing. I was looking forward to beginning my new life. The phone rang as I was packing up my last bag. "Hello."

"Hi, I wanted to say bye before you left." I recognized Lisa's voice and my first instinct was to hang up the phone. We hadn't spoken since I called cursing her out for revealing my secret to Patrick. But I was leaving starting a new life, and there was no need to hold a grudge.

"Thanks Lisa," I said blandly.

"What time does your flight leave?"

"In a couple of hours; I'm leaving in a few because you know how hectic the airport can be."

"Yeah, I know. Tyler I wanted to tell you something before you left."

"What?" my voice sounded indifferent.

"I never said sorry for telling Patrick about the abortion. I know I swore that it was an accident but you were right, it was intentional."

"But why?" Now curious about her truthful confession.

"Tyler you were always the prettiest, and all the guys liked you. Although I never understood why you dumped Chad for that deranged Trey; but anyway then you had Patrick and you had no time for anybody else. You were always showing off the ice he gave you or the shopping sprees he took you on, and I was sick of you flossing in his Benz all the time."

"So basically you were jealous," I said abruptly.

"Yeah I was jealous. I knew Patrick would dump you if he found out the truth, and I wanted to make sure he did. I know that is malicious Tyler and now I feel terrible. I feel like because of what I did you're leaving, and I don't want you to leave." Part of me wished Lisa would've kept her confession to herself because it wasn't going to bring Patrick back to me; but then maybe I needed to hear this to finally close the last door on my life in Georgia.

"Lisa I don't know what to say. We've been friends forever and you are like a sister to me, but I have to leave. There are too many painful memories for me here and I'm in search of happiness. I can't get that in Georgia. But Lisa I accept your apology and I will always love you."

"I love you too Tyler, and please don't forget about me. Pick up the phone and call sometimes."

"I will." I hung up the phone feeling a sense of closure. I looked around my room and stood admiring the Barbie collection I began when I was five years old. It made me revisit all the dreams I had growing up as a little girl. This was the first step to accomplishing the life I had visualized. Even with all the drama I engaged in, I always wanted to be somebody. Staying focused was my biggest obstacle. I continuously went back and forth being with some man in some relationship that kept me off course, but for the first time I had a preliminary sketch. All the details weren't mapped out, but I was letting go of the past and opening a new door and was full of anticipation of what could be waiting for me. Maybe my world hadn't been perfect but I decided that I would go to NYC and make the place the color I wanted it to be; and you know the only color for me is pink.

Chapter Five: Just Got Off

(The Pink Bus)

I don't know if you ever heard the phrase "Just Got off the Bus," you know when a person comes into a new town, not that bright, naïve and easy to take advantage of? Well that was me. I felt that way on the inside, but I tried not to let it show on the outside because I never wanted to be anybody's victim. When I arrived in New York I tried to leave the past behind me. Inside I felt like I had "Just Got off the Bus," but I knew I had to put my game face on. There were endless opportunities here for me, and though I had made a ton of mistakes thus far in my journey the mistakes were still mine to make. I take full responsibility for all of them. Always remember one thing. If you take responsibility and blame yourself that means that you have the power to change it. If you put responsibility on someone else, then in retrospect you are giving them the power to decide your fate in life.

January 8, 1999 I reached my destination with hopes of making my dreams come true in NYC. Once I got off that plane I had stars in my eyes and money to burn...so I thought. Ella let me stay in her dorm style apartment with her two other roommates until I found a place of my own. I wasn't able to get campus housing which I didn't want anyway. I figured I would get an apartment of my own. I later found out that apartment hunting in New York City wasn't quite that easy. Instead of getting a part time job, I opted to whoop it up with Ella all over town. We splurged on shopping sprees, wined and dined at fancy restaurants, reveled in Broadway Shows; we just balled. There was almost twenty thousand dollars in the envelope Patrick gave me, but we all know that if you have no money coming in and you are running around spending, then twenty thousand dollars is no money. Hey I was young. The best thing I did was spend the last bit I had on securing a cozy room in an apartment building on 77th and Broadway similar to dorm-style rooms for students. Within a month, I had gone through all my money and was broke.

I was attending NYU and pursuing my dream of becoming an Actress. I figured my big break was right around the corner. Ella and I were sitting in her room watching TV and she asked me about my future plans.

"So Tyler now that you're here what exactly do you want to do, I mean while attending school, because of course that comes first."

"Well I figured I would concentrate on the books and juggle acting auditions. Maybe do the Broadway circuit, and then get into film; I mean how hard can it be? Look at all the no talent faces in the movie and music business today."

"Yeah, that's true, but there are a lot of beautiful women with a lot of talent on the same mission as you." It didn't dawn on me that there were about a million other girls running around thinking the exact same thing, but Mother instilled in me that I was special. I knew there would always be girls who were prettier and more talented but I felt like I was born to be a star. It was a matter of me focusing and pursing my dream to the fullest extent. I just hadn't figured out how I should go about making it happen because I was basically grabbing in the dark.

On my way to an audition I was walking down the street and came across a flyer about the hot new label 'Get Money Records.' I had flashbacks to when I was in Georgia and was in awe of the guy named T-Roc who I saw in a music video. He was sexy and Lisa laughed at me when I told her one day I'd be in his bed. Now here I was in his city looking at a flyer about his new label. I'm a true believer that if you visualize something, want something, and put that energy out there you will bring it to you and make it come true. It may not come out exactly the way that you envision or want it too, but it will happen and this was no different. That is why you must be careful about what you want and try to reserve your energy for something positive and productive. It took me many years to finally understand that.

After having a delicious lunch with Ella at the *Pink Tea Cup*, I felt energized. Not only did she pay for the fried chicken and pancakes I devoured, but she gave me a week's worth of subway tokens, which I desperately needed. I was strolling down the street counting my blessings on the way to an audition and to my honest surprise, it happened to be the same block where T-Roc's office was located. I only realized that because one of his many workers was standing outside and he struck up a conversation with me.

"What's up cutie, what's your name?" The ultra iced out guy said.

"Tyler," I sneered continuing to prance by until I heard him say.

"My names Ritchie, I work at Get Money Records." My antennae instantly went up since I knew that was the label T-Roc owned. Not wanting to seem impressed I vaguely nodded my head like I hadn't heard of the hottest independent label out.

"I just moved to New York, so I don't know anything about record labels."

"Well that's okay; you hang with me maybe you can learn how to run one," he said with an 'I'm so sure of myself' laugh. "I have an idea. There's a private party tonight where you can get your first taste of the music industry. How bout it?"

"Sure," I said calmly. I gave Ritchie my phone number and he said he would call around seven. Strolling down 23rd street and 7th Avenue all sorts of possibilities were flashing in my mind. Could I actually see or better yet meet T-Roc and I haven't even been in NYC for two months? Could I be that lucky? When I gave Ritchie my number I didn't think he would actually call, but by the time I reached home, he had left a message. I called him back and he said he would pick me up in an hour.

To say the least, I was elated about the possibility of meeting my crush, but at the same time I was extremely nervous. I didn't know what to wear so I played it safe and went with a simple pair of tight black pants and a cream top, dabbed on my favorite *Mac* lip gloss, '*Oh Baby*,' and headed out the door.

Ritchie pulled up in a white Range Rover with dark tinted windows and chromed-out rims. Before I even got comfortable in the car he said, "We have to make a stop on our way to the party." I didn't ask any questions about what, where, or who the party was for. Instead I chose to stay quiet and go with the flow. It's always

been my philosophy, that when you are around people that you don't know, it's always better to remain silent and observe.

To my delight we met up with T-Roc (a young mogul quickly on the rise) and his friends to head to the private affair. Just like that, I was on the red carpet with paparazzi taking T-Roc's picture. He was a huge star and basked in all the attention. He was the hip hop King of New York. Everyone wanted a piece of him and I was caught up. I couldn't conceive that this person who I had seen in heavy rotation on *BET, MTV* and doing interviews for *Entertainment Tonight* was actually just a few feet away from me and we were going into the same party. Little old me; Tyler Blake from Georgia, was in the mix about to rub shoulders with the movers and shakers of the hip hop industry.

The event coordinators escorted T-Roc's large entourage into the VIP section and the next thing I know they were popping bottles and I'm drinking *Cristal*. Yes I had champagne a million and one times before but never like this. Eyeballing the room, I felt out of my element. All the ladies seemed glamorous and different from the girls I was used to back home. With my simple black pants, and cream shirt, and curly bob; I didn't fit in with these chic ladies, but in the bigger scheme of things it didn't matter because I was in touching distance to the man I always wanted to meet, which hadn't formerly happened yet.

That night I partied, had a couple glasses of champagne and began living out one of my dreams. Those days of being back in Georgia partying with my girlfriends, thinking we were whooping it up was no comparison to how the rich and famous partied. Arriving home at the crack of dawn I kept replaying every moment of that night and feeling butterflies in my stomach. This was the most fun ever and I wanted to savor every moment. Although T-Roc hadn't even noticed me, I was overjoyed by the whole experience. There were so many other celebrities there too and all of them looked so much shorter and thinner in person, which was a little shocking but exciting all the same.

The next day to my surprise Ritchie called. "What's up Georgia Peach?" That's the nickname Ritchie gave me after I casually mentioned where I was from. I wasn't expecting to hear from him so soon, but was elated he called.

"Nothing much, I had a blast last night."

"Cool, which means you're up to doing it again tonight?"

"Of course," I said knowing good and well I needed to study for my English test.

"What you doing right now? How would you like to come by the label and see for yourself how Get Money Records is bringing in the millions?"

"That would be great cause I've never been inside a record label before." This was all new to me. Plus any opportunity to meet T-Roc I was taking it. Working with what I had, I selected a pair of low rise jeans and a cropped turtleneck revealing my toned stomach.

Ritchie picked me up an hour after our conversation and we headed over to the label. No matter how much I wanted to scream with enthusiasm, acting laid back was--and still is one of my strengths. When I walked through the doors the atmosphere seemed hectic and fast paced. The energy was strong and everyone was all about the hustle and bustle. There was something alluring about the chaotic atmosphere and I understood why so many people wanted to be a part of this world, including me. Ritchie told me to have a seat and he would be right back to show me around.

As I was sitting there attentively watching people running back and forth like they were developing a cure for some life threatening disease, I heard someone say, "I'm T-Roc, what's your name?" He reached out to shake my hand, and I tried to remain calm so he wouldn't see the dreamy stars in my eyes. Inside my heart was pounding so hard, I thought the building would start shaking. Gazing into his persuasive eyes I knew I was in deep infatuation. By this time I had enough experience to know it certainly wasn't love, but the best type of infatuation I had ever encountered.

"Hi I'm Tyler." I remained cool thinking he would then walk away, but instead he began flirting with me.

"Tyler, that's a pretty name for a very pretty girl." This was better than any Barbie story I had ever made up.

"Are you coming out with us again tonight?" I realized he had noticed me the night before, which made me feel like a Gold Medalist.

I innocently said, "If you would like me to."

Later that night, I was at it again; partying with the hip and chic, taking note that I simply must invest in a New York themed wardrobe. In Georgia I was in style and used to being the center of attention. Here, in my mind I stood out like a sore thumb--and not in a good way. It wasn't the time to dwell on that because I was simply having too much fun. They were playing *Hate Me Now* by Nas and T-Roc grabbed me by my waist and escorted me to the dance floor. He was grinding against me from behind with his face against the side of my cheek and the essence of his cologne had me caught in his rapture. Up until that very moment, I wasn't sure T-Roc was attracted to me in a sexual way.

You have to understand that although I felt cute, my confidence was a little low. Here I was in a new city at these industry parties surrounded by women who looked like they just stepped out of *InStyle*

Magazine. Everywhere you turned there was a beautiful lady but yet T-Roc was dancing with me. I felt special because I'm dancing with the man that every other girl wanted. Why wouldn't they? Not only was T-Roc on top of his game business wise, he was also a very clean cut and sharp looking guy. Nobody possessed his style and his star presence was undeniable.

"How about you come home with me after the party?" T-Roc whispered in my ear before turning me around so we were face to face. It took all my strength to resist his offer but I knew what would happen and I wasn't quite ready yet.

"I want to but I can't."

"Why can't you?" He asked while still in his grip.

"I really have to study. I have an English test coming up and if I don't pass I might fail the class." T-Roc gave me a bizarre look like bitch you can't be serious, but I was. No I wasn't going to fail my class over this test, but I had to say something to get out of going home with him.

"I tell you what pretty girl, you take your test and I'll catch you the next time around." As T-Roc let go of my waist and left me standing on the dance floor, I felt my Prom King had left his Queen.

I laid in bed dreaming about how it would be for T-Roc to make love to me. I wondered how he would feel inside me and if my body would get caught up in ecstasy. It had been months since I had been intimate with someone and wouldn't it be the icing on the cake if it was T-Roc?

A couple of days passed and I hadn't heard from Ritchie. I was a tad disappointed but at the same time I needed the time to concentrate on school for a minute. Once again I wasn't focusing. More and more I was thinking that school wasn't for me. Until I found something more productive, I figured I needed to stick it out. Tired of calling my parents asking for money every other week, I decided I needed a job.

During one of my rare moments of studying, the phone rang and it was Ritchie saying that he was on his way to pick me up. That was fine by me, I was never into studying and I was more than happy to close my English book and take an extended break. I hoped my mogul told Ritchie that he wanted to see me because last time I saw T-Roc he seemed a little put off that I declined his invitation to come to his crib--as I'm sure he hadn't gotten that type of brush off often. He obviously was over it or Ritchie wouldn't have called.

We went to the label, where I sat for awhile without T-Roc saying two words to me. He was running a label and I started to wonder what I was doing there. It was amazing to see him at work because he was a very hands-on type of guy who was an extreme perfectionist. When something didn't go exactly the way he wanted, he had no qualms about having a tantrum right there in front of everybody. After two hours of no one saying a word to me, Ritchie emerged, "Are you hungry?"

"A little bit," actually I was starving but that was too much information.

"Cool, we're going to pick up some food and stop by my friends to chill for awhile." That was Ritchie's favorite word, "cool," I thought to myself.

My mind was made up. If I was presented with another invitation by T-Roc, I would not decline because I had a strong inkling that he was the friend's house Ritchie was talking about. We stopped at this soul food restaurant called *The Shark Bar* and Ritchie picked up the food he had ordered to go and a short time later, we pulled up to a brownstone in the city. I took a quick look around the quaint neighborhood while Ritchie rang the doorbell. Bubbling over on the inside, when T-Roc answered the door, he greeted me with a sly smile and said, "Hello Tyler, how did you do on your English test?" His opening statement threw me off balance but I quickly regained my composure.

"It went great;" I said shyly and gave a smile. On the outside, the building looked historic and old fashioned. On the inside it was all high tech and ultra modern. Here I was sitting and eating with my crush. It was too good to be true. The three of us were laughing, joking, and enjoying the delicious food. After a couple hours Ritchie said he had to run an errand and would be back. That was fine with me, because I could finally have some alone time with T-Roc.

"Tyler what school do you attend, not high school I hope." I tried to get a read on his face because I couldn't tell if he was serious or playing.

"NYU," I responded.

"What's your major?"

"Journalism."

"Oh, you look very young, how old are you?"

"Eighteen, I'll be nineteen later on this year," I said eagerly not wanting to seem so young.

"Don't rush it pretty girl. There will come a time when you'll be wishing you can push your age back, not up." As T-Roc was talking, my mind began drifting off thinking about the hundreds of cute girls he had conquered and the many more that would follow me, but you know what I didn't give a shit. I could have cared less. As I mentioned in the past, when I want something that is what I want--no ifs, ands, or buts about it! At this particular moment in my life, I wanted to know what it felt like to make love to T-Roc. I didn't care if it turned out to be a one night stand, because personally, I thought that would be more romantic. This guy was a known ladies' man and I wasn't naïve enough to believe that I could change him or that I would be 'The One.' Every girl he slept with was probably trying to lock him down so I figured I'd do one better and treat him as a casual sexual encounter. This was about me fulfilling yet another one of my fantasies no more and no less.

We began kissing and I started feeling myself getting aroused, "Tyler how about we go upstairs where we can get comfortable." He took my hand and led me upstairs to his bedroom where a huge plush bed awaited us.

Leaning back on his bed he said, "I want to watch you undress."
My mind began racing and the shy, insecure, and self conscious side of
me took a seat as the other side, the bitchy, fiery and confident side
showed her face. I looked at him like *oh please I'm not taking off my
clothes for you.* You have to understand all these episodes in my life are
like movies to me and I've created scripts that have to be exciting and
fun. I knew sleeping with him was going to happen, but I couldn't let
him think that he would just snap his fingers and my clothes would fall
off. I had to make him believe that he somewhat coerced me.

"No baby, I don't think so. This isn't Scores and I'm no stripper."

"Pretty girl, I just want to see you naked, please." I did have on a
soft pink *Natori* bra and panty set that I wanted him to view. If I wasn't
comfortable with anything else, I pretty much always liked my figure
and felt comfortable showing it off in cute undergarments. I didn't want
to seem too eager to please, and this was my script, so I needed to start
setting the pace. In my mind I was telling T-Roc to back it up buddy, I'm
running this show. I sauntered over to the bed and began kissing him
again. His lips were so soft and his skin so smooth. He was being very
gentle with me and taking his time letting me explore his body. He led
my hand down to his hardness so I could feel how aroused he was. His
hands were slowly moving up my skirt and he began gently squeezing
the flesh of my thighs and buttocks. He got anxious and started to
unbutton his pants trying to push my head down to give him a
professional.

Now ladies, I might do a lot of things, but I was not about to give
him head. That performance is strictly executed for my man and he
definitely wasn't that. Let's back it up for a moment. Some women
prefer to give a professional over sex, but I think that it is way too
personal and should only be shared with a selected few.

"Nah, that's not happening T-Roc, I don't know you like that to
be giving you head." After a little back and forth, he finally accepted that
it wasn't going to happen and we moved on to finally taking off our
clothes and making love. Although he wasn't well endowed, he made up
for it in passion and intensity. He was a good lover and the experience
was pleasurable.

Once he reached his climax I could now close this chapter. It was like wanting something and getting it and then being done with it; because most of the time it's never what you think it's all cracked up to be. This sexual encounter with my crush was no different. I got up and began putting on my clothes because I was ready to go. I never like to sit around and engage in small talk after having sex with someone unless it's my man.

"Where you trying to run off to?" T-Roc asked with irritation in his voice.

"I'm sure Ritchie is coming back soon and I wanted to be ready by the time he got back."

"You wanted to be ready for what, to leave?" He asked like he was surprised and offended by my suggestion it was time to go.

"Well, aren't we finished here? You got yours and I somewhat got mine, what's left for us to do, talk? I don't really care for all that."

"Aren't you a feisty little bitch; who the fuck do you think you're talking to?"

"Unless I was misinformed, your name is T-Roc and I know exactly who I'm talking to." I'd fulfilled my fantasy and wanted to leave before reality set in, which by now was too late.

T-Roc walked towards me and firmly grabbed my hair pulling my neck slightly back. "You pop a lot of shit for an eighteen year old brat from nowhere. You need to decide whether you want to remain a nobody with your schoolbooks and test, or if you want to be somebody and keep me as a friend."

"Oh," I said, with my head still titled back. "That choice is easy." T-Roc smiled and relaxed on the grip to my hair, assuming the crucial decision was a thumb up in his favor.

"I'd rather be my own nobody than your somebody." Ritchie walked in simultaneously when T-Roc had the look men get when they're about to bitch slap you. T-Roc released me, as if he didn't have a choice due to Ritchie's earlier than expected arrival. I was relieved and couldn't get out of his house fast enough. Unbeknownst to either of us, this was hardly our final encounter. Our lives would intertwine in ways neither of us could have expected.

After my brief but memorable encounter with T-Roc, I decided to focus on school and my pursuit of stardom. Eventually securing a part time job at a cute restaurant in my neighborhood which was very convenient, I needed to make some money. I was running out of excuses for my parents as to what I needed all the extra money for. It was basically for clothes. I decided after my brief introduction to the glamorous life I had to invest in some new designer outfits. I also went on a couple of auditions here and there but I wasn't being consistent with the grind work necessary to get any sort of break.

Early one morning my agent called about an audition for a music video for a hot up and coming R&B group. He explained it wasn't one of those typical music videos with every girl running around naked so I said, "Okay, why not try." I got the lead, playing a waitress/girlfriend of one of the group's members. The next day we started shooting and it was inspiring sitting in the chair having professional people do my hair, makeup, and style me. My invocation was this could be the beginning of better gigs to come.

While on set, both the owner who was also a Rap Star named Tah Tah and Mark the CEO and co-owner were at the shoot. Tah Tah, coming off his fourth multi platinum CD seemed to be such a gentleman and Mark was charming too in his own way. But he definitely had an over inflated ego. The shoot wrapped for the day but they summoned me to be back early the next morning, so I yearned to go home and crawl into bed. The moment I stepped outside on the pavement Mark was standing in front of his white Benz with an 'I've been waiting for you demeanor.'

"Hi, can I talk to you for a minute?" Mark gestured his hand for me to come over.

"What's your name again?" Mark asked as I made my way to his car.

"Tyler Blake," I said not wanting to be bothered with the egotistical record honcho, but remembering he was the CEO of the label and overseeing the music video.

"What do you do besides music videos?"

"Actually I don't do videos, I'm an actress, but my agent thought this would be easy work and it pays decent money. I also attend NYU, my major is Journalism." I basically ran down my entire bio because I didn't like Mark's attitude. I deemed it necessary to make it clear I wasn't some dumb, desperate industry ho whose greatest ambition is sucking his dick for a part in a video.

"That's cool, but have you every thought about getting into the music business?"

"The music business?" I paused "In what capacity?"

"A rapper."

I bust out laughing, "I can't rhyme."

"Never say can't. Female rappers are big shit right now. Look at Lil Kim, Foxy Brown, and Eve. We're trying to find a bad ass chick right now to be the first lady of our label. You fit the look perfectly. With your face and that body you'll be the hottest chick out there."

"I don't think you heard me, I can't rap."

"Baby I got this. You have an excellent tone to your voice and speak well. I can have Tah Tah or one of our other rappers write your rhymes, all you would have to do is make a sellable delivery. You think all those female rappers out there is writing their own shit? Hell no! You know how many niggas got Jay Z on their payroll as their ghost writer?"

I was listening to Mark wondering if he was serious or was this some type of over the top ploy to get me in bed. But then again there was at least ten pretty girls on the video set that would have dropped their panties for him without any type of coercion, so all this gassing wasn't necessary if he wanted some pussy. But me as a rapper, that was a stretch. I finally said, "I don't know Mark, I never really envisioned myself as a female MC."

"Think about it tonight, and we'll talk further in the morning." I agreed to do that and headed home." On my way I stopped by the newsstands and picked up the *Source Magazine*, *Vibe* and *XXL*. I sat on my bed flipping through the magazines seeing who the hottest female rapper was and what music producers were lacing their tracks. As I inspected Lil Kim being ghetto fabulous with the *Christian Dior* and the bling bling, I thought being a female rap superstar may not be all that bad.

"Did you think about what we discussed last night?" Mark asked without missing a beat upon my entrance on the video set.

"Actually I did. I'm curious to hear what your game plan is."

"We're wrapping up early today, so how bout coming with me to the office so we can iron a few things out."

"Sounds like a plan to me." I shot my last scene around two o'clock in the afternoon and was dressed and ready to leave with Mark within twenty minutes. When we got to his office there were platinum plaques everywhere and the setup was immaculate. I sat down on a plush red couch as he was going through some papers while handling a business call. Obviously 'LaFamilia Records' was on top of their game and Mark knew it.

"My head A&R is going to join us so we can throw some ideas around." The next minute a tall skinny guy walked in.

"What's up Mark?"

"What's going on Cassidy, this is Tyler the female rapper I was telling you about." The guy checked me out and nodded his head with approval.

"Yeah, she's hot; we can do big things with her. What's the name looking like?"

"I wanted you to help me come up with a couple of ideas; something hot and sexy like the artist herself." The two of them kept going back and forth like I wasn't even in the room. Not once did Cassidy ask to hear me rhyme or even if I could. Their only concern was image and packaging.

"Yo I got it," Cassidy belted as if he just had a brilliant idea. "Her name should be Citrus, you know like the fruit."

"A fruit," I retorted, put off by the name. They both scanned me in unison as though they forgot I was in the room; then without hesitation disregarded my statement.

"That's hot," Mark was nodding his head in agreement. "Citrus," he repeated about five more times. "Sweet, juicy and sexy, that's it Cassidy."

"I hate it," I said with a serrated edge to my voice.

"Tyler baby, let us handle the business side; we're pro's at this. All you have to do is stay looking beautiful and keep that body tight. You do what I ask and everything will be copastetic."

"Copastetic, is that even a word?" I said examining him with confusion.

"Yeah, it's my word."

"What the hell does it mean?" I asked not believing it was in the dictionary.

"I don't know what the definition is in the dictionary but in the Markionary it means everything will go smoothly. So remember that," he warned after winking his eye.

After my unsettling meeting with Mark and Cassidy, I callcd Ella to tell her about my new found profession.

"Hi Ella, it's me Tyler."

"I know my own sister's voice," Ella snapped with a slight attitude. We'd both been so busy and I hadn't talked to her in awhile. I was only giving her a friendly reminder.

"Sorry but check this out, while I was doing a music video I met the owner of LaFamilia Records and he wants to make me into a rap superstar."

"What, did I hear you correctly, a rapper. You can't be serious Tyler?"

"Actually I'm very serious."

"What happened to your acting career?"

"I can still pursue that after I get my first platinum CD."

"You sound crazy; did you call Mother about your new music career?"

"We keep playing phone tag."

"I guess that means you don't know about the separation or the fact that Father has basically gone broke."

"What are you talking about?" I asked surprised. Father made an excellent living as an Investment Banker, how could he be broke.

"Mother said that Father claims he made some bad investments and was broke. She believes after revealing she wanted a divorce he is trying to keep all the money to himself. No money, no alimony."

After I got off the phone with Ella I called Mother but there was no answer. I left a message telling her to call me ASAP. I began to get worried, but then I remembered this was Mother. She probably already had a new husband lined up.

Early the next morning the phone rang shaking me from a deep sleep, "Hello," I uttered not quite awake.

"Yo Citrus wake up," the voice screamed realizing it was Mark. That comment definitely made me alert because I simply detested that name.

"What's up Mark, can I call you back in a couple of hours I'm still sleep." I glanced over at my clock and it was eight thirty in the morning. Today was Wednesday and I always slept in late because I had no classes.

"Can't do that, you've got work to do. Meet me at my office in an hour, don't be late." I heard the phone click, and put the pillow over my face not believing Mark was summonsing me to his office so early in the morning. I was under the impression that music cats sleep all day and work all night. I managed to get out the bed, take a quick hot shower and head out the door. I stopped by *Starbucks* and got a Caramel Frappuccino to completely wake me up. By the time I reached Mark's office I was wide awake and bright eyed.

"Very good," Mark said as he eyed his watch realizing I was on time. We have a lot to do today. Cassidy is taking you over to the studio so you can listen to Tah Tah lay down some vocals. I want you to pay attention to his delivery and his breathing method. Those two elements are key; your flow has to be tight and you have to control your breathing."

"Okay, I think I can manage that."

"I also brought a stylist and a fitness trainer on board. I want you to be perfect at all times. Once we announce you're the first lady of LaFamilia, you're going to be under a microscope. They'll be inspecting everything from what hair style you're rocking to what color polish you used for your pedicure. You have to be on point because when you make your grand entrance you're bodying all these other bitches."

"Mark you're not a little bit skeptical about all of this. I have no experience as a female rapper. What if I suck?"

"That's a possibility, but you have the hardest quality there is to find."

"What's that?"

"That X Factor. It's what I call true star quality. When you first walked on the set for the music video I knew it immediately. It's the same quality I saw in Tah Tah. That is rare. Many people have talent and good looks, and they even have successful careers. But very few entertainers have the aura of being a Superstar. If you follow my lead I promise, you will be a huge Superstar. Whether it is TV, movies, or whatever, it's all yours."

I nodded my head imagining my life as a Superstar. I definitely wanted it, but I was still trying to swallow the whole Citrus rapstress thing. Continuing with my dream, Cassidy walked in interrupting my thoughts.

"What's good this morning Citrus?"

"Cassidy can you please call me Tyler."

"No," he said firmly. "You have to be in Citrus mode at all times. That's your life until you go to sleep at night. But first thing in the morning when you wake up, it's back to Citrus so get used to it." Cassidy turned to Mark and handed him a folder full of pictures.

"These are a few fashion ideas the stylist came up with," Mark was attentively going through each picture tossing some to the side and putting others in a neat pile.

"These work right here."

"Yeah those are the same ones I like too," Cassidy chimed in.

"What were you thinking about as far as producers go?"

"Maybe Money B, he just blessed Tah Tah with a blazing track."

"Okay that's cool, who else?"

"What about Track Masters, Timbaland and maybe Dr. Dre, you know all the hot producers," I wailed, wanting some say so with my project.

"Damn baby you talking about big names which mean big budgets."

"You said we're doing Superstar status, well then I need Superstar producer's right."

"No doubt," there was a slight pause. "By the way do you have an attorney?"

"No,"

"Don't worry about it; I'll hook you up with one I'm familiar with, he's excellent."

Cassidy and I left Mark's office and headed over to Right Track Studio. I'd never been in a music studio and it was cool to watch Tah Tah in the vocal booth spitting his rhymes. His lyrics were sick and his delivery was crazy. Everybody compared his sarcasm to Jay Z, his poetic lyrics to Nas, and lyrical gift to the late great Biggie. He was like damn all across the board. When Tah Tah stepped out the booth he headed straight towards me and introduced himself.

"So you're the first lady of LaFamilia," he said with a smile. "I'm Tah Tah and welcome to the family." He gave me a hug like we'd known each other forever. A couple of weeks ago I was taking an English test and slaving waiting tables, now I was in the studio hugging one of the biggest rappers in the business.

For the next couple of weeks I practically lived in the studio. I was either studying Tah Tah or practicing my flow and delivery. I was constantly trying to mimic Tah Tah and make my voice a little deeper. He'd get frustrated and scream on me and say, "Rap in your natural tone, stop trying to imitate me and tighten your own shit up."

That was easier said than done. Developing my own style was not as simple as I thought it would be. Probably because I wasn't an authentic rapper; I was a packaged product that Mark was creating. If I wasn't in the studio then I was meeting with the stylist selecting clothes that would be ideal for Citrus or I was in the gym trying to get my body perfectly tight. I wasn't enjoying any of it and was having second thoughts about the whole concept. My cell phone rang disrupting my rationalization and I noticed Mark's name and picked up dreading to hear what was on the itinerary for the rest of my day.

"Hi Mark," I said trying to sound cheerful although I was becoming increasingly miserable.

"Listen baby, I know you've been working hard and might be feeling a tad stressed," that was an understatement I said to myself.

"I'm taking you to dinner tonight, so you can relax and discuss the plans I have laid out for your future. I'll pick you up at eight." Dinner sounded nice, but I would've preferred an all day spa pass. Sitting with

Mark discussing my future as a rap star wasn't exactly appealing to me. Maybe tonight I would use this opportunity to explain that to Mark. I hadn't signed anything and the lawyers were still working out the terms of my contract for the label, which all seemed suspect to me. When Mark originally introduced me to the attorney he hooked me up with, he was rushing me to sign the papers without explaining shit to me. I opted to go with an attorney Ella was dating, and he basically told me my deal was garbage and I would be signing away my life and my first born. I heard Mark's specialty was fucked up contracts and I told him to forget it. He tried to pacify me, so my attorney and the label's attorney have been in heavy negotiations ever since.

Mark picked me up right on time, which pleased me because that meant I could make our dinner short and be back home in a couple of hours.

"You look beautiful tonight Tyler." I was happy to hear him call me by my birth name and not that ridiculous Citrus, although I was somewhat dressed like a citrus. I had on an orange chiffon baby doll dress that the stylist picked up from *Versace*. She decided that my entire wardrobe needed to reflect the whole Citrus flavor. I was basically going to look like a fruit all year round. The whole concept was ludicrous.

"Thanks Mark, have you decided where we're going for dinner?"

"I had my chef prepare an intimate dinner at my place. There we can have privacy and talk about your future with LaFamilia." That actually sounded good to me. Maybe I wouldn't be home in a couple hours like I planned, but at least I didn't have to be in a restaurant around a bunch of people. Plus I wanted some privacy when I broke the news to Mark that I no longer wanted to pursue the whole female rapper profession.

We pulled up to Mark's elaborate house in New Jersey. I had never been to his home before but heard how beautiful it was. When we walked inside, it was undeniably stunning, but I had lived and been around houses like this since I was a little girl. It was going to take more than this to impress me. We walked to the dining room where the table was perfectly prepared. Mark poured me a glass of champagne as the Chef fixed our plates. After finishing up the delicious gourmet meal, Mark and I stayed at the table and continued making small talk. After an hour, Mark excused the Chef and his two helpers telling them they were no longer needed for the evening and would see them tomorrow. I was also ready to leave, but I hadn't yet discussed my plans to end my new profession. Mark came back to the table after seeing the Chef and his helpers to the door and making sure it was locked.

"Tyler we finally have the house to ourselves," Mark said in a Mac Daddy voice. I gave him a bewildering stare because I wasn't yet sure if the tone was purposeful. When he swaggered over to my chair and caressed his fingers through the loose curls in my hair I instantly became uncomfortable.

"What are you doing Mark?" I asked while shifting my head letting him know his behavior was inappropriate.

"What do you think I'm doing Tyler?"

"I don't know, but you're making me very uncomfortable so please stop."

"That's what I love about you Tyler, you have entitlement issues. You truly believe that you have a right to do and say whatever you want. I'm going to enjoy teaching you otherwise. Once I break you down, our working relationship will be so much easier."

"Excuse me!"

"I didn't stutter. It's time to introduce you to the real world and get you out of that fantasy Princess shit you live in."

"Mark you sound real crazy, so I'm ready to go, now."

"See what I mean? You're under the impression that you can leave just because Tyler wants to. It doesn't work like that. You leave when I tell you too. But before you go anywhere, I want you to come over here like a good little girl and kiss daddy's dick."

I watched Mark in disgust. This was all the fat fuck wanted from the start. Did he really think I was going to suck his dick? He was sorely mistaken. I would bite the shit off before I would suck anything.

"Mark maybe the champagne has you a little tipsy, or you've just lost your fucking mind but regardless none of that is jumpin' off."

"If you want to become the next big thing you better make it jump off. Understand Tyler I make you, you don't make me because I'm already made. I've got my millions and I will make millions more. I can go out tomorrow and find another Tyler Blake and turn her into Citrus. Nobody would know the difference. So if I was you, I would crawl on my hands and knees and suck this dick until I beg you to stop or your career as a Superstar is over. Do you understand me you ungrateful cunt?"

I laughed uncontrollably and couldn't stop. I could tell Mark thought I was on something and wasn't sure if he should shake the shit out of me, or ask for whatever I was on so he could laugh too. But once he realized I was laughing at him, his attitude shifted back to what it was. I continued to laugh before turning serious.

"You think I care about being your quote Superstar. Baby I'm already a star, the world just doesn't know it yet. But look at you, you're nobodies star. You're just a fat fuck with an over inflated ego that nobody would give a shit about, if it wasn't for the fact you bamboozled your way in this business with your drug money and riding the coattail of a real talent like Tah Tah. Nigga I don't need you or LaFamilia Records. As a matter of fact, I was going to tell you I wanted out of this farce of a career. I'm no rapper never was. I let you get me caught up in some bullshit dream that I never wanted to be a part of. When I do become a star and make my millions it won't be by sucking the dick of a clown ass wannabe Berry Gordy cat like you."

I picked up my purse and pulled out my cell phone to call a cab to get the hell out of Mark's house. I knew the look he had on his face and it meant trouble, but it wasn't happening tonight. There was a champagne bottle sitting right in front of me on the table and if Mark stepped any closer I was busting it over his head. Somebody was going to die tonight if that motherfucker put his hands on me. The thought of being raped again was too much for me to handle. At this point I would rather take my chances catching a case than letting another man violate my body.

"Mark whatever you're thinking, rethink it fast. If you put your hands on me, you better kill me; because if I make it out this house alive not only will I file criminal charges against you, I will make it my mission to destroy whatever respectable reputation you think you have in the music business."

By the intensity in Mark's face he knew I wasn't bluffing. "Have it your way Tyler, but we will cross paths again, and next time I might not be so willing to let you go. I'm sure you'll have no problem finding your way home."

With that, Mark went upstairs and left me alone. I called a car service and finished drinking the last glass of champagne while waiting for my ride. Once again I was back to square one trying to figure out my life. I wondered how much longer I would have to battle for my rightful place. Until the answers were revealed to me, I would keep fighting for the little girl in me that needed to be protected.

After my awful experience with Mark I couldn't seem to find my niche and needed to take a step back and gather my thoughts. The course I was on was leading me nowhere and I couldn't seem to get on track. I decided I needed to go home and be around my own surroundings in order to regroup and regain my strength. While in Georgia Mother nor Father were anywhere to be found so I did a lot of soul searching and decided that no matter what, I would make it in NYC and wouldn't be coming back to live here for nothing in the world. If I wasn't anything else I was a survivor and determined to be a success. The day I had to come back to Georgia would mean that I failed and that wasn't in the cards. After a week of regrouping I headed back home to New York.

As soon as I walked through the door my friend Chrissie called. She was a cute petite white girl who put you in the mind of a younger version of Sarah Jessica Parker. She was my nightclub sidekick. We both went to NYU and were waitresses at the same restaurant.

"What's up Chrissie?" I was actually happy to hear her bubbly and cheerful voice on the phone.

"Nothing much, I wanted to go to *Lot 61* tonight, do you feel up to it?"

"I actually just got back from Georgia, and like literally just walked through the door. But I've been kinda in a funk and going out to party might brighten my spirits."

"Yeah Tyler this is exactly what you need. You know we always have a blast when we go out."

"Okay, I'm going to jump in the shower and get dressed. Meet me here about eleven."

"Cool, I'll see you then."

After taking a quick ten minute shower, not my normal thirty-minute one, I looked through my closet trying to decide what to wear. From the clothes I bought myself after being intimidated by the stylish New York ladies, to the clothes the stylist bought for my new life as female rap superstar Citrus, I had a ton of outfits to choose from. I opted on these sexy tight leopard pants I bought from a boutique on Columbus Avenue with a black fitted shirt and black snakeskin boots, dabbled on my favorite *Mac* lip gloss and went downstairs to meet Chrissie. I loved my neighborhood because it was surrounded by so many cool spots, from clothing boutiques, restaurants, theaters and clubs. Everything was just a step away. When Chrissie saw me she ran and gave me a hug and kiss, "You look hot tonight Tyler, I love those pants."

"Thanks, you look pretty damn sexy yourself." Which she did, Chrissie not only looked like Sarah Jessica Parker but she had the style of Carrie Bradshaw and the body. We hailed a cab and were on our way. We'd been to *Lot 61* a couple times before and we always had a fantastic time because the deejay played great music and we both loved to dance. But tonight I was going to have fun of another kind. After shaking our asses to the sounds of Jay Z, Chrissie and I went to the bar to get some drinks. When I was about to pay I heard a gentleman tell the bartender it was on him. I turned around to look at who made the offer because the last thing I wanted was some dork sniffing around me all night because he paid for a couple of drinks. I would rather pay for them myself.

"Hi I'm Ian," the tall gorgeous caramel complexioned vision said. I stood there with my mouth wide opened until Chrissie nudged my arm so I would snap out of drooling over the flawless creature.

"Hi I'm Tyler and this is my friend Chrissie."

"Nice to meet you," he and Chrissie both extended their hands and shook. He then turned back to me with a smile that was worth at least a million bucks.

"So Tyler do you live in New York or just visiting?"

"I actually go to school here; Chrissie and I go to NYU."

"Oh that's cool, well I'm just visiting but I would love to spend some time with you. Do you mind sitting with me at my booth?" I glanced over at Chrissie to make sure it was cool with her and she gave me the 'I'm okay' wink and I followed Ian to his table.

What attracted me to Ian besides his athletic build, beautiful smile and gorgeous caramel colored skin was that when he introduced himself to me, he came off as kind of shy and innocent although I'm sure he wasn't either of the above but all the same the disposition was very becoming. We sat down, began to talk and we instantly clicked. I hated how when people first meet you they always ask what do you do, so I never asked that question. I waited for the person to volunteer the information. Ian didn't mention his profession but with his beautiful face and tall lean body I thought maybe he was an up and coming supermodel like Tyson Beckford. I didn't care though. All I knew was that he made me feel at ease and I felt a connection with him, so when he asked me to go to his hotel, I didn't hesitate and said, "Yes."

Ian's limo pulled up to the *W Hotel* and I was excited about what would happen when we got to his room. I expected that as soon as he opened the door we would begin passionately kissing and taking off each other's clothes, but he didn't. All he wanted to do was talk and eventually we fell asleep in the bed and he just held me all night. I went to sleep full of disappointment. I hadn't had any good loving in so long and I was about to burst. I was on tension overload and needed to release myself. I had to settle with dreaming about an earth-shattering, mind blowing sexual experience.

The phone rang early that morning waking us up. After Ian hung up he said, "I have to leave and go to Philly for a basketball game but I would love for you to come with me." When Ian mentioned his profession I was impressed and it all made sense. I didn't recognize him because I wasn't up on basketball players. The only one I was educated on was Michael Jordan.

"Ian thank you for the invitation, but I can't go. I was in Georgia for a week and I haven't even unpacked my bags. Plus I'm scheduled to work and more importantly I'm determined to hit the books and concentrate on school. I hope you understand."

"I guess, but I have to admit I'm disappointed. I was looking forward to spending some quality time with you."

"I want to spend time with you too, but right now the timing is terrible." Although I was extremely attracted to Ian, for the first time I was trying to have some priorities and stick with them. By the vexed look on his face it was obvious Ian didn't take the rejection well but he still asked for my number. I wrote my cell number down on a piece of paper from a hotel notepad so I wouldn't miss his call.

During a break at work I flipped through the newspaper to the sports section to acquire some information about Ian. That's when I discovered he was a franchise player and the league had very high aspirations for him. I kept fidgeting all day waiting for his call and nothing came and I soon realized I hadn't received a call all day. To my dismay that very same day my cell was cut off, so I concluded maybe it wasn't meant to be. After meeting Ian I began to follow basketball more frequently hoping to find out what was going on with him on and off the court.

A month later Chrissie and I were sitting in the Student Union. I was reviewing my notes for an upcoming test and Chrissie was reading the *New York Post*. "Oh my goodness Tyler, Ian is in town!"

"How do you know?" I asked full of hope that maybe I would see him again.

"It's right here in the sports section, the Pistons are playing the Knicks tomorrow night. That means Ian is probably here right now."

"Do you think he will be at the club tonight?"

"There's only one way to find out." I decided to go back to the same club where Ian and I first met and if he really, really liked me, he would be there looking for me…like I was looking for him. That night turned out to be hectic because my waitress shift lasted longer than expected and at the last minute Chrissie canceled and couldn't go to the club with me, which meant I had to go solo. I was running late, and ran home unbuttoning my shirt and pants while on the elevator. Once I reached my apartment I basically jumped out of my clothes, grabbed my low rider *Seven Jeans* and pink tank top. I slicked my hair back in a pony tail, dabbed on some lip gloss and ran out to catch a cab. I figured Ian would be long gone by the time I got there, if he had come at all. All the same, I was anxious so I screamed to the taxi driver to speed it up. As I was walking into the club I saw groups of drunken guys staggering out but none of them were Ian.

Then my eyes lit up, and I swallowed hard when I noticed a tall muscular brown skinned guy wearing a huge platinum and diamond chain about to leave, and realized it was Ian. Luckily he noticed me too, and grabbed my arm. The first thing that came out of his mouth was, "You gave me the wrong number."

"No I didn't my phone was..," While trying to explain, Ian cut me off mid sentence and continued to vent.

"I've been in this club for two hours waiting for you to come. I was about to leave and go to my hotel because I didn't think you were going to show up."

Of course, you already know how romantic I thought that was. I was like "Wow," this guy really likes me. He likes me! "I'm sorry, I would've been here hours ago, but I had to work later than expected. I'm so glad you waited."

Ian grabbed my hand and said, "Let's get out of here." Once again, I was feeling special based on some guy wanting me. That night, we left the club and went back to his hotel and of course we made love. No! I did not see fireworks. I was not madly in love and I wasn't overcome with passion, but there was something about Ian that made me feel safe and that was enough, for now. The next day he had a game, so when he asked me to attend I was delighted.

It was my first time going to Madison Square Garden to watch a New York Knicks basketball game. Ian left two tickets so I took Chrissie. Chrissie was from California, so like me she had never been to a Knicks basketball game. "This is so exciting! Tyler I can't believe we have floor seats at a Knicks game."

I couldn't believe it either. Usually these types of seats were reserved for the home team. I knew that because Patrick had a friend who played on the Atlanta Hawks and would only be able to get him prime seats when they were playing at home. When Patrick moved to Chicago he said his seats were only semi when the Hawks played the Bulls.

"Isn't that Will Smith seating across from us?" Chrissie said enthusiastically.

"Yeah it is, but Chrissie please calm down before you embarrass both of us."

"I'm sorry Tyler but I'm from Temecula, California and I never saw any celebrities back home."

"Chrissie you're so sweet, I love your honesty." Chrissie was sweet and honest. I felt that I could trust her, as much as I was capable of trusting anyone. She didn't seem to be jealous of me the way Lisa was. I got the feeling she was genuinely happy about my new relationship with Ian.

"Chrissie how do you think the life of a star NBA player's girlfriend or wife is?"

"I would think totally cool. Like unlimited shopping sprees, the best restaurants, everything just first class all the way."

All those things were cool, but Chrissie's mind set was so limited. I wanted bigger things in life than that. I already experienced designer clothes and fancy restaurants; I wanted to live like a star. After the game I met Ian in the section for family and friends and we said our goodbyes. He promised he would call soon so I could come to Detroit to visit. I made sure he had my home number this time and hoped that he would keep his promise and he did.

After talking to Ian everyday for a week while on the road, when he was finally headed home he said, "Tyler do you think you can get away for a couple of days? I really want to see you."

"Sure," I said excited about seeing Ian again."

"Cool, I'll have my travel agent book the flight. Is tomorrow good?"

"Yeah that's fine; just make it an afternoon flight."

"Okay I'll call you later on with all the details. Tyler, I miss you."

The next day I was on a plane to Detroit. It was thrilling. Here I was flying high in the sky first class all the way on an *American Airlines* flight to Detroit. All I wondered was could Ian really want to be with me, because I was totally digging him.

Ian pulled up at the airport in a silver big body Benz and greeted me with a sweet hug and kiss, "Baby you look even prettier than I remember."

"Shut up Ian, don't try to pump my head up," I giggled.

"No baby it's the truth. Maybe I just miss you so much."

"Not as much as I miss you."

"Why do you say that?" Ian asked as he cruised down the highway.

"Because if you missed me as much as I missed you that would mean you are smitten, and I'm sure you're not smitten."

I smiled as I said those words and Ian smiled back. With a look of love in his eyes he said, "I think I'm just that."

Something about Ian was so childlike and it only added to his charm. When we arrived to his house I was surprised by how modest it looked. I was expecting some huge mansion on an estate. He explained that this was his temporary house while his permanent house was being built. Of course he had that standard flunky that all basketball players have; you know the one that live with them and builds their whole life around kissing their asses. Ian was no different, but TJ was cool. After we got settled, we went out to dinner at an Italian restaurant and we spent the majority of time stealing kisses and Ian playing in my hair. We seemed like two love struck teenagers.

The next evening, I attended Ian's basketball game and sat in the section where the girlfriends, wives or whatever you want to call them were sitting. It was cold so some of the females had on their long fur coats and were all done up. I had on a pair of sleek black *Richard Tyler* pants, a red fitted sweater, and a simple black leather jacket. I definitely wasn't looking like bimbo Barbie. I was more subtle and sophisticated. The Nia Long look alike and her girlfriend were staring me up and down with that '*die bitch*' look. I heard one of them whisper, "She is sitting in Ian's seats. Is that supposed to be his new girlfriend? She looks like she belongs in the library." They laughed loudly to make sure I knew I was the butt of their joke.

"As opposed to a Brothel," I turned around to get a load of both women. The older white man sitting beside them bust out laughing, and when the women turned and gaped at him with hate in their eyes he quickly turned back to the game while stuffing popcorn in his mouth.

"You must have misunderstood us, because we weren't talking about you."

"Oh, then I apologize. I assumed because I didn't look like I just stepped out of a Pimps and Ho's video then you all were making catty remarks about my attire."

"Excuse me, are you trying to say we look like ho's?" The Nia Long look alike snapped.

I sat back and put my finger to my mouth and glanced up as though contemplating her question, "Yeah basically." I turned back around in my seat, waiting to hear a response from the two haters but they sat there mum for the rest of the game. I figured my comment must have shut them up.

After the game, I went in the back to wait for Ian. That was the first time I saw how women throw themselves at athletes. They are like vultures! I mean, there were grown ass women standing out in the area where fans and kids were waiting to get autographs with their best clothes on, hair and makeup done to perfection, with long fur coats just waiting for these guys; hoping that they would catch their attention. I don't condone what Kobe Bryant did as far as cheating on his wife, but I can definitely understand how it happens. I mean there is only so many times you can pass on some pussy that is just thrown in your face on an everyday basis. It made me wonder why Ian wanted me. I wasn't all glamorous and dolled up like them. Once again it didn't matter because he chose me. I had something pink, and innocent about me; I don't know, but whatever it was, he was with me and not with one of the girls standing on the sideline with their Sunday best on trying to throw him their number. I was relieved when we finally left the building because although he was with me, at the same time I was sickened by all the fake glamour surrounding me. It was enough to make me choke.

"Did you enjoy the game?" Ian asked like a kid wanting approval.

"I enjoyed watching you."

"Perfect answer."

"It's the truth," I said giving Ian a peck on the cheek. He made me feel like a young girl experiencing puppy love for the first time.

On our way home we picked up something to eat and took it back to his house. We went downstairs and sat down on his tan sectional to chill out. We were drinking, he was smoking weed and at that time, let's just say that I had a little alcohol problem, I was a drunk! I never knew when enough was enough. I was a drunk and he was a pot head and a drunk too. Now let's just keep this all in perspective. A drunk and a pothead don't mesh at all. As I was saying; we were downstairs at his house and I was drinking and he was smoking weed. TJ was there and we were all bugging out, laughing and Ian brought up how when we first met I told him one of the reasons I moved to New York was to pursue an acting career and the whole entertainment thing. But I was still surprised when out the blue he said, "Tyler Baby, stand up there and sing a song or perform a monologue or something for me."

"Baby you so silly," I said playfully slapping my hand on his shoulder.

"I ain't silly, I'm dead ass serious," Ian babbled sounding like a drunken sailor.

"Baby I'm not really a singer and I definitely don't feel like doing a monologue," I said slightly laughing. I told Ian 'no' for a few reasons, one I was drunk; two, I was in no mood to put on a show for him and three; let's just say that sometimes I can be shy.

"You better get up there and perform," Ian was shoving me off the couch as to hit the stage. He put me on the spot but I still thought he was playing until to my horror, it turned into a huge argument.

With a drunken slur he yammered, "You better get up there and do something or you gonna make me smack that ass up." I was on the edge of the couch glaring at him like are you for real? Ian went on to preach about how his cousin was some big time music guy and if you're not able to perform at the drop of a dime you can't be an Entertainer. All of that could be very, very true, but I mean really....if I said no, couldn't we like just move on. But noooo...it had to escalate and get even more out of control because hey, I was drunk and he was high.

My eyes were glassy and Ian's were blood shot red. His body seemed to be pulsating as he began ridiculing me and putting me down, yelling all over a dumb song. It escalated to the point where I felt dizzy like the room was spinning. Oh, now I get it— the dizziness came after Ian lifted me up and threw me against the wall. Unbelievable!

"Ouch," I screamed as my back hit the wall. "Why the fuck did you just do that dumb shit; because what, you're bigger and stronger than me, and I'm in your house?" Ian had the audacity to throw me around like he was on the court passing the ball--all over a stupid song!

The fact that I weighed a 115 pounds wet and he was robust, it seemed as though I was literally flying in the air when he threw me. I could hear my back crack when I hit the wall. I was now popping shit especially because of my drunken state, I was pissed!

"You should have done what the fuck I asked you too, making some simple ass shit all complicated," Ian hissed.

"You know what? I'm so out of here. I'm not about to deal with you and this bullshit. I don't give a damn how many endorsement deals you have you're fucking crazy!" Ian's eyes seemed cold and distant as he stared me down like I was the disturbed one. I ran upstairs and started packing up my shit so I could get the hell out of there. It was one o'clock in the morning, but I didn't care. After getting my belongings together I went back downstairs and told Ian I was ready to go.

"Puh, I ain't taking you nowhere. You sound stupid right now," he scolded as he walked back to the couch to sit down.

"I want to leave now. I rather sleep in the airport than stay in the same house with you. Now let's go!"

Ian reluctantly drove me to the airport and we were cursing each other out all the way there. "You a dumb ass chick leaving my house in the middle of the night. Where the fuck is you going, to sit in the damn airport by yourself?"

"Exactly, that idea is a lot more appealing than being anywhere near a cocky sonaofbitch like you."

"Yeah, we'll see if you still feel that way when you start freezing in that cold ass airport."

By this time Ian had totally fucked up my high and I was considering clawing his eyes out before I got out the car. He continued to call me names and I tossed names right back. When he pulled up to the airport terminal I jumped out the car, slammed the door, and didn't look back. I went inside to find out the earliest flight back to NYC. The next flight wasn't until 6:30am and it was now maybe 2:30am. I found myself a comfortable chair, closed my eyes and instantly fell into a deep sleep. An hour later, I felt a forceful hand shaking me. I opened my eyes to find Ian standing in front of me.

"Tyler baby I'm so sorry. I was so fucked up and acted like a real ass. Will you please forgive me?" Of course my initial reaction was *this is so romantic*. Instantly I forgot about the explosive incident that brought me here in the first place. I kept saying to myself....he came back for me, he missed me, and so he must care. That's me, the dreamer, always playing some romantic scenario in my mind.

"Of course I forgive you, I should've just sung a damn song," I said with a slight smile on my face. When Ian held out his hand I grabbed it lovingly, and he picked up my suitcase with the other hand as we walked back to his car and drove home.

That night we made passionate love and our kisses were so intense. As I straddled Ian, he kissed my neck and brushed his hands across my breasts before putting my nipples in his moist mouth. I couldn't feel him deep enough inside of me. My fingernails pressed deep into his warm back and we both moaned with desire. As we gazed into each other's eyes, for the first time Ian said, "I love you Tyler, would you please have my baby?"

"Yes. I would love to have your baby Ian," I moaned, momentarily falling prey to my sexual desires.

Sidebar...Ladies when a guy tells you that he loves you and wants to have babies with you, means that he likes to have sex with you for free! All the same I was like "Wow," he loves me. He didn't have to come back for me. He could've sent me packing back to NYC and never spoke to me again. Ian Addison was a superstar athlete. He had his choice of any woman that he wanted but he came back for me.

The next day Ian cooked me a big breakfast, and took me on one of those shopping sprees Chrissie dreamed about. We talked, laughed, and got to know each other better. I loved how sexy Ian looked when I asked him a question and right before he responded he would lick his lips and smile. I was becoming more smitten with him everyday. When we got back home I dashed upstairs and rumbled through my bags so I could admire all the new outfits and shoes he got me. For the first time in so long I felt like a Princess again. Maybe I finally found my prince charming with Ian.

The following day, I was back on the plane to NYC. When Ian kissed me goodbye, I longed for the day I would be with him again, but he reassured me it would be soon, "I'll be in New York in a couple of weeks, so be a good girl until I come. Call me when you get home." Ian gave me a loving kiss before saying goodbye.

While sitting on the plane waiting for takeoff I admitted to myself I was falling for Ian. No I hadn't forgotten that he threw me against the wall but at the same time I had been through a lot worse. Plus I was excusing his behavior on being high and not acknowledging the fact that he was high a lot. But I'd never dated a professional athlete and he was exposing me to a whole other life, and I relished in it.

Once I got back to NYC reality set in and it was time to hit the books. I wasn't bored, but it was more like I was going to school but definitely not into it. Some of the classes were fun, but I never really enjoyed school. It could never hold my attention, ever! I was going to a few auditions but nothing was panning out. I would get extra work here & there, but I was like why do I have to sit around sets for hours and hours and basically for what......enough money to buy myself something to eat. It couldn't pay my bills!

I found it exhausting because I needed money. New York is extremely expensive and something had to give. Although Ian had plenty of paper it was much too soon to ask for a handout. I definitely didn't want to come off as some hard up gold digger even though before I left he told me if I needed anything to just ask. I figured if the relationship continued on the path we were on, soon he'd start handing over whatever money I needed.

I was meeting Chrissie at the restaurant *Cafeteria* for lunch and we were seeing each other for the first time since getting back from my visit with Ian. Chrissie was exuding her normal *Sex and the City* getup mixing shorts with a bustier and standard four inch heels. Besides Carrie, Chrissie was the only person I knew that could get away with wearing such eyebrow raising outfits and actually look good doing it. After sitting down at a corner table and sipping our usual glass of wine Chrissie dove right in with the questions.

"So how was your visit with Ian?" Chrissie asked inquisitively.

"Let's just say I'm totally crazy about him. We did have a minor altercation at first, but we managed to work things out."

"What type of altercation?" I gave Chrissie the play by play on the incident while she sat with her mouth wide opened.

"Oh my gosh, I can't believe that; what an egomaniac. All his money has made him a pompous ass. Josh would never behave like that." Josh was Chrissie's broke boyfriend who always had his hand out begging her for a dollar.

"Don't get me wrong, Ian's behavior was a tad irrational but he's still a great catch. At the end of the day you can fall in love with a rich man just as easy as a poor man, because underneath both men are still the same. They are going to want to control your life and tell you what to do. Men are dominating by nature, so why would you want to be bothered with some broke ass man running around trying to drive you crazy, when you can have a rich one that can at least give you a better life."

"Tyler you're so jaded, Josh doesn't try to control me."

"Yeah because you do whatever he wants you to do anyway. Just wait until the word no comes out your mouth, and then you'll see just how compliant Josh really is."

Chrissie like so many other women had this game all confused. In her meager mind a non ambitious wuss like Josh was somehow a better man than Ian because he never asked anything of her but money and time. Most women are so desperate for companionship that they will give their last dollar and the time they need to put towards themselves on a man whose only interest is how they can benefit from you. I refused to let that be my existence. Ian had his flaws and was far from perfect, but since getting off the bus he was the closest form of perfection for me.

Chapter Six: Holding On To My

(Pink Fantasy)

A lie is so much easier to believe than the truth. Someone can tell you they want you to be honest, but then everyone hates honesty. It's highly overrated. You want that person to stop before they say something that you may regret hearing, only to then accuse them of deliberately misleading you. All my life I created a fantasy because I didn't want to face reality. But sometimes reality slaps you in the face and you can no longer run from the inevitable.

I kept eyeing my watch as the lady blew my hair straight at the Dominican spot. Two weeks seemed to fly by and Ian was picking me up in a couple of hours from my apartment. We were going to some party tonight and I had no idea what to wear. Ian didn't give me any details he just told me to look sexy. I was debating on whether to wear my red *Narciso Rodriguez* dress or my silk animal print *Jenny Packham* dress. Both were extremely seductive and Ian would like either one since he picked them both out. I heard my phone ringing from the hallway but managed to catch it right before the answering machine picked up. "Hello," I said out of breath.

"Where the fuck have you been I've left you three messages."

"I went to get my hair done. Why didn't you call me on my cell?"

"Because you don't ever answer that shit. You should've called and told me where you were. I don't have time to try and track you down."

"I'm sorry."

"Yeah, you should be," Ian said then instantly jumping to another subject. "So what are you wearing tonight?" Ian was becoming more of a tyrant everyday. Since I left, we would speak everyday and he would basically want a detailed report of my day. If he'd call at a certain time and I wasn't home he would scold me like I was a five year old.

"Either the red *Narciso Rodriguez* or the silk animal print."

"No, wear that nude color *Gucci* dress, I love the way it hugs your ass."

"Okay, whatever you say."

"Hurry up, because I'll be downstairs in twenty minutes."

"Twenty," I heard the phone go dead before my thought was completed. With no time to waste I did a quick fresh me up, applied my makeup the exact way Ian liked, put on my shoes, grabbed my purse and zoomed downstairs. His limo was downstairs right on time. The driver opened the door for me and Ian was on his cell phone not appearing to have noticed as I got inside. I reached over to give him a kiss and he put his hand up gesturing me to wait. Ian finally finished his conversation and I was anxious for him to acknowledge me.

"Come sit over here," Ian patted the spot right next to him. "You look so fucking sexy I'm ready to do you right here in this limo, but I want you to stay looking perfect; maybe on our way back to the hotel."

"I forgot to bring my overnight bag,"

"Don't worry about it; you can pick some things up from the store in the morning. I have a surprise for you."

My eyes brightened up, "Really, what is it?" Ian handed me a *Jacob the Jeweler* box with the most beautiful diamond necklace I had ever seen. I couldn't take my eyes off the sparkler.

"This is for me," I said full of shock.

"No doubt, turn around I want you to wear this tonight with your dress. Now you look perfect," Ian said as he examined me from head to toe. We pulled up to a penthouse on Madison Avenue and there were limos lined up down the block.

"Whose party is this Ian?"

"My cousin's, he's celebrating his birthday." My mind was spinning wondering who the hell his cousin was. When we entered the townhouse, the layout was magnificent.

"This is your cousin's place?" I was in awe because it was breathtaking.

"Yeah, he's doing big things. Come with me I want to introduce you to him." I followed Ian up some wraparound stairs that led to a huge open space where about fifty people were lounging on big cream plush couches. Everyone from Russell Simmons, Mary J. Blige and Martha Stewart were socializing and taking glasses of champagne from the waiters sauntering the room. Ian finally came to a cloud of people and stepped through and I heard him saying,

"What's up cuz? Happy Birthday." There were a couple of models blocking my view so I still couldn't see Ian's cousin. People began dispersing as Ian pulled me in and the guest realized the Superstar basketball player and the guest of honor wanted a private moment. As my view cleared and I glimpsed up before completely focusing I heard Ian say, "Man this is my girlfriend Tyler, and Tyler this is my cousin T-Roc."

My heart dropped as T-Roc extended his hand, "Tyler, that's a pretty name for a very pretty girl." The same words he used the very first time he introduced himself to me.

"Thank you," I said dryly.

"You're a lucky man Ian. How long have you been together?" Ian glanced at me as for me to answer, but I was to numb to say a word.

"About a couple of months, but it seems longer. I think she's the one," Ian beamed. T-Roc was undressing me right before his cousin's eyes, but of course Ian was oblivious.

"Ian I need to go to the restroom."

"Do you want me to show you where it is?"

"No, I can find it." I darted off before letting either one of them speak another word to me. This was too much. I found the bathroom, shut the door and sat on top of the toilet overwhelmed by the turn of events. Should I tell Ian that I slept with his cousin or will T-Roc tell him. Maybe I should just keep it to myself and so will T-Roc. But the way he ogled me, like we shared some sordid secret. I gulped down the two glasses of champagne I picked up on my way to the bathroom and inspected myself in the mirror. I applied fresh lip gloss, fixed my hair and adjusted my dress prepared to go back to Ian like nothing was wrong. When I opened the door, T-Roc pushed me back inside and locked the door.

"What are you doing?" I protested. T-Roc put his finger to my lips.

"Shh, there is no need to get upset," T-Roc managed to say in a cool, calm, collected voice.

"First me, now my cousin, you're turning this into a real family affair Tyler."

"I didn't know he was your cousin, if I had…" My words faded.

"What? You wouldn't have fucked with him? I seriously doubt that. The two of you seem very much in love, but then from our past encounter I can tell what type of woman you are; and you're not capable of love."

"You don't even know me, you have no idea how I feel about Ian."

"A great part of my success is attributed to my gift of interpreting people from limited time spent with them. My diagnosis of you is that you're an Ice Princess."

"I don't give a damn what you think of me,"

"Maybe but I'm sure Ian may feel differently."

"What do you want from me T-Roc?"

"I want us to pick up where we left off." T-Roc peered in my eyes and when his lips touched mine; my body became weak and I gave in to him. His hands glided up my dress and he slid my panties to the side as his finger easily slithered inside me. I moaned as he kissed my neck, and then my breast. In what seemed like one quick motion he lifted me up on the sink, lifted my dress and scooted my body forward so he could taste all of me. Right when I was about to reach my climax, T-Roc stopped. Handing me his business card he said, "You better call me tomorrow no later than two o'clock or I'll be having a heart to heart with my cousin about his new girlfriend."

"I can't. I'll be with Ian tomorrow."

"Well you better get creative." T-Roc exited the bathroom, leaving me to wonder how I got myself in this predicament.

I woke up spooned under Ian dreading the rest of my day before it had even started. I tossed and turned all night due to T-Roc's face flashing through my mind. It was too late to come clean with Ian about my past encounter with T-Roc, especially after our bathroom episode last night. But at the same time I wasn't going to let T-Roc dangle our relationship over my head. I had to settle this situation with T-Roc once and for all, which meant I needed to get home and get my mind right before my two o'clock phone call. Right when I was about to slide out of bed, Ian's erect penis was rubbing against my butt, meaning it's time for his morning fix. As I slowly moved out the bed Ian grabbed me pulling me towards him, "Where you think you're going?"

"Baby I have a million things to do this morning I have to get home."

"What, you better get your pretty ass back in this bed." I fell back in Ian's arms giving him an impetuous kiss and jumping out the bed.

"Ian you know I have finals this week, please don't give me a hard time," although finals were actually the following week, but he didn't need to know that.

"Damn, I have a photo shoot for my *Reebok* Ad and I wanted you to come with me."

"How about I call you after my final and I'll meet you there. Is that cool?"

"Yeah that works, but you better come."

"I will, I promise."

I sat in the cab replaying exactly what I planned to say to T-Roc. There was no way I was going to let him ruin my relationship with Ian. He was the best thing to happen to me in so long, and T-Roc wasn't going to suck me in to whatever sick game he was trying to play. By the time the cab pulled up in front of my building I had my T-Roc speech all worked out.

I paced my living room back and forth as the clock ticked closer to two. I knew T-Roc said to call him by two, but I figured if I called him closer to the cut off time then maybe he wouldn't know how shook he had me. I took a deep breath before picking up the cordless phone and dialed his number. The phone rung once, then twice and then, "Hello," a distinct voice said.

"Hi can I speak to T-Roc?" I asked although I knew it was him on the phone.

"Speaking, who's this?"

"Tyler Blake."

"Right at two, I'm sure you purposely pushed the time."

"No, I just walked in the house."

"Whatever you say Tyler," his confidence aggravated the hell out of me. I wanted this conversation over with so I could forget I ever had a crush on a man named T-Roc.

"Listen, I'm gonna make this quick because I have somewhere I need to be. Last night was a big mistake. I had a few glasses of champagne which made my cogitate skills zero. As far as what took place a few months ago is in the past and that is where it should stay." There was a long silence before T-Roc spoke.

"Tyler you're right and I apologize for putting you in an uncomfortable predicament," T-Roc said with what seemed like genuine sincerity.

"Does that mean you won't be telling Ian about our connection?"

"Is that what you think we have a connection?"

"You know what I mean," becoming flustered.

"If you're asking me if I'll keep our past relationship a secret from Ian the answer is yes."

"Thank you I have to go now." I hung up the phone before T-Roc lured me in. It blew my mind how cooperative he was. How obliging he was confused me and it had me on edge. The ring of my cell phone jarred me from my thoughts. It was Ian and I scurried to pick up. Before

I got a word out Ian belted, "Where the fuck are you and why aren't you here yet?"

I stuttered trying to explain myself, "I'm so sorry, here I come right now" It was almost three and I told Ian I would be to him no later than two thirty. He hated waiting, especially for me.

The traffic was terrible getting to the east side and by the time I arrived Ian was standing in front of his limo talking to an older white guy in a business suit. I waited until they finished before walking up on him. "Hi baby, sorry I'm so late." Ian strong armed me in the car and slammed the door.

"Where the fuck was you at?" Before he let me answer he smacked me in the face. My hands went up in defense mode because he marked me as if about to strike again.

"Ian don't," I sighed feeling perplexed because the driver was surveying us from the front seat; Ian was too preoccupied scolding me to notice or he just didn't care.

"How you gon have me waitin' for you. When I tell you to be somewhere that's where you be; do you understand?" I pondered his words and Ian belted again, "I said do you understand?"

In a soft lost tone I said, "Yes." Ian leaned back and put his head down as though I ruined his day. For the rest of the car ride and even when he shopped in *Jeffrey,* he didn't say two words to me. The silence was driving me nuts and I'd become so desperate for his approval that I blurted out, "I'll never disappointment you again. Whatever you want that's what I'll do."

"You promise," Ian commanded.

"I promise." With my pledge of assurance Ian tongued me down and led my head to his hardness. I pleasured him for the duration of our ride believing that I had earned his love again.

The next morning Ian left and I missed him already. Luckily school was almost over and I could spend my summer with him. Until then, studying was my number one priority. While listening to my answering machine messages I was surprised when I heard my agent saying it was an emergency and please call him back. We hadn't spoken since I went through my whole rapper phase and was curious as to the urgency. I replayed the message one more time before dialing his number. "Hi, Chris it's me Tyler Blake."

"Tyler, Tyler, Tyler sweetie, I've been trying to track you down." Chris's usual grumpy voice was upbeat and friendly.

"Yeah, I got your message what's so urgent?" I asked with suspicion in my voice.

"I got a call today from a guy that heads up the new female clothing line 'Be Me.' Some photographer hired to shoot the ad campaign saw you on that video you did for LaFamilia Records and thought you'd be perfect. He presented his idea to the owner and she loved it."

"So are you saying I got an ad campaign for a clothing line?" Not believing it to be true.

"Exactly, the shoot starts first thing tomorrow morning. The ad will consist of you and two other ladies, but you'll be the lead. Isn't this fantastic? I'm negotiating for top dollar."

"But Chris I'm no model. I'm an actress."

"Actress, smactress who gives a fuck, it is money. They want you. They're paying you, so let's do it. I'll call you in an hour with all the logistics. Congratulations Tyler." I had to put this whole situation on odd, or maybe I was just lucky. But then I always thought luck was for people that served the devil and blessings came from God. So was this a blessing?

Early in the morning a car service was waiting downstairs to take me to a studio in Soho. When I arrived the atmosphere was chaotic and Marvin Gaye's greatest hits were blaring from the speakers. There were a couple of other models, I guess the two Chris spoke of, some executive types and Sasha McIntire the owner of Be Me clothes. She was some Ex Supermodel turned Designer. She had great success with her lingerie line and was now branching off into women's clothing, shoes and accessories. Sasha pranced towards me as though on the catwalk. "Hi, you must be Tyler. It's a pleasure to meet you," Sasha said in some fake Hollywood tone. She was the epitome of over indulgence at its finest with enough bling to put *Fred Leighton* out of business.

"Thank you, I appreciate the opportunity to be included in your ad campaign."

"Don't be silly. You're gorgeous and that body of yours will look perfect in my designs."

"Thanks."

"Follow me over here so I can choose your first outfit for the shoot." Sasha picked out some tiny pale pink satin shorts, that no one but my friend Chrissie would have the balls to wear in public, with a matching white and pale pink tube top. Thank goodness I had nothing for breakfast because a dry piece of toast would have added ten pounds in this getup. While pulling my outfit Sasha formally introduced me to Brianna and Sierra. Brianna was a tall Brazilian looking chic, and Sierra was a mix of Asian and Black. Both women were tall and gorgeous and I still wondered how I fit in this mix.

During the shoot, the photographer placed me in the center and had the other girls behind me like how they do Kelly and Michelle in Destiny's Child. I felt like Beyonce' and they were the step sisters. During a break, Sierra and I were in the middle of idle chatter when I viewed Sasha and Brianna tonguing each other down in the corner.

"Isn't Sasha engaged to some big time movie honcho?" Sierra was now viewing the spectacle that warranted my comment.

"Oh, she's bisexual but so is her fiancé. They're swingers so they'll have the perfect marriage." Sierra responded like this was normal and acceptable behavior.

"Oh okay, whatever works for them."

We worked from 8:30am to 8:30pm until the last picture snapped and it was a wrap. It was hard but the easiest work I'd ever done for the amount of money they were paying me. Plus the exposure would be priceless. Maybe Sasha's husband would see the pictures and think I was perfect for a role. I put my street clothes back on said goodbye to Brianna and Sierra and the rest of the crew and darted downstairs. That whole scene wasn't for me. They had basically turned the studio into a club. Everyone was drinking champagne and snorting coke. I had no problem with the bubbly, but I stopped short fucking with the white girl. I exited the building feeling a warm spring breeze and a silver Bentley Azure was parked in the spot I assumed the town car would be. The driver stepped out and opened the back door and there was T-Roc, "Tyler get in the car." I scanned the area seeing where I could run for cover but the street was isolated and deserted. With hesitation I got in the car and the door slammed behind me.

"How was your shoot today?" T-Roc questioned with authority.

"Who told you about that?"

"You're not that naïve are you Tyler?"

"Ian?" I asked looking puzzled. Last night I called Ian excited about the gig, and of course he didn't share in my enthusiasm, but why would he tell T-Roc? But how else would he know? As the answer was coming to me, T-Roc rained on my parade.

"I wanted to give you something that would make you happy."

"No you want me to owe you."

"I already have that. This was just a gift to you."

"How in the hell did you maneuver that? Did you beg Sasha for a favor?"

"I don't beg for anything. I'm a silent partner. I own fifty percent of the company. But you're a beautiful girl Tyler and once I showed Sasha your picture, she had no problem hiring you for the job. See it's all about who you know."

"Why, why did you do this?"

"Because I can, and I want you. The best way to win a woman over is to give her what she wants the most. You want to be a star and I can make that happen for you."

"T-Roc I'm in love with Ian, your cousin," I said sarcastically, reminding him because he seemed to have forgotten.

T-Roc slightly chuckled, "Tyler you're not in love with anyone and I doubt you ever have been. But what I can give you is a whole lot better than love anyway and it will last."

"Forget it I don't want any part of it."

"Have it your way," T-Roc said nonchalantly.

"I guess that means you're scrapping me from the Be Me ads."

"Tyler like I said before you're perfect for that ad. I only gave you an opportunity that most people never get because they don't have the necessary relationships; but you do, we're family. Well here we are." I peered out the window and we were in front of my apartment building. I moved since first meeting Ritchie and wondered how T-Roc had my new address; but then again, T-Roc probably knew everything.

"Thanks for the ride and modeling job," I said feeling a twinge of gratitude. T-Roc just nodded his head not speaking a word. That night before I went to bed I spoke to Ian for about an hour, but when I fell asleep I dreamed of being with T-Roc.

After my final exam, I took a break to spend some time with Ian. When I arrived his dream house was completed and he was living in a fabulous mansion on acres of land that had its very own lake. His home was truly spectacular and Ian knew it. He especially loved his custom made Steinway grand piano that stood in front of his living room window with a view of the lake. He said it soothed his mind. Unfortunately not to the point that we were able to get along, the visit turned out to be another very volatile encounter.

Ian was pissed I'd gotten the modeling job and still wanted to pursue a career in the entertainment industry. On several occasions we discussed me transferring to a college in the Detroit area so we could be together year round. But I had bigger ambitions than being some basketball player's girlfriend or wife. Having a successful career would give me a sense of purpose and direction that I longed for. Being with Ian was a one sided relationship which was becoming increasingly annoying.

The next evening we had dinner with one of Ian's teammates and his girlfriend at The Whitney. In the middle of relishing in my chocolate glazed bombe dessert the conversation turned bothersome. Ian boasted saying, "No matter how bad a man fucks up, the woman is suppose to stand by his side and hold her position. The man is the leader. The sooner women understand that, the more content they'll be."

"You sound like a complete male chauvinists," I trilled.

"Get over yourself Tyler; you know who controls this relationship." Ian gave his rookie teammate a pound. The wet behind the ear rookie obviously idolized Ian and would agree with anything he said. I stared at the rookie's girlfriend to get a read on what she thought, but the sexy Spanish girl sat there with a blank expression.

"So my opinion is baseless."

"Basically," Ian laughed still showing off in front of his rookie flunky. Was this my life; trailing behind an arrogant, overpaid, egoistical maniac.

After dinner we said our goodbyes to the empty couple and headed to the car. Once inside Ian exploded, "Don't you ever question what I say in front of nobody."

"Ian you were being a complete asshole in there."

"You better watch your mouth or you'll be footin' it back home."

"How can you talk to me like that, like I'm nothing?"

"Don't get all sentimental with me; you know what time it is. Everything you got on I paid for. That rock on your finger I just bought that, the new apartment you're living in, I pay the rent. You were a struggling student when I met you, now you don't want for nothing. So if that means you better keep your mouth shut when I say something you don't like, then that's what you do."

"You bastard! Fuck you and your damn money," I screamed. Ian cursed me out, calling me bitches, whores, and sluts. You know, all of the names that men throw at women when they can't put together a coherent sentence to express themselves. Instead of saying something that makes any sense they call you everything but your government name. Ian was driving all crazy, swerving into the other lanes. I thought we were going to crash.

With fear I squealed, "Ian slow down, this argument is not worth dying for." Ian had all this built up frustration from the presumption that I wasn't putting him first in my life. Ian wasn't interested in me pursuing a career. He wanted a twenty four hour sex slave at his beck and call and damn the bitch who wasn't down for the cause. Luckily we made it back to the house in one piece, but the argument continued. This time, there was no him coming to the airport and saving me, there was no him being my knight in shining armor. I was annoyed and disgusted with his attitude! Never one to hold my tongue, it was my pleasure telling Ian what an idiot he was.

That night there was no making up and making love. Ian was sprawled out on one side of the king size bed and I slept on the other. He woke up in the morning, and left without saying goodbye. I stayed home and surmised where this relationship was going. Circumstances were different this time. At the end of the day, what could we really do? We were two different people. I wanted to be successful in my own right. I wanted to have my own money, my own possessions. Ian wanted a doormat. Our personalities were on complete opposite sides of the spectrum.

I lounged by the pool waiting for Ian to come home dreading our talk. He finally made an appearance five hours later.

"Where have you been?" I asked part missing him and hating him for leaving me for so long without even a call.

"Out," Ian snipped.

"Out doing what?" Feeling that maybe he had been with another woman.

"Doing me," Ian said totally throwing me shade and the conversation was going nowhere.

"That's cool, your overt stank attitude is speaking volumes. You obviously feel that whatever is out there is better than what you have right here, so you win."

"What you mean I win," finally getting more than two words out his mouth.

"It means that the relationship is over, finished."

"Finished?"

"Yeah finished, you do know what finished means? Over…To bring something to an end, which in this case is our relationship."

"What are you going to do without me Tyler? I'm the best you'll ever get."

"Well then you must have a low opinion of me, if you're the best that I can get." I cruised past Ian with contempt. How dare he insult my intelligence as if he is the end all, be all. Ian remained at the pool smoking his weed and drinking some *Hennessy*. He was in his own zone and didn't realize or probably care that I packed my bags and left. It was goodbye to Detroit and hello to New York.

Chrissie and I were laying out in Central Park soaking up the sun in our pink bikinis. It was a beautiful Tuesday afternoon and we both needed the relaxation. I was dosing off to sleep when Chrissie had to strike up a heart-to-heart chat.

"How are you dealing with the whole Ian situation? I know you must miss him." Chrissie knew that I didn't want to discuss Ian any further, but insistent was Chrissie's middle name.

"Actually I'm doing okay. I talked to him yesterday but his attitude hasn't changed. He is totally stubborn." When I first got back to New York Ian had left numerous messages berating me for leaving; it wasn't until he went upstairs two hours later and noticed all my stuff was gone that he realized I left and was furious. He finally calmed down and gave me a half ass apology, but his views on our relationship hadn't changed.

"I agree Ian is a tyrant, but I know how much you love him," Chrissie debated.

"Yeah I do love him. He's coming to New York sometime this week for a couple of days. We're going to try to work things out."

"Great, but Tyler don't let him pressure you into conforming to his barbaric ways."

"Okaaaaay," I gestured. Chrissie was right I had to remain strong because Ian could be so persuasive, but I didn't feel pretty and pink with him anymore.

No longer was I on cloud nine and caught up in the excitement of being with a star athlete. I was maturing and trying to grow up. Although the ad campaign was courtesy of T-Roc, making my own money was liberating and a natural high. I wasn't getting that same high attending basketball games, or eating at fancy restaurants, or shopping. At the end of the day how many designer bags do you really need? It was becoming a bit repetitive. Plus Ian wasn't the brightest crayon in the box and I was craving for intellect. I felt inadequate with Ian because my opinions didn't matter. I was there to strictly please him when he beckoned. We were no longer connecting. When he met me, I had really, like you know, just got off the bus. Initially being exposed to the excitement of the NBA was thrilling. Bragging to my friends that I was dating Ian Addison superstar point guard for the Detroit Pistons, or to see him on a commercial and know that I was in his bed last night would pump my adrenaline. I felt privileged to get on a plane and malinger in a big old mansion, lounge and be glamorous. But at the end of the day, that wasn't my plane, it wasn't my pool and that damn sure wasn't my mansion. I was a visitor!

"Tyler I'm ready to go. This sun is burning me like a piece of toast."

"That's cool because my head is killing me." Chrissie and I were gathering our shoes and zipping up our cut off jean shorts when I heard the chiming of my cell. I finally located the miniature phone but didn't recognize the number.

"Hello."

"Tyler."

"Yes this is she."

"Hi, it's Sasha."

"Hi Sasha, how are you?" Surprised to hear her voice.

"Wonderful, your pictures came out fabulous. I can't wait for you to see the final product. But that wasn't what I was calling about. I'm having a small get together at my penthouse in the *Trump Tower* and would love for you to come."

"Party at your penthouse in the *Trump Tower*," I repeated out loud. Chrissie nodded her head yes again and again.

"Sure, I would love to come. Is it okay to bring my friend Chrissie?"

"Of course, so I'll see you around nine." Sasha gave me her apartment number and hung up the phone.

"This is so cool. I've never been in the *Trump Tower* before and it's in a penthouse. Your life is so cool Tyler. Thanks for bringing me along."

"Chrissie if it wasn't for you I probably wouldn't even be going." I had a feeling T-Roc would be there and I wasn't up to seeing him. T-Roc gave me a powerless sense of being that scared me.

I didn't know what to wear. It was burning up outside, so I wanted something sexy but not too revealing. My lime green satin halter dress by *Miguelina* would be perfect. I sleeked my hair back in a bun and wore the strappy *Emilio Pucci* heels Ian purchased for me a couple of weeks ago. Not to keep Chrissie waiting, although she came fifteen minutes early I gave myself the once over and I was the vision of summer perfection.

"Chrissie why didn't you come upstairs instead of waiting outside," I wondered.

"Because I needed to smoke and I know how much you hate the smell of cigarettes."

"Oh yeah, you did the right thing," Chrissie knew I was damn near allergic to the cancer sticks.

"Oh my gosh Tyler, you are unbelievable in that dress. You bitch," Chrissie said in her teasing cute way.

"Look at you Chrissie! You're putting Carrie Bradshaw to shame in that skintight powder blue one piece short suit." Chrissie loved to wear micro minis and micro shorts to show off her toned curvy legs. Besides bottled blond perfect ringlets, her legs were her next best asset.

Entering Sasha's penthouse in the *Trump Tower* was like hitting the lottery for Chrissie. I hadn't seen her this excited since she got the deal of a lifetime on a vintage *Chanel* dress. When Sasha told me a small get together I figured ten to fifteen people, maybe twenty at the most. It was like forty people scattered around and I assumed there were at least ten more lurking around the corner somewhere. Sasha immediately strolled over with her kisses on both cheeks and counterfeit hug.

"Tyler I'm so glad you could make it, and this must be your friend," motioning to Chrissie with the same fake kisses and hugs.

"Come have some champagne and relax. We also have excellent blow and ecstasy available if you like."

"Champagne would be great." Chrissie and I followed Sasha over to a couch in the corner where the waiter placed a bottle of Cristal and glasses.

"Cheers ladies," Sasha chirped before going off to mingle with her other guest.

"Her penthouse is amazing," Chrissie said gazing around. Sasha's place was no doubt beautiful, but couldn't come close to touching T-Roc's grand townhouse. I scanned the room, but I didn't see him and was actually disappointed. After thirty minutes of having three glasses of champagne and dissecting every person in the party with Chrissie, I was actually having a great time.

"Here comes Sasha again," Chrissie complained.

"Tyler I have a proof of your ad shots in my bedroom. You should go up and see them and tell me what you think."

"That's okay I can wait," not feeling all that comfortable going in Sasha's bedroom.

"No you have too. I really want to get your opinion."

"Well if it's that important to you, I'll go. Chrissie come with me." As Chrissie was standing up to follow me, Sasha grabbed her hand.

"Actually there's this actor that wanted to meet her."

"Really," Chrissie said with eyes beaming.

"Yes, he's extremely cute too," Sasha added to sell the idea.

"You two go head, I'll go look at the pictures and let you know what I think." Sasha gave me directions to her bedroom, and once again I put her on odd. Her aura rubbed me the wrong way. When I finally made it upstairs to her bedroom the door was slightly ajar, a dim light was on and the sounds of Lenny Kravitz was playing. I peeked around the door and gawked at the spectacle I faced. After a full sixty seconds of digesting the scene I stood in the hallway against the wall to catch my breath. There was no way I saw what I just thought I saw. I closed my eyes, reopened and scrutinized the spectacle one more time. The picture didn't change, it was still the same. Brianna and Sierra the step sisters from the ad campaign were having a ménage trios with my prince charming, Ian. Brianna was giving him a professional and fingering Sierra at the same time. My, what skills she had. Ian was sucking on Sierra's breasts and then flipped and started fucking her doggy style while Sierra munched on Brianna's bush. It was all so sick and disgusting.

I wanted to scream, break shit, and fuck all three of them up but my mouth wouldn't open. My body was numb and my heart was frozen. What was it with men and ménage's anyway? One piece of pussy wasn't enough. They had to indulge in two. Ian didn't even call and tell me he was here. Instead he rushed over to Sasha's party for some fucking and sucking. I closed the door choosing not to interrupt the private party. I drifted down the stairs knowing the tears were coming and wanting to leave this place now. I searched the room for Chrissie and to my disillusionment she was at the table snorting coke with some soap opera actor. It was time for me to go, and when I turned to leave there was T-Roc.

"Tyler are you okay, you seem slightly distraught."

"No, I'm not okay. I feel terrible." I put my head down, not wanting T-Roc to see the tears in my eyes. He gently lifted my chin and gazed in my eyes full of concern.

"Baby what's wrong?"

"Can we leave here please?"

"Sure, where do you want to go?"

"Anywhere but here," there was complete silence until we got inside his Bentley that was waiting outside.

"Tyler are you going to tell me what's wrong?"

"I don't want to talk about it. Can we go back to your place? I'm not ready to go home."

"Are you sure that's what you want to do?"

"Positive."

That night T-Roc and I made love as if it were our last night here on earth. My emotions were disseminated all over the place; which caused me to grasp on to him for dear life. Making love to T-Roc overshadowed the pain Ian caused me. With every stroke T-Roc entered my body and Ian left my mind. We fell asleep in each other's arms and Ian's once warm and secure embrace was now replaced by his cousins.

"Rise and shine pretty girl, I know you must be starved." T-Roc had breakfast with fresh flowers on a tray."

"Is it some sort of family trait cooking breakfast for your women friends?"

"Only the special ones," T-Roc smiled. T-Roc was an excellent cook and I devoured the French toast and home fries and downed it with a Bellini.

"That was delicious!"

"I see! You didn't even come up for air. So are you going to tell me what happened last night?"

"What's there to tell?"

"Why you were so upset at Sasha's party."

"I wasn't upset; I was just ready to go." In the middle of answering T-Roc's question my cell phone started ringing and it was Ian. I tossed the phone down not wanting to see his name or hear his voice.

"That's my cousin calling. You're not going to answer?"

"For what, I'm here with you aren't I."

"Talk to me Tyler," T-Roc demanded as he sat at the edge of the bed looking at me. Observing him in his white terry cloth robe, there was a sense of sincerity that prompted me to open up to him.

"At Sasha's party I walked in on Ian having a ménage trios with these two model chicks."

"I'm sorry Tyler."

"Why are you sorry? Ian wasn't using your dick to fuck those two bitches."

"I'm sorry, because I know how devastated you are."

"I'm over the devastated part. Now I'm just empty. Can you hold me? I just want to feel loved." I fell back asleep in T-Roc's arms wishing I could erase the revolting images of Ian. He completely ruined my pink fantasy and I didn't know if I could ever recapture that. As T-Roc held me closely I thought maybe all hope wasn't lost.

Chapter Seven: Exposed

(Secrets in Pink)

*W*hen you have a secret you know more than likely it will come to the light. You may cover it with layers of disguises, but eventually any secret worth keeping will be exposed. All you can try to do is prepare for the ramifications once it's unburied.

"Tyler what would you like to order?"

"Nothing, I'm not hungry. I'll just have a glass of Chardonnay."

"Baby you need to eat something," T-Roc stated in his typical 'I'm your daddy listen to me type way.'

"Fine I'll have a salad. Is that good enough?"

"I see you're in one of your moods. Take this. It always makes you feel better." T-Roc handed me this tiny white pill I had been taking for the last couple of weeks. I nicknamed them dolls. Like from Jacqueline Susann, *Valley of the Dolls*. I didn't know what was in it or even the name, but it always relaxed me and kept my mind free of bullshit, which meant not thinking about Ian. I hadn't spoken to him since my peep show and he still didn't know why I wouldn't accept his calls or see him. I only went home once to get some of my belongings and had been staying with T-Roc ever since. I almost broke down a couple of times to call him, but I would take a doll with a glass of champagne and forget all about Ian for the moment. Sometimes I felt addicted, but hey it was just dolls. It wasn't like it was coke or something. But I was a tad curious.

"Baby what's in these dolls?"

"All natural herbs and stuff, it just relaxes your muscles so you can feel good." I knew there was more to it, but I preferred hearing the bullshit so if things did go bad, I could pretend as though I was in the dark and unaware that I was willingly taking narcotics.

"Okay, that's cool," smiling as if I fed into his garbage.

"Don't forget tomorrow you have to meet with the photographer to take a few shots for the promo ads."

"How can I forget? You remind me every other hour."

"Tyler baby don't get smart. You know how I detest when you're loose with the lips." T-Roc was exactly like Ian, but more subtle with his controlling ways. Ian would hit me or scream to make me follow his commands; T-Roc would try to bribe me by using logic. If that didn't work, he'd simply hand me a pill. T-Roc excused himself to go to the restroom and as I began feeling the affect from the pill my cell rang and it was Ian. I scanned the room and when no T-Roc was in view I answered.

"Hello."

"You finally answered my call. Baby why are you mad at me?" Instead of the bellowing I expected from Ian, he was calm and mild mannered on the phone.

"I can't talk about it right now."

"When can you talk about it? Baby I'm going crazy without you."

"Ian don't do this, I have so much to say to you."

"Then say it," Ian pleaded.

"Not now."

"Come to Detroit and be with me for a few weeks. Whatever's wrong I know we can work it out Tyler." T-Roc stopped and chatted with a gentleman after leaving the bathroom and was now on his way back to the table.

"Ian I have to go, but I'll call you tomorrow so we can discuss everything." As I was hanging up the phone I heard Ian saying he loved me. Could Ian love me though? I mean all men cheat. The ones that don't are because they can't find anyone to cheat with. But a woman is never supposed to know. My ideal man is so discreet and tactful with his indiscretions that it would never get back to me. Because if you don't know, although it may linger in the back of your mind without proof technically it didn't happen. Unfortunately I caught Ian red handed and there was no escaping that. In my heart he was still my prince charming and we belonged together.

"Who were you talking to?" T-Roc asked before even sitting down.

"Just Chrissie telling me about her problems with that soap opera guy."

"How's that relationship panning out anyway?" T-Roc asked knowing good and well he could give a flying fuck.

"Excellent if you call fucking and snorting a relationship."

That night after T-Roc fulfilled his oral fix and we made love, I laid in the bed mulling over what I should do about Ian. I wasn't ready to let him go, but I definitely couldn't see Ian and T-Roc. They were cousins for goodness sakes. This was too much to deliberate. I'd revisit the issue in the morning.

I dreaded getting up in the morning especially to meet with a photographer. I scrutinized myself in the mirror and I was a vision of shit. My energy level was nonexistent and morale low. Luckily T-Roc left two dolls to help me through the day. After throwing on some sweats and a t-shirt I hopped in a cab and headed to the photographer's studio.

"Hi Dave, what's it looking like today?"

"In and out; Sasha left two outfits for the promo ad and she wants one with low cut jeans no shirt."

"Cool, I can handle that."

"I got something if you need a boost."

"You're a sweetheart but I'm good." One sure thing in the fashion business, you can always count on having your choice of anything in the candy store.

Thank goodness T-Roc did leave me a couple of dolls because I was completely drained and wanted to crawl back in the bed. When I thought my morning couldn't get any worse, Sasha came prancing in with her typical over the top attire. Even at eight o'clock in the morning she was in full glamour girl mode.

"Hi Tyler, I've missed you. We haven't spoken since my party."

"Yeah, I've been busy."

"So I hear; with T-Roc no doubt," she grinned. I cracked a half smile, hoping Sasha would take the hint I was in no mood to talk. But of course she didn't.

"You must be awfully special for T-Roc to go through so much trouble for you."

"Trouble…What kind of trouble?" Although I'd rather eat shit and die than talk to Sasha, I was aroused with the basis of her statement.

"Actually between me and you, because T-Roc might get a little pissed if he knew I was telling you this. But personally I think it's flattering that he went through all the trouble." By this point I was going to strangle Sasha if she didn't come right out with it.

"Well T-Roc asked me to hook up his cousin Ian with Brianna and Sierra and have you catch him in the act. Can you believe he went through all that trouble so he could have you? You must be amazing in bed." Sasha stood their telling me this psychotic story with a big smile revealing her perfect porcelain veneer teeth as if I would feel lucky.

"I knew you were a despicable bitch," I sneered. Sasha did a catwalk stand as if she didn't hear me correctly, so I repeated myself. "You despicable bitch; how dare you make me a part of you and T-Roc's game. That whole 'Go upstairs and look at your pictures,' was nothing but a ploy to catch my boyfriend fucking the nit wit twins?"

"Tyler you're taking this way too seriously. T-Roc obviously cares about you a great deal if he would turn on his cousin just to have you. Instead of being upset, you should be honored that someone of T-Roc's status went through the trouble."

"Sasha there is no sense reasoning with you, because in your pathetic mind you can't even comprehend how foul this is." I put back on my sweats and t-shirt to get the hell outta this hell hole while Sasha stared at me with confusion written on her face.

"Where are you going Tyler? You have a shoot to do."

"Sasha, I won't be doing any shoots for you ever again."

"You can't just leave. This is the biggest break of your life. You will never get another chance like this."

"Sasha dear, your never and my never is two different things. Your type of never, you right I hope I never get a break like that again. It comes with too high of a price." As I stormed out the building I heard Dave calling for me to come back not knowing why the confusion was taking place. I was boiling over inside and reached in my bag to get my *Dasani* water and last doll. T-Roc was playing God with my life and that was unacceptable.

I arrived at T-Roc's office demanding to see him immediately, but his Assistant told me he was in a meeting so I just barged in.

"I need to talk to you now," I demanded.

"I'm in a meeting Tyler can you wait for a few minutes?"

"No, I can't." T-Roc with extreme annoyance asked the two men and one woman to step out for a moment. After he closed the door, fire was in his eyes, but it was no match for the fire that was brewing inside of me.

"You look like shit. Why aren't you at the photo shoot?"

"Oh I guess you haven't spoken to Sasha."

"Sasha? She actually did call a couple of times but I told my secretary that I would have to call her back. Why is there a problem with Sasha?" T-Roc was fishing, but I was more than happy to deliver him the bait.

"She told me everything. That bitch had the audacity to think it was somehow cute the way you all set me up."

"Tyler what are you talking about?"

"Don't patronize me. You planned for me to catch Ian in bed with those women. How dare you play God with my life?"

"You don't need Ian, he will never appreciate you. My cousin is just an overgrown kid. You deserve so much more than that Tyler."

"I deserve what, someone like you?"

"Yes, I can make you happy. I will provide the success you crave so badly. Ian will never give you that. He'll want you stuck in the house barefoot and pregnant. You have so much more to offer than just that."

"I hate you. I hate you so much. You stomped all over my heart just so you can win and tear me and Ian apart."

"Tyler you don't love Ian. He is a safe and sure thing for you. There is so much more out there. That's all I wanted to show you. I see so much of myself in you Tyler and I want to expose you to the world. Is that so wrong?"

"T-Roc you don't own me. I'm my own person who can make her own decisions. I don't want to be a part of the life you are creating for me."

"So what are you going to do, go back to Ian? It will never work. He isn't the man for you Tyler."

"Neither are you."

"You say that now, but I guarantee you'll be back. I'm the only person that will ever understand you and accept you for who you are."

I left T-Roc's office feeling more confused than when I arrived. Although I hated T-Roc he had an undeniable hold on me. I opted to walk home instead of taking a cab so I could use the time to reflect. Once I reached my apartment, the first thing I did was take a long hot shower. That had now become a ritual when I needed to wash away my pain. I put on Sade, had a glass of wine and lay on the couch contemplating what I should do next. Over the music I heard what seemed to be a slight knock at the door. I took my phone off the hook, not to be disturbed and hoped it wasn't T-Roc at my door. I peeped through the hole and to my pleasant but shocked surprise it was Ian. As soon as I opened the door, Ian wrapped his arms around my waist and lifted me off the floor.

"What are you doing here?"

"I figured if I kept waiting around for you to come to Detroit, It would never happen." As Ian put me down, he zoomed in to kiss me. I turned my face away because I hadn't forgotten why I stayed away in the first place.

"Baby you still mad at me, what's got you so vexed?" Ian had no idea what I witnessed and after my conversation with T-Roc I almost wanted to forget that it ever happened, but I couldn't. No matter what role T-Roc played; nobody forced Ian to fuck those two chicks.

"Ian a few weeks ago I went to a party and saw you dickin' down two bitches," I said point blank.

"What?" Ian was obviously stunned as his upright position turned humped over.

"You heard me. Does Sasha McIntire ring a bell? You were at her penthouse in the Trump Tower and you were fucking two model chicks named Brianna and Sierra."

"Tyler I..."

"Don't bother trying to deny it, because I saw it with my own eyes."

"Baby I'm so sorry. I know you must hate me." Ian shook his head still trying to digest what I witnessed him doing.

"Baby I'll do anything to make it up to you. It was a mistake. I met them ho's at T-Roc's place. We were all heading to that chick Sasha's party and they hit me off with an E Pill. That shit had me so open by the time we got in home girl's crib they were all over me and I couldn't resist. Baby I had no idea you were going to be there. How do you know those chicks anyway?"

"The ad campaign I did was for Sasha's line, those girls are in the ad with me."

"What? Yo I had no idea you even knew them."

"Ian none of that matters, the point is I can't trust you. If you did it with them, then you're probably doing it with mad other bitches."

"Baby I swear I'm not. I was so out of it that night. My mind wasn't working clearly. I wasn't myself. Tyler please don't let some worthless tricks ruin what we have. We belong together, you know that." Ian was now holding me and he was wearing the cologne that I loved. I missed how safe I felt in his arms.

"Ian will you promise never to hurt me again? That pain was too overwhelming; I couldn't go through that all over again." Ian stroked my hair and kissed my forehead in that special '*baby I love you way*' that I craved more than anything.

"Tyler I promise I will never hurt you that way again. You're my baby, I never want to cause you pain."

"You mean that?"

"I put that on my life. Baby why don't you come to Detroit and live with me? I know you love me and I want to be with you all the time. There is nothing in New York for you; your life is with me."

"I don't know Ian. That's such a big step."

"I tell you what, come for a few weeks and see how you like it. But I guarantee you; I will make you so happy you'll beg me to stay."

"You're that sure of yourself?"

"Positive." Before I could say another word, Ian silenced me with a kiss. He scooped me up leading us to my bedroom. He slipped off my bathrobe as I wrapped my legs around his back. I rocked back and forth feeling his arousal through his jeans. After a flurry of loving kisses Ian slid out of his clothes and laid me down on the bed. He lightly sprinkled kisses until my entire body shivered. Then he wrapped my legs around his shoulders and his tongue entered me. It felt so good that my hands tightly gripped the bed sheets but I couldn't choke back my moans, yelps or squeals.

"Baby I want you inside of me," I said breathlessly.

"Tyler," he said in a serious voice. Do you love me? Do you want to be with me for the rest of your life?"

"Yes I do, I love you so much."

"Then let's make a baby. Will you do that for me?"

"Yes, whatever you want. Just please make love to me right now." With that Ian entered me, and I buried my face in his neck to get a faint smell of his cologne. With every thrust I felt our connection coming back to life. Maybe his home was where I belonged.

When I woke up in the morning and Ian's arms were still wrapped around my body I knew this was where I belonged, with him. Watching him sleep I examined every tattoo, every defining muscle and how beautiful his caramel colored skin was. I don't care what T-Roc said. Ian and I are meant to be together.

"Baby how long you been up?" Ian asked still half asleep.

"Not that long."

"What time is it because I have to get back to Detroit today? You're coming with me right?"

"No doubt; it's ten fifteen."

"I'ma stop at the hotel, pick up my bag and then come get you. Can you be ready by two?"

"Definitely, give me a kiss goodbye."

"I'll see you in a few." Ian threw on his clothes and headed out the door. Today was starting off to be a good day. Having Ian back once again made me feel complete. On my way to the kitchen I noticed my phone was still off the hook and put it back on the receiver and no sooner did it start ringing from a private caller.

"Hello."

"You turned off your cell and had your phone off the hook all night. Are you avoiding me?"

"That's a stupid question, especially since you know the answer to it."

"I understand that you're angry with me, but don't go back to Ian. Take some time for yourself and figure things out."

"It's too late. Ian and I are back together and I would appreciate it if you stay out of our relationship."

"When did you have time to reconcile with Ian?"

"He flew in from Detroit and came over last night. We talked about everything, except for you. Which is exactly how I want to keep it. I'm going back to Detroit with him today and I don't want to speak to you anymore T-Roc."

"You think you can erase me from your life that easily. Tyler I control your mind more than you know. You're making a mistake going back to Ian, but like you said it's your mistake to make. But when you need someone to help you pick up the pieces, call me."

There was silence on the phone and I realized T-Roc hung up. What did he want from me? I knew he wasn't in love with me, but he was determined to own my mind. Whatever it was, I prayed that he would let it go so Ian and I could be happy together.

"Baby I should call my doctor and have him stop by. You've been sick for a week straight."

"I'll be fine. I think I have a minor virus, no big deal."

"Tyler if you're not better in a couple of days, my doctor is coming to see you. I'm serious."

"Ian your concern is so cute. If I'm not better in a couple of days we'll call your doctor."

"I'm heading out to get something to eat with TJ; you want me to bring you something back?"

"No, I'm good," I replied. Ian kissed me on the forehead and walked out of the bedroom. I pulled the covers over my face racking my brain trying to figure out how I was going to get myself out of this mess. I'd been in Detroit for two and a half weeks, sick. First, I assumed it was because my period was about to start. But then I back tracked and realized I was three weeks late. I began rationalizing out loud, "There is no doubt in my mind that I'm pregnant, but I have no idea who the father is. I didn't use protection with T-Roc or Ian. If Ian discovers I'm pregnant he will assume it's his baby and want me to have it, unaware that it might be his cousin's. I have no choice but to terminate this pregnancy immediately. But before I drive myself crazy, I need to be sure."

I dreaded getting out of the bed, but I had to go to the store and get a test before Ian came back. As I drove to the store a cloud of depression fell over me. Unlike before when I was pregnant with Patrick's baby, I knew I didn't want his child. But the circumstances were different this time. If part of Ian was growing inside of me, then I would want to hold on to that. But there was no way I could take the chance that this baby was T-Roc's. Not only would it destroy Ian, but T-Roc would probably end up destroying me. I ran into the store, purchased the test and speeded home. When I pulled up I was relieved not to see Ian's car, but when I took out my keys to open the front door to my dismay there stood Ian.

"Oh my goodness, you scared me. What are you doing here? I didn't see your car out front." My voice was shaky and I hoped Ian didn't sense my nervousness.

"TJ is running an errand for me and I let him hold my car. Where are you coming from and what's in the bag," Ian asked as he reached for it. Before I could yank it away from him he was already opening it up.

"*EPT*, you think you're pregnant?" Ian asked mixed with shock and excitement.

"I'm not sure."

"But you must think there's a chance. Maybe that's why you've been so sick. Tyler this would be incredible."

"Baby don't get keyed up yet because it could very well be a false alarm."

"Well damn no sense standing down here discussing it, let's go see."

Walking up the stairs to the bathroom seemed to be the longest walk of my life. I took each step like it was my last. By the time I reached the bedroom Ian had the box opened and test out. At first I considered dipping the stick in some water so the test would come back negative, but Ian fucked that up, because he wanted to see the process from start to finish. He actually held the cup when I urinated. He kept saying, "I know you're carrying my son, I know that's my son in there."

It was too much to stomach. Ian set his stop clock and when the buzzer went off, with a gleeful smile he said, "It's time." When he came out the bathroom, lifted me up, and wrapped his whole mouth around me to the point I thought I was going to choke; I knew the test was positive.

"Tyler you've made me the happiest man on earth. I have everything now; a beautiful woman and a beautiful child growing inside of you. We have to get married, baby I'm serious. Let's go pick out the biggest rock ever."

"Ian calm down. You're moving way too fast."

"Are you kidding me? I have to call my Moms and Pops and let them know they're going to be grandparents, and they're getting a new daughter. Tyler I love you so much, I can't explain how happy you've made me." Ian gave me one last kiss before he picked up his cordless and made calls to share the news with his family and friends. I wanted to put down the emergency brakes but this car was on cruise control and now driving itself. Right now I would give anything for a doll, but I was carrying a baby inside of me one that it seemed I would be having. I opted for a glass of juice. I was walking towards the stairs and could hear Ian yelling but couldn't make out what he was saying. Then I heard a loud crash. As I ran closer to the top of the stairs, Ian was running up them with all the color drained from his face. Sweat was trickling down and his body was trembling.

"Baby what's wrong is everything okay?" Ian moved closer to me up the stairs and his eyes were stinging.

"I just got off the phone with T-Roc. You were fucking my cousin? Tyler tell me that bastard is lying, tell me damnit!"

"Wait baby wait, wait please wait." I was breathing so hard I couldn't hear anything.

"He said that baby growing inside you could be his. Tyler please tell me there is no chance that our baby could be T-Roc's... Tyler why aren't you saying what I need to hear?" Ian and I were now face to face and I could clearly see the tear coming from his eye.

"Ian I can explain." But there would be no explaining. In what seemed like a split second I was free falling down the stairs. In one quick shot Ian lifted his right arm and gave a blow that knocked me unconscious as I hit the bottom floor.

Chapter Eight: Finding Love

(My Pink Heart)

Finding Love...My love life was in shambles and between Ian and T-Roc I believed I was walking around with the Scarlet Letter emblazoned across my chest. I convinced myself mentally that I wasn't worthy of love and would never truly experience it. But then again, being the optimistic person I am, when one door closes in love another is sure to open.

"Tyler it's so good to see you out and about again. I was beginning to worry that you would never come out your apartment," Chrissie said.

"Yeah, well there was nothing out here I wanted to see. My life is basically empty. Ian hates me and I hate myself." It had been over six months since I actually came out the house looking halfway decent. After my tragic incident with Ian I went into mourning and always came out the house looking like shit. It was now 2000, and half of the new millennium already seemed to have passed me by.

"How can you care what Ian thinks. He pushed you down the stairs and caused you to loose your baby. You should've brought him up on criminal charges."

"Chrissie what do you expect? His own cousin told him that the baby I was carrying could be his. Talk about being devastated, I'm surprised he didn't kill me."

"Hello...that was his intention. You just so happened to live. Or maybe he wanted to guarantee that your baby never saw the light of day because he wouldn't be able to handle it if it turned out to be T-Roc's.

Whatever the reason, he is fucking crazy and you should be grateful he is out of your life."

"Maybe, but I don't feel that way. I'm lost and I don't know what to do to find my way."

As Chrissie lectured me about getting over Ian while we ate lunch at *Da'Silvano*, some unassuming gentleman walked passed me, made purposeful eye contact and turned back his head to smile. Here was another creep trying to undoubtedly get in my pants. I didn't take it seriously. I mean this is New York City and seeing men flirt with just about everything that had a pulse became the norm. Not thinking too much of the crafty glance I continued chatting it up with Chrissie and drinking my Kir Royale.

About ten minutes later the waiter sat the flirtatious guy and his friend's right behind me. One of his friends' that was sitting the closest to me sparked up some half ass conversation.

"Hi sexy, would you and your girlfriend like a drink?"

"You mean besides the one that is already in my mouth?"

"Excuse me miss, I was just offering you and your girlfriend a drink."

"No thank you, we're fine."

"Yeah you definitely that, so can I buy you a drink or what?" After responding sarcastically to his question I recognized that he was some up and coming 'would be' Rapper. At this point anybody remotely in the music industry was a major turnoff. I was hoping the 'would be' Rapper picked up on my cynicism and ended our little chat.

A few minutes later he got up and I heard someone else say, "That's an interesting tattoo, what does it mean?" I had on low rider jeans so the Japanese symbol on my buttocks was impossible to miss. I turned around and studied the man who made the comment and saw it was the unassuming gentleman from earlier. His eyes were enthralling and from using that topic of conversation he somehow maneuvered a seat at the table with me and Chrissie.

"So what does the tattoo mean?" The boyishly handsome gentleman asked.

"Freedom."

"Freedom...that's interesting. Who are you trying to be free from?"

"Who said I was trying to be free from somebody?"

"Just a thought, so what's your name?"

"Tyler and this is Chrissie." Chrissie gave a slight wave to show she was mad this man was interrupting our lunch. Normally I would be giving the wave too, but something about his subtle cool demeanor was engrossing.

"I'm Brian. I would love to call you Tyler."

"I'd like that too, I responded." Chrissie was burning a whole through my sweater with her intense glare. I wrote my number on a napkin and was actually looking forward to hearing from Brian.

I was sitting on my red canvas couch engrossed in a juicy Jackie Collins book when Brian called.

"Hi, it's Brian. I don't know if you remember, but I met you yesterday at *Da'Silvano*."

"I remember you silly."

"Oh, I was just checking. I don't know how many guys you know with the name Brian," he said being funny. I thought it was cute.

We ended up having a meeting of the minds for hours. He seemed to be everything that I needed in order to put my guard down with a man. Nothing about him was threatening and that was refreshing. His spirit was unlike any other man I had ever met.

The next day Brian and I became absorbed in another two hours of non-stop chatting. With the conversation never seeming to end we decided on no more phone talk. We needed up close and personal talk. As I was waiting in front of my apartment building, I kept trying to remember how he looked physically because he had on a hat when we first met. I was pleasantly surprised when I opened the car door and saw the cinnamon complexioned guy with the smooth bald head. He greeted me with a mega watt smile with a dimple on his right cheek. His body frame was small but with strong muscle definition.

Mary J. Blige was playing on the radio, and I was humming along as he drove down Broadway. "Are you a singer?" Brian asked.

"No why?"

"I'm always looking for talent, I'm a Music Producer." As the walls seemed to be closing in on me, I realized throughout the hours of conversations not once did we discuss his profession. I didn't ask and he didn't volunteer the information. The last person I wanted to get involved with was another industry cat. Maybe he was new to the scene and wasn't turned out yet. His ride was fly, but niggas can buy that after they sell their first track; which most do.

"So you're a Music Producer? Who have you worked with?"

"Jay Z, Jennifer Lopez, Mary J. Blige, Nas," and the list went on and on. He definitely wasn't new to this. There was only one Music Producer named Brian that I heard of in this industry and I was hoping he wasn't him. But I had to ask.

"Are you Brian McCall?"

"Yep, you've heard of me?" He said with a big smile.

"Who hasn't heard of you? You're like one of the biggest hip hop producers in the business. Your beats are classics."

"I'm flattered. Are you in the music business?"

"Hell No!"

"Why you say it like that?" Brian asked with his faced frowned up.

"Actually if I knew you were in the music industry. I would've run in the opposite direction. But then again I should've known. This is New York, you're driving a hundred thousand dollar car and you're young and black. I haven't seen you on the big screen or any sneaker ads, so you're not an Actor or Athlete. What else can you do but be in the music business. You don't really strike me as a pharmaceutical dealer."

"That's a little cynical, wouldn't you say?"

"Call it what you like," I said fidgeting in the car seat.

"Does that mean you won't go inside with me for a minute?" I glanced out the window and we were on West 54th street parked in front of the *Hit Factory.*

"Oh, no thanks I'll wait in the car for you."

"What's the problem? Who is it that you don't want to see?"

"Brian, go handle what you have to do. We'll talk when you get back." He shut the door a bit put off with my attitude. Between T-Roc and his flunkies, and Mark and his flunkies I was bound to run into somebody I knew at the studio. I wanted to avoid any encounter at all costs.

Brian was gone for about fifteen minutes but came back with the same attitude he left with. He didn't say two words to me until we were sitting down at the *American Park* restaurant at Battery Park.

"Talk to me Tyler. Tell me what ghosts are haunting you?"

"Excuse me?" Brian's question threw my mind in a tailspin.

"To be so young, you are so intense. What has your mind so damaged?"

"I seem damaged to you?"

"To be quite honest, hell yeah; but I want to help you."

"Help me? I'm beyond help."

"Everyone can be helped Tyler but you can't be afraid to let people in who want to help."

I spent the rest of the evening divulging all my skeletons to Brian. My disastrous relationship with Ian and T-Roc, my momentary bout as a Rapper under the guidance of shady Mark, and I even shared the nightmare I have every night of Trey blowing his brains out. His face truly did haunt me.

Brian sat and listened without interrupting me once. He was so sweet and attentive. With other industry cats I dealt with, it was all about them. Their attention came with strings attached. Brian seemed to genuinely care about the demons I was fighting. He was extremely humble and down to earth, especially for a Producer of his status. Not once did he make a move on me. He never so much as tried to kiss me and unlike Ian, Brian was intellectually stimulating. The combination of his mind and the physical attraction drew me in.

When we pulled up to my apartment I couldn't hold back. "Brian will you give me a kiss goodnight?" I asked wondering if the question came out as innocent as I felt. Brian leaned towards me and when his lips and tongue touched mine the chemistry was undeniable. I got butterflies in my stomach and that tingling feeling. It was amazing.

That night my mind was ambushed with all sorts of thoughts. I kept tossing and turning thinking maybe he wasn't any good in the bed because he wasn't putting the moves on me. I wondered if maybe he was lacking in the area where it counted. I decided it was time to nip my thoughts in the bud. I needed to find out once and for all what was going on down there. If he was lacking, there was nothing I could do for him besides be his new best friend.

Some might disagree, but in my opinion if two people aren't sexually compatible, the relationship is dead before it has even started. Several elements go into making a relationship work, but at the end of the day when you all are having problems like every relationship will—sex is important. If the two of you don't have enough passion and lust to make love and forget your differences for just a moment then how are you ever going to get through any real storms? I had to know if Brian and I were compatible sexually because I was falling for him.

"It's beautiful out here tonight," I said as Brian and I took a nighttime stroll through Central Park. We were laughing and holding hands when I suggested, "Why not play a game of Truth or Dare?"

"Truth or Dare... you're taking it way back to junior high school."

"We can play the adult version."

"Which is?"

"Truth or Dare and take off your clothes."

"We can skip all that. How bout I just dare you to strip down right now." I glanced around the park and not a soul was in sight. I went behind a tree and reappeared in my midnight blue bra and panties. Brian scanned me up and down and said, "That's not naked you basically have on a bikini."

"Really?" with that I unclipped my bra and slid out my panties. The whole episode was turning me on.

"That's more like it," Brian said with greed in his eyes. Although I could see how much he wanted me, I respected the way he took his time crossing my path. His hands were touching my skin and gently exploring my body. He obviously had never done any sort of manual labor because his hands were as soft as a babies. His touch was sending chills down my spine. His lips melted on my neck and the nighttime summer breeze on my naked body escalated my arousal. The kisses became more and more passionate and I wanted to be with him right under the tree. I rubbed down his pants for a spot check, but with his big baggy jeans, it was impossible to get a read. I was like fuck it. I'll take my chances. This had to happen tonight.

Between kisses and heavy panting I managed to say, "Brian I want you now, I can't wait."

"Right here under the tree? Tyler there is nothing but dirt and grass here."

"Well let's go back to my place." I threw my clothes on and we headed to his car. Once inside we could barely keep our hands off one another. I was so anxious and overcome with desire that I demanded he pull over.

"You want me to pull over?" Brian asked in disbelief.

"Yes please," I said in an 'I want you so bad' tone. After comprehending the seriousness in my voice he scrutinized the area for a quiet place to pull over.

I chewed over the possibilities of what was waiting for me underneath his pants, or the major disappointment. I stripped off my clothes as Brian parked the car. Luckily he was pushing a Range and neither one of us were massive so it was plenty of room to make it happen. Once he was in the backseat the fervent kisses back and forth were in full swing. My curiosity was driving me wild. For a flash I reminisced about LL Cool J's song *Back Seat of My Jeep*. When I watched the video, I conceptualized playing a part in one of the scenes and now the experience was happening to me.

I eagerly undressed him, starting with his pants. He stepped in and took off his boxers. I ogled his better half for the first time and was like, "Wow." He definitely had nothing to be ashamed of and wasn't holding back out of embarrassment. As a matter of fact he was on point; I couldn't have created a more perfect size. I wanted him inside of me and when he entered we became one.

During our ride home Brian and I continued our fervent kisses and while he ran his fingers through my hair, he grabbed it tightly. He turned my face towards his so we were eye to eye and he asked, "Why are you trying to make me love you?" His mood surrounding the question was eerie but yet powerful.

"Because I need you to love me," I said intensely. You know me, I love intense because intensity spells drama and drama spells stimulation--everything I crave. After our night of passion we were inseparable. Even though we loved to talk and laugh at one another, we loved being in the bed even more; our favorite pastime bonded us.

In the beginning of our relationship I don't even really want to call it making love because it was more like obsessive sex. Our lust for one another absorbed our whole minds. We would do it anywhere at anytime. Brian couldn't get enough of my insatiable appetite for sex. It was never enough for me and I only craved it from him.

Big Pimpin', by Jay-Z was blaring from my CD player and I danced in front of the full length mirror like I was the star of his video. While pretending to be Jigga, I was getting dressed to go to the movies with Brian. When my phone rang, I didn't bother to look at the caller ID because I knew it was him telling me to hurry up. "Brian I'm almost ready."

"Who's Brian?" The serious voice asked sounding exactly like Ian's. The last time I heard his voice was when he came to see me at the *Ritz Carlton* in Dearborn. After Ian knocked me unconscious he had TJ take me to the emergency room. Of course he told the nurses and Doctor it was an accident and when I finally woke up I backed his story. Although the nurses took it upon themselves to call the police because of the bruise on my face from when Ian knocked the shit out of me; I stuck to my story that the lights were off and I hit my head on the stairwell and tripped and fell. The officers didn't seem convinced but they couldn't prove otherwise. Of course the Doctor informed me I lost the baby, which wasn't a big surprise. I stayed in the hospital for a couple of days and when I checked out TJ picked me up.

TJ drove me to the hotel, gave me a room key and told me Ian would come see me later. When Ian arrived he could barely make eye contact with me. It was like going over my ordeal with Patrick all over again, but this time I didn't kill the baby, Ian did. Out came that same envelope. This time there was no cash but a check.

"Take this," Ian said as he handed me the envelope.

"What is this money? I don't want your money Ian." When I spoke those words I meant it. "If this is hush money, you can take it back. I'll never tell the police or tabloids what really happened," I said solemnly. I considered myself responsible for Ian's actions. No way would I bring him further humiliation by letting the world know that he caused me to have a miscarriage because I didn't know if he or his cousin was the father.

"No, it isn't hush money. I know you would never do that."

"Then what is it for?"

"Because I can't be with you anymore Tyler, it would hurt too much. But the baby you were carrying could've been mine, and I was the cause of its death. That will fuck with me for the rest of my life."

"This money isn't going to change that."

"Maybe not, but I'm hoping it will ease my conscious. The rent for your apartment is paid up for the rest of the year. This money will hold you over until you decide what you want to do."

"I don't want it. This is guilt money, and the only one that should feel guilty is me. Ian I'm so sorry, but you have to believe that I love you and I never wanted to be with T-Roc. After I caught you with those girls my heart was broken and I felt alone. T-Roc was there to console me; although I eventually found out he set it up to work out that way. If you could only forgive me, I know we can make this work." I walked towards Ian and put my arms out to hold and feel his embrace; but he motioned his hand for me to stop.

"Don't," Ian quavered. "I don't know what can happen in the future, but right now there's no way I can be with you Tyler. The whole T-Roc situation is fucked up, but it doesn't change the fact you let my cousin feel inside of what I thought belonged to me. I don't know if I'll ever get over that, but I do ask one thing of you."

"What's that?"

"Under no circumstances do I want you to go back to my cousin. This money should hold you over for awhile, and if you do need something call me. Don't call him. If you ever truly gave a fuck about me, then do what I ask."

"I will do that. I promise I will never have anything to do with T-Roc again." Ian turned around and walked out the door. I opened the envelope and there was a one way plane ticket back to New York, and a check for two hundred and fifty thousand dollars. Once again Ian was using his money to control my life even if he wasn't going to be in it. I considered how I could chill for a minute with this type of money and not worry financially, but then this was blood money. This check was a substitution for the unborn child Ian took away from me. I ripped the check up into tiny pieces and flushed them down the toilet. That was the only way I could free myself from the guilt and pain of my sins. Here it was six months later and Ian was on the phone, questioning me as if he had never left my life.

"Brian is a friend of mine," I answered as if it was my duty.

"Your friend huh?"

"Yeah."

"I was checking up on you because you never cashed the check. Are you maintaining financially, or is your friend handling that for you?"

"I'm okay. I've been working a part time job and going to school."

"Why didn't you cash the check Tyler?"

"I didn't want your money that's all, and honestly I don't want to discuss it any further."

"Well can we discuss us?" Ian said seriously.

"What about us?"

"Tyler I was beyond pissed with you a few months ago, but everyday I wake up in the morning and before I go to sleep at night, you're all I think about. I want to give us another try. I still love you." Ian's words were bittersweet. I questioned whether Ian ever loved me, but it didn't matter because I now loved someone else. Brian had become so important to me. The first few weeks of us talking for hours and hours, I shared my private thoughts and experiences with him--things I had never shared with anyone. When we made love for the first time, we connected emotionally and physically and it was perfect. We clicked and Brian was definitely somebody I wanted to share my life with.

"Ian I yearned to hear those words from you again, but it's too late. The friend I spoke of is more than that. I love him. He understands me and he loves me too."

"Tyler you couldn't share the same love with him that we have."

"I don't even know if what we shared was love. Maybe we fulfilled a void in each other's lives--your need to control and my need to be controlled."

"No matter what you think, I do love you and I want you back. If you believe this other guy can make you happy then I won't try to come between that. But Tyler if you ever need me, call me."

I stared at the phone after Ian hung up. He was supposed to be my Prince Charming but he wasn't after all.

"Yo Eddie Murphy was so funny back then," I giggled as Brian and I sat on my couch watching *Raw*.

"Yeah, he was a funny cat. Now he's white bread All American. He's definitely not the same Eddie Murphy that came in this game starving and had us crying on *Saturday Night Live*."

"You ain't never lied." I hollered agreeing with Brian.

"Losing that hunger is what makes you loose your edge. You have to always go at something like it's your first and could be your last."

"Is that how you should proceed in relationships too?"

"Yes if you believe you've found the one you want to spend the rest of your life with. Just like I think you might be the one, so I'm keeping you under my thumb."

"Oh, that's why we spend so much time together? You want to make sure no one swoops me up."

"Something like that, but to be on the safe side I have an idea…My lease is about to be up on my crib and your lease is about to be up, how about we get a crib together?"

"I don't know Brian."

"What's with all the hesitation? You don't want to live with me?"

"We're having so much fun right now and having a place of my own keeps the relationship sexy and unpredictable. We have plenty of time to move in with each other." I did love Brian but I wasn't in love, and living together would just complicate things. I was also feeling that whole Destiny's Child *Independent Women* Theme.

"I think that's a mistake, but if that's how you want it, then so be it." Brian's statement and delivery was a tad uncanny, but I dismissed it and we continued to watch *Raw*.

"I can't believe you managed to meet me for lunch. Every since you started dating Brian, you never have time for me."

"I'm sorry Chrissie, but you know I love ya baby." I said as we were having a late afternoon lunch at our favorite spot, *Da 'Silvano*.

"Whatever…I hope you're not here to break news of a whole baby, horse & carriage thing."

"No, not yet; Brian actually made the suggestion to move in together but I think it's too soon. But I do have to move. My lease is about to be up and I definitely can't afford the rent."

"Why not ask your new boyfriend?"

"Brian is different from the other guys I've dated. I want to show him that I can be independent and stand on my own two feet. If I can do that, then I can earn his respect."

"Oh brother...you've really fallen hard for this guy. I hope he's worth it Tyler because you're about to do a lot of struggling."

"Tell me about it. I don't want a roommate and I can't possibly afford a place in the city, so I think I'm going to have to take it to the boroughs."

"What! You can't be serious?"

"I have no choice."

"No. You do have a choice. You could always call Ian."

"I'm not going to do that. I'm committed to Brian. I was actually considering moving to Brooklyn. That's where he's from."

"Now you wanna be one of Brooklyn's finest. Where is my friend Tyler? What has happened to her? Excuse me for a minute I have to go to the ladies room." As Chrissie walked off to the bathroom I thought about what she was saying. My lifestyle would change a lot; but I wanted a real relationship, not one that was dictated by money. It was important for Brian to understand that I wanted him for him and not because of who he was or how much money he had. This was my way of doing that.

When Chrissie sat down I noticed white powder under her nose. "I know you're not still fucking with that shit!"

"I had stopped," Chrissie took a deep breath. "But after your confession of this new nightmarish life, I had to medicate myself."

"Funny," but I'm serious Chrissie you need to leave that crap alone."

"It's not that big of a deal. I'm a social user. What about you and those pills you used to take?"

"I'm through with all that. Every since I've been with Brian, I haven't felt any sort of depression. My dolls are a thing of the past," I assured her.

Interestingly enough a few weeks later a friend of Ella's knew this couple who lived in the Park Slope area. They recently had a baby and needed a bigger place so they were subleasing their apartment. Brian went with me to take a look at the place and make sure it was okay. The neighborhood had tree lined sidewalks but the building was a walk-up, meaning no elevators, and it was smaller than the apartment I had in the city. Let's just say I wasn't excited about moving in because it definitely wasn't 66th and Central Park West. But the price was in my range and it was available ASAP. Brian gave his stamp of approval so it was a go. As Chrissie put it, I began the process of being one of Brooklyn's finest. To some people, they would have thought it was a nice apartment, but I was from Georgia and always lived in beautiful homes with pretty neighborhoods. I considered myself to be struggling in the city and now here I was in Brooklyn and I definitely wasn't feeling pretty in pink.

After settling into my new place, Brian had to go to Miami to work with Busta Rhymes for a few weeks. He asked me to come, but between school and work I was hectic. I somehow managed to get a few days off. I looked forward to spending time with Brian in a different place and getting some sun. After my trip to Miami though, I had to reevaluate if Brian was really 'The One.' There are certain traits that I believe a man should have and Brian hadn't learned them yet.

When I arrived in Miami, Brian was at the gate waiting. I had an obviously stank attitude, so he asked, "What's up? What's wrong with you?"

"Brian why would you make me fly coach?"

"Excuse me?" Brian snorted as if he didn't hear me correctly.

"I'm a little...No; a lot bothered that you had me fly coach instead of First Class."

"Come on, let's go." Brian said, ignoring my complaint.

At this particular time I wasn't counting Brian's pockets but I thought he had been in the game long enough that he could afford to put me in a first class seat. So I was furious that I had to fly coach on my way to Miami. A limousine was waiting for us outside, which added to my fury. You have a limousine waiting for us, so then you could have put me in first class. Don't half ass it. I could tell by the way Brian was looking at me he thought I was an obnoxious snob. I wasn't a snob, but when you like something you just like it.

When we arrived on Ocean Drive my eyes immediately became fixated on the tall elegant art deco hotel The Tides. I was thrilled when I realized we were staying there. When we got to the hotel room and Brian opened the door, the interior was luxurious and spacious. The oceanfront room had all soft tones of beige, white, taupe, and sand. The serenity of the room put me in a romantic mood and I was no longer agitated with Brian.

We were spending time luxuriating on the beach, dining at the best restaurants, but once again I became a little annoyed. We weren't doing any shopping. I was sitting in the studio with him all day and became bored with this whole trip. The only purchase Brian made was some roller blades and that was for himself. I was like, "Okay I'm in Miami and you fly me here in coach, and we're not going shopping? This is not looking good for us. The future doesn't look too bright."

My biggest pet peeve is a cheap man. Every man that I dated was giving in terms of knowing that women love gifts. That's part of feeling pretty and pink. That idea goes as far back as to when I was a little girl and one of the few memories I have of my Daddy who was only a Plumber. When he would take me and Ella shopping he would include my friends because he wanted to be fair. I had little room for compromise in that belief. But right before it was about to be curtain time, Brian unleashed his trump card.

On the third night in the *Tides* Hotel I can honestly say that I made love for the very first time in my life. Coming back from a late dinner I was feeling exhausted. I took a long hot shower to relax myself and get ready for bed. After drying off and lathering my body with lotion, the bed was calling for me. Brian was already in the bed watching a movie. The sky was clear and the moonlight and stars were shining through the windows. This was the type of night where fools fall in love.

The crisp sheets felt so good under my naked warm body. Brian turned off the TV and the moment I closed my eyes his hands gently spread my legs apart and his warm tongue entered me. Brian was licking my clitoris with elegant strokes combined with the needed force at the same time. My past boyfriends had tried to gratify me this very same way, but none made me fall into an abyss of pleasure like Brian.

"Baby nobody has ever made me feel this way. I don't want you to ever stop." I said awing in heavenly bliss. Brian's oral pleasure gave me a full flush orgasm. I could feel the powerful gushing of cum leave my body. Without so much as a pause, Brian kissed on my stomach and tickled his tongue in my belly button. He did it just long enough to give me the right affect. With his hands he caressed my breasts and I just luxuriated with my eyes still closed, not wanting this to end. As though he was reading my mind, his hardness entered inside me at the exact moment my body was calling for him. I wrapped my legs around his neck so he could go as deep as possible. His strong arms were pressing down on the bed holding me up as I was clinching his back and my breasts were pressed against his chest.

I never wanted to let Brian go. I couldn't hold him tight enough. With every stroke, a part of my soul became his, until finally it happened. This explosion of ecstasy overcame my body again. I was having my second orgasm in less than an hour by the same man for the first time in my life. At first I couldn't quite grasp what was happening to me, because this was a wake up call. I had to digest the fact that I never had an orgasm. All my other sexual experiences where I just knew I was getting mine were a mirage.

"Brian you have sent me to heaven. This is the most unbelievable feeling I ever had." I realized at that moment every other sexual experience I had was nothing and meant nothing. During the orgasm my eyes literally rolled to the back of my head. I screamed so loud that I startled him.

"You mean that?" Brian asked as if wanting to be sure of the sincerity of my statement.

"I'm a hundred and fifty percent positive. Out of all our many love making sessions this was the first time you ever made me feel this level of pleasure...Baby I want to marry you," I said laughing. I wasn't actually ready to marry Brian, but his love making skills made him the number one contender.

For that brief time I forgot I had flown to Miami in coach or that he hadn't bought me a damn thing except provide food and shelter since my arrival. Contemplating a short lived relationship was out the window. All material gain seemed pointless. All I longed for was that internal calm that enveloped my body.

I hopped on the train rushing to meet Chrissie in the city. I loathed the commute from Brooklyn to Manhattan, but nothing in life is perfect. I didn't want to be late because Chrissie said this meeting was extremely important. In Chrissie's last year at NYU she got an internship at a high profile publicity company. They hired her full time after she graduated and she met all sorts of celebrities. She didn't give me the name, but said she met a celebrity mother who was launching her own styling company and wanted to bring her on board. Chrissie in turn thought it would be a great opportunity for me and we were meeting the woman to discuss a potential job position.

When I reached the office building on 25th and Park, I took the elevator straight up to the 14th floor where Chrissie said she would be. The doors opened directly to the huge loft office space. The layout was still in the beginning stages, but the color schemes were in place and everything was black, silver and white.

"I'm so glad you made it," Chrissie beamed. "With your new Brooklyn zip code, I had my doubts you would get here on time." Chrissie was still giving me a hard time about living in Brooklyn, but I was actually cozying up to the quaint culturally inclined area.

"I'm not coming from the jungle Chrissie. It's Brooklyn."

"Whatever. Follow me. I want you to meet Cynthia White." That name sounded so familiar but the face and the name wasn't clicking.

"Mrs. White this is Tyler Blake. Tyler this is the one and only Cynthia White."

Cynthia White was absolutely beautiful. Her caramel complexion and short auburn hair put you in the mind of an older Halle Berry. She had great style and carried herself with the highest of class. And although she appeared to be nothing but a complete lady, you could also tell she was a woman not to be taken lightly. She knew how to handle herself and didn't tolerate people trying to get over on her in any way. After taking in her beauty, I quickly realized exactly whose mother she was and wanted to wring Chrissie's neck. Cynthia White was T-Roc's mother.

"It's a pleasure to meet you Mrs. White."

"Why thank you. You're a very beautiful young woman and Chrissie tells me you're smart too."

"You're making me blush."

"You have nothing to blush about. When someone pays you a compliment, simply straighten your back, poke out your ample chest and say, I know," she teased.

We all burst out in laughter simultaneously. Mrs. White and I talked for two more hours as though we had known each other for years. We had an instant connection, but I was seriously apprehensive about getting involved in the project because of T-Roc. He would no doubt hit the roof. To say T-Roc was displeased after I cut him off would be an understatement. At this point in his career he definitely got next to little or no rejection in his life. But something about Cynthia White was positively endearing. I knew we were supposed to be in each other's lives for a reason. With all the success of her son, she didn't want to ride his coattail but instead wanted to accomplish her own success. She was smart and savvy enough to do just that and it made me admire her that much more. I could definitely see where her son got his drive from. I decided to take on the project and assist Mrs. White with her new business venture.

Later that night I was lying in bed with Brian and began discussing my new career plans.

"I met with Chrissie today and she wants me to work with her at a new styling company."

"That sounds dope. You have great style and Chrissie has that whole *Sex and the City* vibe going. Whose company is it?"

"Cynthia White."

"I know you didn't just say what I think you said?" Brian snapped.

"Baby I was taken aback at first too, but working with Mrs. White has nothing to do with T-Roc. There's a chance we may never even run into each other."

"Now you're reaching. You need to worry if she's a crook like her son."

"Please. Mrs. White is definitely nothing like T-Roc."

"Okay," Brian said sarcastically. "But he learned his cutthroat business tactics from somebody. I'm sure the apple doesn't fall too far from the tree. How bout this...Instead of working for Cynthia White you can start your own company,"

"What?"

"Yeah, you can do it. I'll fund everything. You said Chrissie was working at some big time publicity company and you're going to school for Journalism. That's a perfect combination. You all can start your own publicity company."

"Brian, I don't have a clue how to run a business."

"I'll have my business manager oversee everything for you and Chrissie. All you have to do is concentrate on getting clients."

"But I have school, and this all sounds so rushed and crazy."

"Listen you can still go to school and work part time while Chrissie is there full time."

"I don't know Brian. Will it bother you that much for me to work with Mrs. White?"

"Yes it will," Brian said sternly.

I knew Brian wasn't offering me this company because he believed in me or even wanted me to have success, but to him it was worth investing thousands of dollars just to have power over the situation and not let me work with Mrs. White. That was just one of many tell tale signs of what extent Brian would go, to make sure he always controlled everything in my life.

After speaking to Chrissie she was positively psyched with the whole idea. We both still had an interest in Mrs. White's company and me in particular with our new budding friendship. I was caught up in the excitement of starting a new company and my relationship with Brian, because although it seemed like we had been together for years, it had only been a few months. With all the commotion I wasn't paying attention to key signs that weren't adding up in our relationship.

For example, when Brian suggested we move in together, after I declined we both looked for our own place. He always spent so much time at my crib or I would be in the studio with him all night; that it wasn't dawning on me as to why I had never been to his new place. Although we were together constantly, something wasn't quite right, but I couldn't put my finger on it.

Sometimes you get so caught up that you don't focus in on indications that are staring you in the face. But I did what I rationalized as a thorough investigation by dotting my i's and crossing my t's. I spoke to a few of my industry associates about Brian and asked them to find out if he was dating anybody, had any kids, or was on the down low. You know sometimes men get selective amnesia and forget to give you the make it or break it information. But his report came back positive. His record was very clean indeed.

With the help of Brian's business manager, Chrissie and I got our new publicity company up and popping in no time. We named it 'Girl Power PR' but for the first few months let's just say a lot of money was being spent but no money was coming in. Chrissie was basically carrying the company solo because between school and being with Brian, I barely had time for anything else. Eventually we landed our first client, a female R&B singer who had the number ten song on the Billboard charts with a bullet.

Right when business was picking up Brian had to be in Upstate New York for a few months to work on tracks for several artist projects and he wanted me to come along. Of course I wanted to be with him but I also had school and a new business to help run. But Brian didn't care, his exact words were, "That Company, I pay for it. So that means I pay your salary. You'll get a check regardless. As far as school goes, you can always go back. I need you with me, so get your shit together and let's go."

Because my heart wasn't into the company anyway it was easy for me to go and as for school I never enjoyed that. My first year at NYU was only fun because Chrissie was there. After she graduated it was whatever.

Off to Upstate New York we went. We stayed in the mountains and the homes looked like cabins. It was a warm and cozy atmosphere. There were tons of artists there like: Nas, 50 cent, some new female group called Diva's and the list went on and on. Brian's plan was to complete all their needed tracks within his four month stay. He had me in his back pocket so we were literally around each other 24/7. Playing house made us grow even closer because we were up under each other all the time. I would wait on him like we were husband and wife. During this period I began to love him deeply. It grew beyond the mind blowing sex, but to an elevated level of respect and praise. Brian was a man that basically came from nothing and had to work for everything he had. When you meet a man like that, you have no choice but to admire the grind work they put forth in order to accomplish what they have in life. But some men who undergo that kind of struggle become selfish and never learn how to truly take pleasure in life and enjoy their success.

After being in the mountains for weeks at a time I would go home for a couple of days, but it still wasn't clicking in my mind exactly where home was for Brian and whether his information was on the up and up. So when he was dropping me off at home, I questioned his story. "Brian where exactly is home for you?" I gazed intently in his eyes searching to see if his answer was the truth.

Without skipping a beat he calmly said, "I've been staying with my business manager Greg. You know he recently purchased a huge home in Jersey and I'm staying with him temporarily until our house is finished being completed."

"Why don't you just get an apartment?"

"That's a waste of money. Greg has plenty of space and most of the time I'm at your place anyway. Then we're in Upstate New York for the next few months. What's the point? You're the one who said you weren't ready to live together. I figured we test the waters Upstate, and by the time we're done there, you'll be ready to make it official." That was the line Brian used on me and that was the line I ran with and fell for.

A few weeks later it was Valentine's Day and we were back in NYC. I stopped by the office to read some pitch letters Chrissie wanted me to take a look at. Brian was on his way and I figured he would take me to a fancy restaurant and surprise me with a nice little trinket or something. When he showed up with some roses, gave me a kiss on the cheek and then said, "Baby I can't stay long, I have to go back to the mountains and finish a track for an artist."

I surveyed him with daggers in my eyes and retorted, "Motherfucker you can't be serious. Because if you are, take your bullshit roses and shove them up your ass."

"Yo what the fuck is all that about?"

"You must think I'm crazy. It's Valentine's Day and you have to rush up outta here to work on some tracks. What...You fucking your track now? That's how you're getting your shit off?"

"You're seriously bugging right now. I swear I have to get this track done for this cat. I'm behind schedule. Don't you think I want to be with you?"

"So why can't I come with you?"

"Tyler I'm coming right back tomorrow. Anyway you told me earlier today you had to meet with Chrissie tomorrow to get some shit done."

"Whatever nigga, your shit is stinking right now. You step in this office with some half ass roses and some bullshit excuses. I don't know what the fuck is jumping off, but something is wrong. And if it isn't, I can't be bothered with someone as unromantic as you."

I stormed out the building, and as I walked down the street Brian followed me in his car pleading his case. There was nothing to discuss. I will let other days slide for someone who is not use to being romantic like Brian. But when it comes to Valentine's Day, a day that is stamped on a calendar to be imprinted in every man's head to get on top of his game; and my man comes with some roses and a goodbye speech. Fuck him!

I went home and I was done with Brian. This shit was for the birds. Not being one to sulk in misery, I picked up the phone and dialed Ian's number, hoping it hadn't changed. I needed to hear a familiar voice and speak to someone who could take my mind off the circus ride I just got off of.

"Hello," Ian answered, and I instantly felt relieved to hear his voice.

"Hi, it's me Tyler," I said not sure of what sort of comeback I would get.

"I can't believe you called me. I'm actually here in town for a game. I would love to see you."

"Ditto."

"Give me your address, I'll come get you. We can have dinner and talk about what's been going on in our lives."

"Perfect, that's exactly what I need."

An hour later Ian picked me up in a Stretch Limo and yeah he had those same tired red roses (but a lot more) that I tossed back at Brian. But it was 10 o'clock at night and he had no idea he was going to see me until the very last minute. Plus Ian had shown me his generous gift giving side in the past so that was never an issue. When I stepped in the limo and saw Ian's face he was as handsome as ever, but there were no butterflies like I felt with Brian.

"Tyler you look beautiful. Give me a hug, I missed you." When I hugged Ian his smell was still intoxicating, but I yearned for Brian's smell.

"I missed you too Ian," I lied and said.

"Baby what are you doing living in Brooklyn? Your man isn't holding it down for you?" Ian couldn't even wait until we made it to the restaurant without starting in on the slick ass comments.

"Obviously I don't have a man if I'm here with you, and there is nothing wrong with Brooklyn," I snapped.

"I'm sorry, I just worry about you. Believe it or not, I want you to be happy." I laid my head on Ian's chest hoping the empty void Brian left he could somehow fill.

While we dined at *Asia de Cuba* my mind drifted to Brian and what he was doing. I looked at the waterfall wondering if throwing a penny in would change Brian into the man I wanted him to be. Ian and I made small talk about what had been going on in each others lives, but my mind was somewhere else. After finishing dinner, I told Ian that I was tired and had to get up early in the morning. Using Ian as my crutch wasn't working. When we reached my apartment Ian was still optimistic that he had a chance.

"Tyler I know you have a lot on your mind, but I can help you through it. Get some rest tonight because tomorrow I have a game and I want you to come," Ian said confident that I would be there.

"Okay, call me tomorrow," and we kissed briefly on the lips before I closed the door.

The silence in the apartment added to my gloom. Being with Ian didn't help me get over Brian. It made me miss him more. At the same time, I knew I needed to let him go because the bottom line was we were too different. I fell asleep with Brian McKnight's *Anytime* playing on my CD player, not giving into the urge to call him.

Early the next day someone was buzzing at my door and to my delight it was Brian. When he came inside the first thing he saw was the red roses on the table that Ian had gotten me. He gave me a quizzical look but didn't question me about them. He simply said, "I love you and I'm sorry. No woman has ever really asked much of me and I'm finding it difficult to adjust. But I know we belong together so I'm going to make it right."

"You mean that?"

"With all my heart Tyler because I never knew I could love someone as much as I love you." I could feel the tears welling in my eyes. Brian's words touched a core inside that I didn't know existed. My heart filled with warmth that only true love could bring.

"Brian my heart belongs to you. The love you've expressed to me is the same love I feel for you." Brian and I made love right there on the living room floor before heading back upstate.

When we got upstate, we had this incredible night to make up for a lousy Valentine's Day. While sitting in the car about to go in the house Brian said, "This is like deja vu, have you ever experienced that?"

"No, what exactly is that?"

"It's a feeling of having been in a place or experienced something before. I just had that with you, so I know this is where I'm supposed to be." We had a heart to heart about many of my concerns. I explained to Brian that I didn't expect him to give me everything in the world, but that he needed to step his romance game up a few notches. He understood that I wanted him to sweep me off my feet, and not just in the bed. The real romance happens outside the bedroom. He was rough around the edges when it came to that, but for the first time I could see that he was willing to try and that was a positive sign.

As winter turned into spring, our love affair continued. Our bond seemed stronger and I loved Brian even more for making such an effort in our relationship. As a surprise to show good faith, he took me on a fabulous shopping spree up and down 5th Avenue and didn't even restrict me with a budget. That was a major leap for him.

My heart belonged to Brian. I was totally pink for him. Our relationship was in full bloom and now I had gotten into a comfort zone. But once again that gnawing pain in my stomach indicating something wasn't quite right was back. The answers always seemed so close but yet so far. One sunny afternoon while walking in Park Slope eating *Haagen-Dazs'* Dulce De Leche ice cream I felt compelled to stop him and speak my mind. "Brian I feel like you're living a double life," I said candidly.

He looked at me with ice cream dripping from the side of his face, smiled and said, "You know everything about me." As I took my finger and wiped the ice cream from his chin like we were an old married couple, my sixth sense was telling me otherwise. I couldn't put the pieces together, none of them seemed to fit, and since I hated to dwell on anything that I couldn't instantly figure out I put my thoughts in the back of my mind. They were all there on reserve waiting to go in their proper places. Here I was with a man that had made my heart so pink. I knew in many ways we weren't exactly compatible, but he made me love him. I compromised in the belief that maybe there was a chance for us.

Chapter Nine: Shattered Love

(Lies Aren't So Pretty in Pink)

I believed I had found true love--not in a perfect package but a very workable one. We'd come so far and it had been over a year in our relationship and I deeply loved Brian. I knew we could be together forever. But then again forever is a mighty long time.

I was sitting in the lounge at the *Hit Factory* talking to a young lady named Melanie, a cute Hispanic girl who was one of Leon's many girlfriends. Leon was Brian's partner and so called best friend. He was a short light skinned cat that wore his hair in long braids and swore he was a ladies' man. Out the blue Melanie looked at me seriously and said, "I don't think that Brian deserves you," which struck me as odd because I thought she and Brian were close. She always referred to him as her big brother; so my antenna instantly went up.

"Why would you say that Melanie?" I asked curiously.

Instead of answering my question she shot back with another statement, "People aren't always the way that they seem." With those words I knew this was the beginning of the end. I asked her point blank what she meant by that. What she said next was chilling.

"Do you ever wonder why you've never been to Brian's house?" I didn't have an opportunity to respond because right after her final words Leon strolled in the room, with his oversized *Sean John* sweat suit. He first glared at me and then at Melanie and back at me. He immediately sensed the vibe was off and rushed Melanie out of the room. But he was too late. The damage was done. I didn't need for her to tell me anything else. I knew! I knew....I didn't have the details yet, but

I knew what that meant. That meant the double life that I thought he had, was a reality. My mind was spinning and I couldn't believe this lousy sonofabitch had played me like a fool for all this time.

I stormed out the lounge and went into the studio where Brian was and spewed out, "You are dead to me. This relationship is over and I don't ever want to see your lying face again."

Keeping with the lie he had the audacity to keep a straight face asking, "What are you huffing about? You need to stop bugging out over bullshit." When I surveyed his face, his eyes were empty and cold. With his right hand he kept stroking his throat as though contemplating his next lie. He then continued, "What the fuck is wrong with you Tyler, and why are you acting like this?" He knew exactly what I was talking about.

"You're a sick fuck and I hope you burn in hell forever for each despicable lie you fed me. If I don't ever see your face again it will still be too soon." He glared at me with torture and agonizing pain. Within an instant, he lifted me up by my white *Luca Luca* leather jacket and slammed me through the door and then slammed me up against the wall. My whole body buckled under the pressure.

This was all unbelievable because he was such a little guy and I couldn't believe that he had such strength. Leon ran into the hallway to get Brian off of me and he reached around Leon and punched me dead in my face. People started running out of the other studios wondering what all the commotion was about. They witnessed Brian ripping plaques off the walls and throwing them on the floor. He screamed, "How the fuck can you treat me like this? I take care of you. You are supposed to be my woman. This is how you repay me?"

I was literally in shock, and pissed and torn all at the same time. Here was the demise of our relationship unfolding at the *Hit Factory* with strangers being privy to our dirty laundry. Brian had done a lot of things for me but put his hands on me wasn't one of them. He had never raised a finger to me. Never! We argued and we had disagreements but he always remained so calm. I had never seen anything in his character to point toward such a violent temper. But then again, I really didn't know this man at all.

After they finally restrained him, I was so overwhelmed, I ran out the building in tears. Melanie followed me outside to get a taxi and said, "I'll call you tomorrow so we can finish our conversation." I reached in my purse and quickly wrote down my number. Leon was lurking in the back and I didn't want him to have a clue as to what we were discussing. I went home feeling dazed and confused. I sat on my bed scrutinizing the bruises on the side of my stomach. My eye was swollen, and my leg was also bruised because Brian kicked me while I was on the floor. That's what they do. They kick you while you're down.

Early the next morning the phone rang and jarred me from my sleep. It was the call that would start to answer so many questions. The soap opera news began rolling out before I could digest it. As soon as I picked up the phone Melanie started spitting out the information.

"Tyler I was in Chicago with Leon a few weeks ago, and the day we were leaving the hotel he asked me to check out. I went to the front desk and they handed me the bill, and I asked for the phone records too which they were more than happy to provide. I handed Leon the hotel bill and put the phone records in my purse. When I got home I started calling the numbers, trying to find the number to his crib so I could blast his baby mother. There was one particular Jersey number that was on the phone records several times, so when I called some chick named Beverly answered the phone. I played it off with her by saying my boyfriend was in the music industry and this number had showed up several times on my cell phone bill and I wanted to make sure he wasn't calling the next chick on my phone. She tried to ease my paranoia by explaining that she was Brian's girlfriend and mother of his child. She went on to say my boyfriend was probably calling to speak to him."

My mouth dropped and I believe for a brief second my heart stopped, if that's possible. The room started spinning and I felt like I was in the twilight zone. I had to sit down because my knees became weak and my stomach was nauseated. I wasn't ready for this. I was still in shock over the fact that he had just jumped on me, and now Melanie was telling me Brian had a ready made family. All this triggered so many mixed emotions. In mostly all of my prior relationships they were abusive and because I too had serious issues within myself, it made me feel closer to a man when they put their hands on me. My excitement free relationship with Brian had now taken on a life of its own. This new side of him was dark and dangerous but at the same time I just got this devastating news that someone who I thought was my man wasn't really my man. He was somebody else's man and they had a child together. All while Melanie was doing her detective work trying to scheme on Leon, she lucked up and came across my man's dirt. After Melanie gave me Brian's number, we hung up and I called to get the Scooby Doo.

After the second ring a woman's voice said, "Hello."

"Hi can I speak to Beverly."

"Who's calling?" The woman asked sounding apprehensive.

"This is Tyler Blake," the woman paused.

"I'm sorry you have the wrong number," the woman said abruptly. But I knew I didn't have the wrong number and I knew it was Beverly on the other end. I said it again, but this time I asked to speak to Brian and she put him on the phone.

Without hesitation, I told him I knew all about his lies and his other life and of course he tried to act like I didn't know what I was talking about and said we needed to talk. When he hung up the phone, my mind was so clogged over the whole situation but I did want to hear his side. I tried to absorb all this new information and replay it in my mind over and over again. It hadn't dawned on me that my heart was shattered and I was truly crushed.

Brian didn't call me that day or night because that is what men do. They play mind games with you. They first try to figure out what you know and believe to be the truth so they can then contradict whatever you think is true with more thought out lies. They plot and they scheme and get all their lies together before they even have a conversation with you. Then they keep you waiting so the anxiety is so built up, that by the time you all do talk you don't know what to believe yourself. That's how fucked up they have your head. I call it the Jedi mind trick and honey once you master it, you are not to be fucked with.

Thank goodness I had 'Girl Power PR' because although I was drained and feeling miserable at least it gave me a reason to put my clothes on and get out of bed. I was confused and I had so many emotions I was trying to sort out. I felt betrayed, used, lied to and that I had wasted over a year of my life. While I was sitting at my desk, the phone rang and it was Brian. He told me that he wanted to come over that night so we could discuss everything. I told him that was fine. When I hung up the phone I put my head on the desk and hoped that I would open my eyes and this would all be a bad nightmare. But this wasn't a fantasy script I wrote to spice up my life. This was my reality. This was me once again having to accept that the world isn't so pink.

Later on that evening, Brian came over and the first words out his mouth were, "Please forgive me for hitting you. I never meant to put my hands on you Tyler." After looking at my bruises his eyes filled with tears and in a sorrowful voice he said, "I'm sorry for hurting you this way. I felt overwhelmed when you said you wanted to leave me, and the built up anxiety from keeping this lie bottled up was weighing heavy on my mind and heart," he divulged.

Sidebar: Do you see how men can turn their web of deceit around and all of a sudden they are the victim? You can be walking around with a broken arm and busted lip, but because of your actions you caused them to react. For all you ladies who are reading this book and you are just realizing this crap for the first time, don't worry about it. You see what type of bullshit I had to go through to finally get it.

I wasn't interested in his words of sorrow. I wanted to know about Beverly and the baby. "Brian who is Beverly," I asked harshly.

"She's an ex girlfriend."

"That you have a baby with? How old is the baby?"

"A few months," he said coyly.

"So you were having sex with her while we were together?"

"In the beginning when we were having problems, I started seeing her off and on and she got pregnant. After she told me she was pregnant I never slept with her again."

"There was no need. The seed was already planted. Were you ever going to tell me you had a baby, or were you going to keep me in the dark until the baby turned eighteen?"

"I knew eventually I had to tell you, but I could never find the right time or the right words. I didn't want to lose you and I still don't. I'm not with her anymore, Tyler I swear."

"Then why is she living at your house, the house you claimed you didn't have?"

"She doesn't live there. She lives in Brooklyn. I got the place when her due date neared. I couldn't live in Greg's house with a baby. She is only staying there temporarily so I can be near my daughter and help her out because she doesn't have any family." When he said daughter I felt a lump in my throat because that was supposed to be our daughter.

"How long is she staying with you Brian?"

"I'm not sure, but it doesn't matter because I'm not in a relationship with her. I'm with you and she knows that. Tyler all I'm asking is that you give me some time. I want to be a father to my daughter and that means having a cordial relationship with her mother."

"Are you sleeping with her?"

"No, I swear I haven't had sex with her in months. I have no desire to sleep with her. Tyler I made a mistake, but when I tell you my heart belongs to you that is the truth."

I believe in my heart that if Melanie would have never told me the truth Brian would have kept the lie going until he got caught in some other way. After we talked, I felt a sense of relief because he still wanted to be with me. I didn't want him to be with me because I loved him, although I did. I wanted him to be with me because he owed me for the year and a half he took of my life based on a lie. This was the same man who was adamant that people don't just accidentally cheat, and a man doesn't just so happen to fall in some pussy. He would beat in my head the importance of commitment, a monogamous relationship, and that your body is your temple and that it is the most precious thing you have. He was the same self righteous motherfucker that I felt I didn't deserve. He appeared to be such a goody two shoe and I was just some recovering wild child. I wanted to prove that I was worthy of his adoration and his affection. This man had convinced me of all that and then some. But yet this was the same man that had been living with another woman and had a child with this woman while we were together. I had given him every opportunity to tell me the truth but instead he chose to say I was the only one. I was looking at a man who was nothing but a liar but I still believed in him. In my mind I couldn't accept that a man who had taught me all these positive and wonderful things could be the scumbag that I thought he might be. To have a child that he didn't acknowledge to me and a life I knew nothing about was crazy. Either way he was going to pay, literally for the pain he was putting me through and everything he took away from me, which was time. Time is the only thing in this world that can't be replaced in any shape or form. Once it is gone it's gone. Even though I was young, I deemed my time as valuable.

That night after telling me more half truths, we made love, and that night was the beginning of the end. In my heart I knew that. No matter what happened from that day on, part of Brian was dead to me. Part of him was nothing to me. I gave that man my soul. I put trust in him that I had never put into anyone else. I believed in him which made me vulnerable to his deceit. He violated my trust in the most unforgivable way, and although I knew I should have left him and never looked back--the other part of me that halfway loved him and halfway wanted to make him pay couldn't let go. I began the process of collecting on my debt, and at the same time I tried to pull it together mentally in order to handle the cards I had been dealt. It wasn't an ideal situation, but under the circumstances it was my only option. Brian was the one that broke my heart it was only fair he put it back together.

Chapter Ten: Picking Up the Pieces

(To My Shattered Pink Heart)

Picking up the pieces to a broken heart is never an easy task. Everyone has different aspects on how they should deal with their anguish, which leaves each individual a few options on what to do to ease the pain. My case was somewhat unique because my heart was broken and shattered, but yet I chose to stay with the man that had deluded me. Faced with the truth, I tried to find a way to bury my distress. Staying with Brian somehow softened the blow.

"I can't believe I'm in Brooklyn, but I have to admit I'm somewhat impressed. It's very cute and hip over here. I was expecting derelicts on every block," Chrissie whimpered. I rolled my eyes and continued packing up my belonging.

"Chrissie, would you please make yourself helpful and tape up the boxes? The moving company will be here shortly."

"Well why don't you have them tape up the boxes?"

"Chrissie I remember when we first met, you were so sweet and down to earth. Hanging out with all those celebrities has made you so New York snooty. Take it down a notch. I mean it's not that serious."

"Alright, alright where's the tape?" Chrissie asked annoyed with my comment; although she knew I was right. Chrissie located the tape on the kitchen counter and continued sizing up my apartment. "I still don't understand why you're not moving back to the city. With the high rent you're paying…I mean Brian will be paying, you can get a beautiful place in the city instead of Jersey."

"Unlike you, I don't want my stomping ground to be my sleeping ground. I'm not up to being bothered with the hustle and bustle of the city. I need peace and quiet. I need trees, flowers and grass. I can't get that in the city."

"I don't agree with your logic but I understand. I'm just happy you're moving out of this dump. Brooklyn isn't as bad as I thought, but you're so above this place. It's about time Brian is putting you in the lifestyle you're accustomed to, even if you had to catch him with his pants down to get it. I knew you were making a grave mistake when you stripped away your beliefs in order to prove you were worthy. It never works. Men don't appreciate that sort of sacrifice," Chrissie preached.

"I can't believe this is coming from you Chrissie. You're the same woman that told me I was jaded for my views on men and relationships. I remember the time when you were sleeping with some Real Estate Tycoon and were ecstatic when he bought you a pair of $900 *Jimmy Choo* boots. I made the comment, "What, you fucking for boots now? Is that all you're getting out the deal?" And you blasted me. Now you're basically telling me that trying to be independent in order to gain the respect of a man is overrated."

"Yeah that's the long and the short of it. You were right Tyler. Men don't think anymore of you for trying to be superwoman or please them by giving into their every need. If anything you'll end up tired and old looking from working so hard to please them, and they'll be luxuriating with the chick that was smart enough to put her energy into maintaining herself."

When the door buzzed and I let the moving people in, Chrissie's words were still weighing heavy on my mind. Is that where I went wrong with Brian? I let all the guilt of my past relationships dictate the direction I went in ours, not feeling worthy of the gifts and money men so freely gave me in the past, in order to control my life and have me obligated to them. Or maybe I so desperately wanted to belong; I sold myself cheaply for momentary doses of love. Whatever my reasoning, I was more confused than ever.

I stepped on my balcony and basked at the beautiful view of the city. I was completely moved into the loft apartment that was located on the Hudson River. As I stared out at in the Empire State Building directly across from me, my mind replayed the heartache that brought me here. I was so full of anger. Actually, I was beyond angry. I was at the boiling point. I tried to medicate the anger by digging my hands further and further into Brian's pocket. While I was spending his money, did it make me feel any better? As a matter of fact, yes it did.

I remember one night in particular when I went to meet him at his office (he was now the President at a major label) because we were going out to dinner. It was rather chilly that night and I decided that I wanted a new coat. This man had deceived me. A little coat wouldn't hurt his pockets. We were walking down 5th Avenue and I saw this beautiful coat in the *Fendi* window. Of course I dragged Brian in the store. I tried on several other coats but my heart was set on the one in the window. Not bothering to look at the price tag, I had already set in my mind that I was getting that coat.

"Excuse me," I said to the sales lady. "Could you please get that coat in the window for me, because I don't see it in the store?"

"Why of course," the sales lady grinned as if she had dollar signs in her eyes.

I tried the camel colored coat on and viewed myself in the mirror. "You look stunning in that coat," the sales lady co-signed on what I already new. "That is a limited edition. There's only twenty like it in the world." I let the lady give me her million dollar sales pitch, but she was preaching to the dead because the coat was already sold and paid for in my mind.

"I'll take it," I said not bothering to ask the price. Brian and I walked over to the sales counter and I lingered on the side waiting for him to pay. He pulled out his newly issued *Black American Express* Card and nearly fell to the floor when the sales lady told him the price.

"Twenty thousand dollars? Are you crazy? You can put that shit back!" Brian paused and looked at me before he said, "I don't have a twenty thousand dollar coat. I don't even have a five thousand dollar coat. That's ridiculous."

I breathed in the idle chatter that Brian just kicked. His words had no substance because I had already made up my mind that I was leaving with that coat. "Darling, I don't care if you don't have a twenty thousand dollar coat. I don't care if you don't have a $100 coat. Hell I don't care if you don't have a coat at all because this isn't about you. I want that coat and I deserve that coat," I said in a sweet saturated bitchy tone.

As Brian reluctantly handed his card over to the sales lady, I put my old coat from last year in the bag and threw on my new money coat and sashayed out the *Fendi* store saying, "Mother would be proud of her Princess." Some people might say that money can't buy you happiness, yeah that might be true, but it can sure make you look damn good while you are disintegrating in misery.

The more money Brian spent on me and the more I asked for, the more resentful he became. Brian felt that if he didn't give me what I asked for and didn't spend his money on me I would leave him, and you know what? He was right. I would make it clear everyday that I really didn't give a fuck about how he felt or what he thought. If he concluded because he had some Baby Mama and a child and their expenses were going to deprive me of what I wanted then fuck him and them. I became bitchy, and said so many despicable things about him, his child, his Mother, and anybody that was affiliated with him. But it really wasn't me talking. It was that other person inside of me that was dying from a broken heart. Overnight I'd become a bitter bitch and I hadn't even reached my mid 20's. I never felt so betrayed in my life and I wanted him to feel the pain that he caused me. I would say and do things just to bring him grief. I was out for blood and he was definitely my prey.

No matter what I did though, I constantly thought about my situation with Brian and my anger continued to brew. I became increasingly curious about who this other woman was in his life. I had visualized all sorts of scenarios and wanted my mind at rest. My dear friend Melanie with her great detective work was able to obtain the address as to where Brian lived. I imagined him living in some elaborate house like the Estates in *Timberline At Alpine* and playing house with a beautiful woman and adorable child. If true, it would give me the strength to just walk away. I know when something is a loosing battle. I can embrace that disappointment and move on. I knew if that was the life he shared with Beverly then I would have to bow out gracefully because no woman can ever compete with a package like that.

Sidebar: All women should know that if you ever meet a man who has a beautiful woman, a beautiful child, and they arc living this ideal life--you can never come between that. Even if he decides to be with you, part of his heart will always be with them. I had to see once and for all if that was what I was up against.

"Melanie pull over. That's the place right there," I said pointing to an average small condo complex.

"Hum, this is where big time Music Producer Brian McCall lives. I thought he would be living a little better than that," Melanie moaned.

"You know Brian, always saving for a rainy day."

"He must be trying to save for a rainy year by the looks of this place."

"It's not that bad Melanie."

"For the type of paper he's making, it ain't that good."

Ignoring Melanie's comment, I glanced at my watch calculating the time I believed Beverly would show up. Brian was at the studio and would be there until late, so I figured she would be home soon because of the baby. Fifteen minutes later we recognized a car pulling up that resembled Brian's and a couple seconds later, a woman stepped out. I was on the passenger side so we were basically face to face. I knew it was Beverly. I politely smiled and said, "I'm sorry. I'm lost this is the wrong address."

"No problem," the woman said after a long pause. As Melanie made a U-turn my blood pressure started to rise.

"This is what that nigga fucked up my heart for? A pathetic life in the cut with this chick. Unbelievable! Take me home. When I got to my apartment I crawled into bed and all I could say was why me?

A few days later we were off to LA for the Soul Train Awards. It was freezing in New York so I knew the LA sun would do me some good. We stayed at my favorite hotel the *L'Ermitage* Beverly Hills. The room had a contemporary décor with a delicate infusion of Euro-Asian ambiance. While I was in the spacious walk-in closet getting dressed for the Awards, the eye spy encounter with Brian's Baby Mother kept flashing in my head. I was rolling my eyes at him, so he finally snarled, "Why you giving me those dirty looks, what's on your mind?" I shrugged my shoulders, avoiding the conversation. But then the idiot had the audacity to say after he took a deep breath, "If you're wondering if she picks out my clothes, she doesn't."

I wanted to scream, "I don't give a fuck whether she picks out your clothes or picks out your ass. That's my last concern. I'm trying to figure out what the fuck is wrong with me, that I'm dealing with a contemptible rat like you." But I knew that would totally ruin our evening. I was thinking it so hard though, I wondered if he could read my mind.

I knew I needed to leave Brian but I wanted to take him down! We were together in the physical form but there was no respect. I had zero respect for him. To guarantee that was clear, at any given opportunity I'd embarrass him in front of his friends by being rude and disrespectful. Hell, they weren't my friends. These were the same clowns in the mountains with me for months and months, hee heeing and ha haaing. But while they were in my face running off at the mouth, none of them bothered to reveal Brian had a girlfriend and a baby on the way. They were probably too busy hiding their own skeletons. At this time I didn't give a damn what they thought about me because it couldn't have been any worse than what I thought of them.

Brian and I were sitting in the third row at the Soul Train Awards, and every time someone would come up to him, he would introduce me as his girlfriend. "Don't you feel like a hypocrite introducing me as your girlfriend when you already have one sitting at home with your baby?" I cracked.

"We already discussed this. Beverly isn't my girlfriend. You are," he howled.

"Oh, so she's just your live in Baby Mother?"

"Temporarily, I'm working on that. You need to stop worrying about Beverly and concentrate on us. She is irrelevant to our relationship."

"You don't care what people are probably saying behind your back? Oh he got his Baby Mother stashed at home and his so-called girlfriend on his arm."

"Hell No. I don't care. The dirty laundry these motherfuckers got stored in their closets makes mine look sparkling clean."

Brian constantly ridiculed his friends and industry peers for their trifling behavior. He considered himself different and of a higher moral standard and would never approve of such indecency. I now had more respect for them, than him because at least they were straight up with the chicks they messed around with. For instance, one of Leon's jump-offs Courtney was in LA too, but she knew her position. When Brian and I went to Leon's room to get him, Courtney answered the door in her pajamas. When I asked her if she was coming, Leon observed me then chirped, "Nah, she ain't going. She's staying right here and babysitting this room until I get back. You think I'm taking the chance getting caught out there and letting it get back to my Baby Mother or one of her friends? Courtney knows what time it is." Courtney kissed Leon as he walked out the door, and told us bye like it was all good.

The next day, Brian and I were strolling around the Beverly Center, when all the built up anger in me boiled over. "I hate you and myself even more for being in this nightmare called a relationship," I bawled, not caring who was around or heard me. These outbursts were becoming frequent occurrences and Brian became so fed up he flipped out and bitch slapped me right there in the Beverly Center in order to shut me up.

There it was once again, the cycle. They hit you once, they hit you twice. They hit you again, again and again. Violence soon became a normal part of our relationship. I would beat him with my words. He would beat me with his fist. The dysfunction continued, but yet, the relationship was more exciting than ever. Can you imagine who knew this guy had so many layers? A liar, a cheat and an abuser....long breath....who would've thought.

No matter how angry I was for all the lies and all the deceit, part of my heart still was very much in love with Brian and felt we would get through this dark cloud and be together. That is what happens when you are in a dysfunctional relationship. You start getting the lines blurred. You don't know what in reality is good for you or what you are just imagining and making up in your mind. I was on that line in my relationship with Brian. To somehow camouflage my fantasy world and feel empowered, I focused my energy on making Brian jealous. And he did everything humanly possible to control my life, which I more than willingly allowed since it made me feel like he loved me. That went back to my childhood. I had always rationalized that it was romantic for a man to have power over your life and dominate your every move. I was constantly going in and out of fantasy and reality! Soon I lost control over making Brian react at my design.

Pacing back and forth at Melanie's apartment arguing with Brian was now a daily routine. "I'm sick of you and this emotional roller coaster that seems to have no end in sight," I screamed as I sat down on the burgundy sofa.

"Save it Tyler, you're the silly bitch that doesn't want to get off; ranting and raving about the same shit over and over again. You think you're fed up? I'm spending more time and money on you than ever before, but instead of being content you complain like an old nagging wife. Fuck that. You're worse than a wife. If we were married, I wouldn't have to put up with half of the crazy ass demands you ask of me. These shenanigans are wearing me down."

"Well you don't have to be bothered with it any longer. I'm done fucking with you. The next man will be more than happy to pick up where you left off." Click, was all he heard as he let out a word to respond.

Forty five minutes later we heard a knock. Not thinking anything of it, Melanie opened the door and standing before her was Brian. He immediately shoved her out the way and with intense rage lunged at me, grabbed my hair and groaned, "We're going the fuck home." Resisting, he reached in his dark blue baggy jeans and pulled out his 9mm handgun, put it to my head and echoed, "I will blast you and then kill myself because I don't give a fuck." I tried to make contact but could barely see his eyes under the Yankees baseball cap. I was panic-stricken at the notion of what Brian would do. Melanie was freaking out. She'd forgotten how demented Brian could behave sometimes. As Melanie darted across the room to reach the phone and call the police she bumped into the coffee table and fell on the floor. Her hands were shaking uncontrollably. Brian peered at her with such hate in his eyes and yelled, "You started this bitch. This is your fucking fault."

After Brian found out it was Melanie who opened Pandora's Box he loathed her. It gave him pleasure to see her helpless on the floor. When Melanie reached for the cordless I begged her not to call the police. She gazed at me with confusion. My heart was pounding, but I didn't want Brian to go to jail and I didn't believe he would actually kill me. For a brief second I closed my eyes to gather my thoughts. I spoke to Brian in a soft and easy, almost hypnotic tone. "Baby I love you; I know that we belong together. Every word I spoke was out of anger and frustration and I apologize. Please forgive me." The words flowed with such ease that I believed what I said. Brian released my hair and put the gun away.

"Melanie I know it's asking a lot to excuse Brian's behavior, but please let us handle this on our own." With a look of fear and disgust she reluctantly agreed.

My life was spiraling out of control and I didn't know how to stop it. Normalcy was desperately needed, but no matter how much drama we went through or how much pain we caused one another, when we made love we became one. Our chemistry was intoxicating and whatever Brian's faults, our connection was stronger and more passionate than we ever shared with anyone else. My heart hungered to go back to the time when I admired him and deducted he had the most beautiful soul in the world. Now our relationship was full of misplaced obsession with no trust or faith. I looked in the mirror, facing my inner monsters. With great stupidity I believed I could use Brian to get over him, but instead my emotions fell into a bottomless pit.

Chapter Eleven: Second Chance at Real Love

(Not in Pink but in Blue)

From the outside it seemed Brian was treating me like a Princess. He would always send truckloads of flowers to the office and Chrissie would complain, "Why can't I find a man to show such adoration." It got to the point that she actually told Brian she was banning him from sending anymore. He had chocolates, balloons, or even all day gift certificates to plush spas delivered. Or sometimes he'd have an invitation sent telling me to meet him at a suite in a five star hotel. When I arrived, rose pedals were everywhere and he'd bathe me, wash my hair in the Jacuzzi while I'd drink champagne. He stepped his romantic game up to the next level. So the night I surprised Brian by telling him I was pregnant he promised he would take care of me as his Queen for the rest of his life.

A few weeks later Brian had to leave for a business trip and would be gone for a week. Being a top executive with a ton of responsibilities, I thought nothing of his traveling plans. A couple of days after Brian left, I ran into Courtney while leaving work.

"What's up girl? I haven't seen you since LA," I said giving Courtney a hug. "What you been up to?"

"Nothing, just working and fucking around with Leon crazy ass. I was going to get a bite to eat. Come with me so we can play catch up."

"Sure," I agreed knowing something was up, but thirsting for the information all the same.

As Courtney sat and ate her turkey burger she casually said, "You know Brian took Beverly and the baby to Aruba for a family vacation." She glanced up at me as she took another bite of her burger waiting for my reaction. I was livid but I wasn't about to let that hating ass bitch know it.

"Really? He forgot to mention that when he slipped this ice on my hand before he left," I said coolly placing my engagement finger under her nose, thinking 'eat this bitch.' Courtney sat there with her mouth wide opened annoyed by my reaction and ring. I finally said, "Dear close your mouth before something flies in."

When I left the diner I was burning up inside, to the point when I opened my mouth I knew fire was going to come out. Walking to the parking garage to get my car I was talking to myself out loud and could see people staring at me as if I was crazy. I screamed to one passing pedestrian, "This is New York City. Don't act like you've never seen someone talking to themselves." I got in my car and slammed the door. As I headed towards the George Washington Bridge my cell phone chimed and Brian's name popped up. Without even a hello I said, "Where are you?"

"You know where I am, LA," Brian said right on point.

"Is that right?" I retorted suspiciously.

"Tyler don't start. What the fuck is up now?"

"I heard you took Beverly and the baby on a vacation to Aruba." There was a pause, and I knew it was true.

"That's a damn lie. Who told you that bullshit?"

"Nigga fuck you. You do you and I'm gonna do me." After hanging up I immediately dialed Courtney's cell. "How about *Mr. Chow's* tonight, my treat I'll pick you up around nine."

When I picked Courtney up I had on my perfect fitting *Blue Cult Jeans* and silk lime green *Plein Sud* shirt. To be four months pregnant, I wasn't showing and my clothes still fit just right. My plan was to have a ball tonight and I wanted to dress sexy for the occasion. Brian had been calling me nonstop every since I hung up on him and called three more times for the short period Courtney was in the car. He blocked his number as if I didn't know it was him. After the fourth unanswered call, Courtney's phone went off. "It's Leon, I need to get that," she said enthusiastically not putting two and two together. I heard him clearly giving her the third degree.

"Where you at Courtney?" Leon demanded to know.

"On my way to dinner," fidgeting with her cell phone.

"With who?"

"Nobody you know, just a girlfriend from work."

"It bet not be Tyler, cause that's gonna cause a serious problem between us." There was a long break and then Leon said, "Did you tell Tyler that Brian took Beverly and the baby to Aruba."

Courtney swallowed hard and replied, "No."

"Alright, I'll call you back."

Before Courtney and I could even discuss their conversation Brian was blowing up my phone again. Of course I didn't answer, so once again Leon called Courtney. But this time he was on three way with Brian. I heard Brian bark, "Put Tyler on the phone." Being the Leon pleaser that she is, Courtney handed me the phone. "Go home now. I don't know why you think I'm with Beverly and the baby, but I'm not?"

I took a deep sigh and squealed, "Go fuck yourself. If you want to take your Baby Mother on a trip then you need to be with her and leave me the hell alone."

"Yo when I get home, it's so over for you."

"That won't be for a few days so it gives me plenty of time to enjoy myself," and I hung up the phone.

Courtney and I dined at *Mr. Chows* and I was enjoying myself. When I tell you I wasn't thinking about what Brian was doing with his Baby Mother, I didn't give a damn. It was all about a party for me. Brian continued to blow up my phone so I turned the bitch off. Then they started calling Courtney and of course she got on the phone, entertaining the bullshit. All while Leon had two kids with his Baby Mother and had about twenty other jump-offs just like her. But in her pathetic little mind, she figured if she acted like the good girl maybe she would be 'The One.' Lies Bitch. I told Courtney to hang up and let's enjoy our dinner and forget them, and finally she gave in to my request.

Just then my friend Rob walked in with a couple of guys and he came over to our table and bought us a bottle of *Cristal* and we started kicking it. Rob was also in the music business and invited us to go to LA to do a little partying, a little shopping, and I was like cool. In my mind I didn't have a boyfriend anymore and I needed to frolic. Plus Courtney was all excited because Rob was the same cat that she told me while in LA she had a crush on. Here was her opportunity, because Rob was a genuine guy and would treat her right—so she eagerly gave him the digits. Rob and his friends were headed to Missy Elliot's party so we tagged along and had a blast. I couldn't help but think I was going through a whole bunch of bullshit with Brian when whooping it up at the club was so much more fun. I partied until 4 o'clock in the morning and by the time my head hit the pillow, the sun was rising. Later on that afternoon, I called Courtney and she was acting like everything was cool, not telling me she had talked to Brian again. My phone beeped and it was him.

"Tyler what do I have to do to prove to you that I'm not with my Baby Mother? You know if I was going to take anybody out of town it would be you," Brian pleaded sincerely.

"Give me the number to your hotel so I can call to see if you are where you say you are."

"I'm in the car driving, but I'll be back at the hotel in ten minutes. I'll call you with the number the minute I step foot in my hotel room." A smiled spread across my face hoping that maybe Brian was telling the truth about his whereabouts, maybe Courtney was just being a nuisance.

Lounging on the plush white sofa, I held onto the phone anticipating Brian's call. It was a beautiful afternoon and the sun beamed through the huge bay windows. I rubbed my stomach fantasizing about Brian and I being a family with the baby growing inside of me when a knock at the door bolstered me back to reality. Thinking maybe it was the concierge personally delivering a package, I opened the door. To my despair, standing before me was Brian with the look of death in his eyes.

Before I could utter a word, one left hook landed me on the thick off white carpet pleading for Brian's mercy. But there would be no mercy. He turned around slammed the door and proceeded to stump me over my entire body with his Timberland boots with the exception of my abdomen. "You were out all night fucking around with Rob, you fucking whore...I set you up. You want to act like a whore, I'm gonna treat you like a whore," he said grabbing my hair and dragging me into the bedroom, feeling the carpet burns on my legs. "You wanna act like a whore, then suck my dick like the whore you are," Brian growled as we reached the bedroom and he pushed down my head forcing me to perform oral sex.

As the tears streamed down my face Brian continued with his tirade, "You deserve to die, you trifling bitch. I'mma show you how whores get fucked." He grabbed my arms and threw me down on the bed and had rage fueled rough sex with me. Tears were strolling down my face and I turned my head to the side praying for the moment this depraved act would be over with. Brian was breathing so hard and his adrenaline was pumping like the repugnance episode was turning him on. After pounding my body he stood up and threw all of my clothes and shoes out of the closet and drawers. He rant and raved for the next 15 minutes, and finally bellowed, "Have this shit cleaned up by the time I get back," and left.

I sat on the bed and cried for hours feeling ashamed until falling into a deep sleep. Later that night Brian's warm body against mine woke me up. He whispered in my ear, "Tyler please wake up."

"I'm up," I said quietly,

"Baby I should've never gone off on you like that, but when Courtney said you were with Rob all night I lost it. You're sacred to me. I put you on a pedestal and the thought of anyone touching you drives me crazy."

"But Brian I wasn't with Rob like that. We're old friends nothing else."

"Well, Courtney said you were going to LA to hang out with him."

"Courtney was saying an awful lot. Did she mention that she gave Rob her number because she wanted to date him?"

"Nah she didn't mention that."

"I figured as much. She was so busy trying to score brownie points with Leon that she sold me out…But Brian that doesn't change what you did to me today or going to Aruba with your Baby Mother."

"Tyler I swear I wasn't in Aruba with Beverly. How the fuck am I going to be in Aruba with her yesterday and be back here today with you." I asked myself the same thing, but for some reason I believed Brian was in Aruba. The idea of me being here and what I would do knowing he was with her drove him so crazy he cut his trip short and came home. It was just as easy for him to catch a flight from LA as from Aruba.

Whatever problems Brian had, I couldn't escape the realization that I had a sickness for staying in this relationship. I was now with child and needed to put the welfare of my unborn baby ahead of the sick relationship I shared with him. But before I could make a final decision there were some questions I needed answered. As days turned into weeks I needed to make a decision and stick to it.

Sitting on the bar stool tapping my finger on the glass table, I picked up the cordless to place a much needed phone call. "Hi. Is this Beverly?" I asked solemnly.

"Who's calling," she responded with underlined attitude.

"This is Tyler Blake."

"What do you want?"

"Listen. I'm not trying to cause you problems, but I need to ask you a few questions. I'm at a crossroads in my relationship with Brian, and I hoped you could clarify a few of my concerns."

"Crossroads?" She paused and smacked her lips. "What do you mean a crossroad?"

"A turning point; I was told that Brian took you and the baby on a family vacation to Aruba. He has adamantly denied that and said that you all's relationship is solely based on your daughter, and there isn't any sort of romantic dalliances jumping off. Is he telling the truth, or is he making you the same sort of promises he's making me?

"I can't speak for Brian because he is his own man, but I will tell you this. I'm the mother of his child, so no matter what you think you have with him doesn't compare to our bond. You know he has a child with me, so you need to just let him go."

"For your information, Brian didn't tell me about you or his daughter, I found out by a mutual friend. After being caught in his lie, he took responsibility and said he only wanted to be there for his daughter. I'm trying to find out if the lies are continuing or is he being honest with me about his relationship with you."

"I'm not about to ease your mind, because now you do know about me and the baby. If you were any type of woman you would let Brian go so he can be with his family. But you're probably nothing but a whore anyway." Do people ever grow tired of throwing the word 'whore' around? It's so juvenile and pathetic. It's like if you can't extend your vocabulary and think of anything better to say let's just use the "whore" word, whatever. After hanging the phone up with Beverly, I was more torn than ever. Brian had her so programmed that she wouldn't reveal any of his dirt. But she still managed to leave me with a feeling of guilt because of their daughter. But I too was carrying Brian's child, and our son or daughter deserved a stable life. I was so confused and couldn't comprehend any of it. What you don't understand is what you fear the most and I was tired of being afraid of the unknown.

As Brian strolled through the front door, my legs became weak and I sat down. When he walked down the hall towards me I admired his perfect cinnamon complexion and beautiful smile; and visualized the gorgeous baby he would give me.

"Hi baby," Brian said as he kissed me on my forehead. He walked back towards the kitchen and went in the refrigerator and pulled out a *Heineken*.

"Brian we need to talk."

"If it's about your conversation with Beverly, I'm not mad. I understand you have some concerns and questions. Did you get the answers that you need?" I was surprised by Brian's laid back attitude and almost lost my train of thought. I quickly regrouped and continued.

"Actually I did." Brian's eyebrows raised and he ogled me quizzically, assuming that Beverly hadn't told me a damn thing; when in actuality what she didn't say spoke more volumes than anything else.

"Really, what was that?"

"Brian I still love you very much and always will, but we can't be together anymore. I want you to be a part of our baby's life, but our relationship is over." I let out a long sigh, feeling relieved the words finally came out.

"Tyler if you're concerned about my relationship with Beverly it's almost taken care of. I'm going to let her have the condo and we're going to get a house together. I was trying to be diplomatic with her because you know how women can get sometimes. I was afraid she'd wile out and threaten to keep my daughter away from me and take me to the cleaners for a whole bunch of child support. But we've worked past that now, and she's accepting the fact that we're not getting back together."

"I don't believe you, because the woman I spoke to hasn't accepted anything. But for argument sake let's just say you're telling the truth. It's too late. The damage has already been done. I should've left you when I first found out about Beverly and the baby, but I couldn't let go. I was determined to make you suffer and feel the same pain that you caused me. You ripped my heart out Brian and I wanted to rip out yours. But it didn't work. All I accomplished was further destroying me.

"Tyler just stop, stop this nonsense. You know we belong together and no matter what you say you'll never leave me."

"I believed that to be true at one time, but it isn't the case anymore. When I look in the mirror, I don't like the person staring back at me. I continue to go from one abusive relationship to another and it has to stop. This relationship is so twisted that you actually recorded my phone conversations so you could know my every thought. You're sick, and so am I. Somewhere in my life I stopped loving me, and I have to find that again, because without it, I'll never be happy." Brian moved near me and stroked my face, as he knelt his head down to place a kiss on my lips I turned my cheek."

"Baby I love you," Brian whispered.

"Sometimes love isn't enough," I said pushing Brian out the way.

"Are you sure this is what you want Tyler?"

"Yes, this is what I need to do for me and our baby. Our child doesn't deserve to grow up in a household full of so much dysfunction. We owe it more than that." Brian stood there shaking his head speechless. "I do want you to be a part of the baby's life and mine, but as friends."

"That's funny. You honestly believe that with all we've been through we can somehow be just friends? I don't think so…And I'll tell you what else. I'm not going to make it easy for you to walk out of my life. That baby you're carrying is mine. I own it, just like I own you. By the time you give birth, you'll be begging me to take you back because you'll have nothing."

"What are you talking about? Are you saying you're not going to give me any sort of financial support during my pregnancy?"

"You're fucking right. You think I'm going to pay you to leave me?" Brian grabbed my hand and snatched off the engagement ring he gave me less than six months ago.

"This isn't about you. This is about the child I'm carrying. How am I supposed to support myself?"

"You should've thought about that when you stepped on your soap box." Brian turned his back on me and walked away. I sat down to digest the conversation. Would Brian really leave me pregnant with no sort of financial assistance? I couldn't fathom that reality.

The phone rang early in the morning and to my dismay I had fallen asleep on the couch. The microwave clock said it was only eight thirty and for a brief moment I wish I had taken the phone of the hook. When I answered the phone, Chrissie was hysterical. "Tyler what the fuck happened? I came in the office this morning and the locks were changed. All my stuff was packed up in boxes and stacked outside the door. When I called the building manager to find out what the fuck was going on, he said Mr. McCall told him the company was under new management and change the locks."

"What!" I said stunned by the dialogue coming out of Chrissie's mouth.

"You fucking heard me! When I called Brian he said my services were no longer needed and any further questions should be directed to you. So what the hell happened?" By this point I laid back on the floor spread eagle style, looking at the ceiling believing I was caught in a nightmare.

"Chrissie I'm so sorry."

"I don't want your damn apology. I want to know what the fuck is going on. I put my heart and soul into this business and Brian in a blink of an eye can just pull the rug from up under me? This is outrageous!"

"It's a long story, but Brian and I broke up. The decision was mine and I knew he wasn't happy with it, but never did I think he would go this far."

"This man is turning my life upside down over some girlfriend slash boyfriend drama? You have to be kidding me. He's not going to get away with this. I will sue that psychotic motherfucker."

"Chrissie wait," I said but she already hung up the phone. Brian sent his message loud and clear. If possible he would take everything from me and leave me with nothing. Immediately my mind kicked into survival mode. I called my bank to check the balance in my savings account. I had ten thousand dollars which would barely cover two months rent. I looked down at my ring less finger and went to my jewelry box to see what items I could sell. I had a couple of tennis bracelets, diamond studs, *Chopard* watch and the diamond necklace Ian bought me. The items would bring me a nice piece of change, but my bills were long and on top of that, I had medical expenses to have the baby. My head was spinning and I needed to calm down. Without a second thought I called Mother.

"Mommy," I shrilled sounding five years old when Mother picked up.

"Tyler, what's wrong and why are you calling so early?" Mother was never an early bird, but this couldn't wait.

"Mother I told Brian that I didn't want to be with him anymore but I wanted us to remain friends for the sake of the baby. All has gone downhill since then. He shut down me and Chrissie's business. He has threatened to cut me off financially and leave me with nothing."

"Pull it together Tyler and stop all that crying. What did you expect for Brian to do, roll out the red carpet? You need to swallow your pride and tell him you want him back," Mother stated firmly.

"But Mother, he's abusive and I don't know what his relationship is with his Baby Mother. It's too many things that are making my life miserable."

"Get over it...Brian is an excellent provider and you're carrying his child. His Baby Mother is irrelevant as long as he continues to give you everything you want and need. It's time for you to get your priorities in order."

"But Mother, I want someone to really love me."

"Stop living in a fantasy world Tyler. Brian does love you, the best way he knows how. I'm not saying he is perfect, but he treats you good and will always take excellent care of you and the baby. What more do you want?"

"Self respect, honesty, and a little loyalty would be nice," I said sarcastically.

"I gave you my advice. Take him back, enjoy your pregnancy and relax. You're making this way too complicated."

"Mother I don't want Brian back. Our relationship isn't healthy. I need you to help me Mother. Would you please send me some money?"

"No." Mother said point blank. "I'm not going to fund your stupidity. You have a man right there, who can give you anything that you want, call him."

"Don't you hear me? I hate myself when I'm with him. I'm begging you to please help me."

"Sorry Tyler you're on your own. I hope you will come to your senses and reconcile with Brian because I will not be sending you any money. And don't even think about calling your Father because he is in the South of France with his new wife."

"Mother don't do this to me."

"Stop being so dramatic, it will all work out. You and Brian will be back together in no time. After the baby is born, I'll come visit you. Now dear, I really want to get a couple more hours of sleep. I'll speak to you later."

I called Brian and pleaded with him one last time to do the right thing and help me financially. He simply said, "You should never bite the hand that feeds you," and hung up.

I sat back for a minute trying to determine exactly when my life went to shambles. Here I was six months pregnant, contemplating all my financial resources to get through my horrendous circumstances. I scrolled through the yellow pages calling all jewelry stores that bought merchandise, seeing who offered the best prices. I narrowed my search down to three, gathered my goods got dressed and headed out.

"Ms. Blake, Mr. Dunn will see you now," the pretty receptionist said escorting me through the glass doors. When Brian refused to budge financially after pleading with him three more times Chrissie said it was time to get an attorney. She referred me to some top dogs in Woodbridge, New Jersey and luckily I got a decent amount of money for the jewelry I sold, to afford them.

"Good morning Tyler, it's nice to finally meet you," the distinguished older gentleman smiled and said.

It's nice to meet you too Mr. Dunn."

"Stop with the formalities, call me Richard." We shook hands and I sat down on the antique leather chair. I was immediately intimidated when I first entered the building. Forget about having a whole floor, they owned the whole damn building. There was glass and marble everywhere, with wrap around staircases and just plush, plush and plusher. They were way out of my league and it would take every cent I had to retain them.

"Okay Richard," I said meekly.

"Let's get right down to it. I went over the notes from our conversations and the one with Mr. McCall's attorney."

"He has an attorney already?"

"Yes. As a courtesy to you I mailed a letter to Mr. McCall to see if he was willing to sit down and come up with an amicable solution; and his response was a phone call from his attorney Ted Armstrong."

"What did he say? Are they willing to try and work things out without a court battle?"

"Unfortunately not; it's actually going to be a longer and more complicated procedure than first anticipated."

"What do you mean?" I asked confused.

"Not only does Brian want a paternity test, but he is also seeking custody of the child."

"What? There has to be a mistake."

"I'm afraid not. It could well be a legal ploy, but Mr. McCall is his own man. He doesn't have to do anything that he doesn't want to. From what you told me and my conversation with his attorney, your ex is trying to make this as difficult as possible. I'm sure he's counting on that you can't survive a long drawn out battle, and will throw the towel in. From what you stated your finances are extremely tight but we can try to schedule an emergency hearing to get you temporary support. I'm not sure how successful it will be since you all aren't married, but he has been your sole means of support so it's worth a shot."

"Can he actually try to get custody of my child?"

"New Jersey law states that he can, but in all likelihoods, he will not prevail. But a custody battle is costly and time consuming."

"So where do we go from here?"

"As I said, I will file an emergency hearing to try and get you temporary support, but I don't know how successful that will be. It is important however for you to stay at your current residence and maintain your expenses."

"Why?" I asked puzzled, wondering if he was trying to make me go broke.

"Because your expenses will be an indicator on just how much child support you're entitled to. When you fill out your 'CIS,' the higher your monthly cost of living the more you can ask for in support."

"But Richard I'm living on a hope and a prayer right now. The last bit of money I have is going towards your retainer."

"I understand Tyler, but see what you can do. Your baby will be here in a couple of months and after the paternity test, the case will pick up in pace."

"Push Tyler, push…I can see the head. Come on now push a little harder," the Doctor instructed.

"I can't, it hurts too bad," I screamed breathlessly falling back down on the hospital bed.

"You can't stop, you're almost there. I'm going to count to three and I want you to take a deep breath and push harder than you ever have before." I glanced down at my swollen hands and sweat drenched body feeling that I had nothing left in me to push with. I had been in labor for twenty eight hours and now the head wanted to finally appear. I was tempted to tell the Doctor that I did my part and the baby was going to have to maneuver the rest. Realizing that wasn't an option, I closed my eyes, called on the angels above and mustered all my strength for one last and final push before hearing the cries of joy. The last words I remembered was, "Tyler it's a boy," before passing out.

When I woke and the nurse brought my angel to me, I gazed into his dark eyes, and surmised that he was the most beautiful baby I had ever seen. He was perfect. I nicknamed him Poncho because he resembled a little Indian. With his dark reddish complexion and jet black straight hair, I was in awe and couldn't believe he was mine. I held my angel and he naturally latched on to my breast and in an instant our bond ensued. As I smelled, touched and held my son all I could think of was Brian, and that he made this possible. February 12, 2003 I received the greatest blessing in the world, and because of that Brian would forever hold a special place in my heart.

Chapter Twelve: The Battle Begins

(Pink vs. Black)

Don't ask me why, but for some reason people like to fuck with me. They get the impression that I'm weak and soft. They didn't understand like Thomas Jefferson said, "Walk quietly but carry a big stick." If I didn't get it exactly right, the point is--don't ever let them see you coming. I like it when people make the usual assumptions because that means they always underestimate me.

"Tyler he is gorgeous," Chrissie grinned as she held my baby. This was her first time seeing him because as always, Chrissie landed on her feet. She gave up her fight with Brian and was now heading up the publicity department at *MTV* and traveled constantly.

"Who would have thought that something so beautiful could cause so much pain? Honestly I didn't think I was going to make it. But then I concluded that if I didn't pull through, Brian would raise him so I found the strength." I halfway joked.

"But wasn't he worth it?" Chrissie asked in baby talk.

"Yes, and then some."

"You still haven't told me his name."

"Christian Andrew Blake."

"That's beautiful Tyler. You're so blessed to have such a beautiful baby."

"I am blessed, especially since everything else is going downhill. After not paying my rent for four months, I finally got an eviction notice."

"I'm surprised they let you get away with it for that long."

"I know, but the Building Manager felt sorry for me. When I finally revealed why my life was spiraling out of control, she said she would hold off on the eviction process for as long as possible. I figure it will take another two months for them to actually put me out and by that time, hopefully the Judge would've ordered temporary support."

"You still haven't received any temporary support from Brian? What the hell is the hold up?"

"Brian's attorney keeps having the case postponed, using a million and one excuses. In the court of law one thing money can surely buy you is time. Brian is still probably trying to figure out how I've been able to survive for so long. He didn't count on the fact that I'm a child of God and with faith he will deliver me from any dark path."

"Praise the Lord to that Tyler. Honestly I don't think I could've been so brave. Your strength is amazing. I know I've told you that I admired you in the past, but it was always for superficial reasons. But now I admire you for being the strongest person I know. You had this baby against all odds and now look at you. This is the happiest I've ever seen you."

"I am happy. Throughout this pregnancy I had a lot of time to do some serious soul searching. For so long I was yearning for love from every man I was with. Then it finally dawned on me that everything I need to be happy is inside of me. The greatest love one truly possesses is self love. I have that now. It took a lot of bullshit to get here, but now that I've found it, I'll never let it go."

"Oh Tyler I love you," Chrissie cried as she gave me a long tight hug."

"I love you too."

"Tyler did you receive the documents that I mailed over?" Richard asked as I tried to eat, read and talk to my attorney before Christian woke up from his nap.

"Yes, I'm still stunned and haven't quite digested all these lies."

"Well, Mr. McCall is definitely playing hardball."

"Could you please call him Brian?" I said quickly interrupting. "Calling him Mr. McCall makes him sound like a respectable human being, which obviously isn't the case."

"I apologize Tyler; but calling him by his last name is my way of keeping it impersonal. I'll be more than happy to call him Brian if you wish."

"I understand, please continue with what you were saying."

"With the allegations he is making against you, he's definitely hitting below the belt. I must ask you though Tyler did you have a coke addiction?"

"Hell No! I briefly dabbled with pills but that was way before I even met Brian and I surly wasn't addicted to them."

"What about the allegations that because he found out you were a stripper and call girl you all broke up and that is why he is demanding a paternity test?"

"More lies. Why would I need to be a stripper and call girl when he was taking care of me? I didn't need the money."

"He's saying it was to support your costly coke habit."

"Whatever. That is a bunch of crap!"

"Have you seen Brian at all?"

"As a matter of fact, he has been over here just about everyday since Christian was born."

"Really? What has the conversation been like?"

"I don't really talk to him. I let him spend time with his son and then he leaves."

"Interesting...he is demanding a paternity test but yet he is coming over to see a son he says he doesn't know is his."

"Don't you get it? Brian knows this is his son. He is trying to drive me crazy. Aren't you wondering why Christian is six months old and he still hasn't taken the paternity test?"

"Tyler, I never doubted that Christian is Brian's son. I assumed Brian would play the, 'I'm not sure that's my son,' card until we at least got to court. By visiting Christian on a regular basis, his actions are reflecting he believes your son to be his. That's not going to sit well with the Judge, especially since he isn't giving you a dime."

Two weeks later, we finally took the paternity test and to no one's surprise Brian was the father. It still didn't motivate him to write a check, but he insisted on seeing his son. None of my friends understood why I was allowing Brian to visit with Christian when he refused to come off any paper. I tried to explain that when you keep a man away from his child to punish him, it doesn't hurt the man. In all actuality it hurts the child. Whether or not women want to believe this, if you keep a man away from his child long enough, he will get over it. Especially if he has another child that he is able to be with and see whenever he wants. The first couple of years are the most important because that is when men and their children bond. I didn't want my antipathy for Brian to interfere with the bond I hoped he would share with his son.

After talking to my attorney I was weary and needed some fresh air. I was on my way out the door to take Christian for a walk when the phone rang. "Hello."

"Girl turn your radio on to 107.5," Ella shrieked.

"I can't, I'm one foot out the door with Christian. Why what's up?"

"Wendy Williams is talking about Brian on her show."

"What! What is she saying?"

"She is blasting him. She's talking about how he threw his first Baby Mother Beverly out the house with no car, no money, and sent her packing back to Brooklyn. Now she's talking about the court battle he has going on with you, and that he needs to check himself because when you do dirt, dirt comes back to you."

"Are you serious?"

"As a heart attack; but that's what his trifling ass gets. Brian needs to get over his God complex. He thinks because he has money and a little fame he can walk all over people. Nobody has obviously taught him about Karma."

"I can't believe Wendy blew him up. But that's why women love her, because she's all about female empowerment."

"You got that right," Ella co-signed. "Well I have to get back to work. I just wanted to let you know that Brian's secret is out the bag. Everyone knows what a jackass he is."

Brian was on his way over to see Christian, and I hoped we could resolve our problems and put this nightmare behind us. When I opened the door the first words out of his mouth was, "You ready to end this useless battle?" Surprised by his attitude, there was a glimmer of hope that this would be easier to resolve than I thought. Or maybe he didn't like the fact that the 'Queen of Radio' put him on blast.

"Always have been," I said coolly.

"No, you wanted to be Miss Free and Independent. But I've brought you to your knees so I'm sure you're ready to end this."

"Excuse me," I said shocked by his cocky and over the top attitude.

"Tyler listen, I always knew the baby was mine but I needed concrete proof. You never can be one hundred percent sure with women these days. But now that I have my proof it's time to move forward and end this bullshit. You read the documents and you know I've got you in a fucked up predicament. Why don't you stop with all this 'I wanna be a single mother' bullshit and come back to me. I still love you, never stopped."

"Brian you never loved me and if you did, you have a bizarre way of showing it. And whatever predicament you think you have me in is a figment of your imagination. I've never done coke and definitely wasn't a stripper or call girl. No Judge is going to believe your lies. By the time we do go to court, the Judge will be so turned off by your theatrics; you'll be begging me to settle."

"I see you're still the same naïve bitch I met three years ago. Do you not know who I am? I already have my witness list prepared. They will all testify about your out of control drug habit and how you sold your body to maintain it. Baby you're in the big leagues and money can pay for any lie you need. A broke bitch like you just needs to count your blessings that your baby daddy got long paper. So you can either enjoy the benefits of having some of my paper, or you can watch me win custody of my son and you have nothing."

"Do you think a Judge will give custody to a man who has put a gun to my head and beat me throughout the duration of our relationship? I don't think so."

"So what if I did those things," Brian said arrogantly. "You'll never be able to prove it. And if you think you can get Melanie or one of those other dizzy ass broads to testify on your behalf, dead it. Leon has those dumb bitches so wrapped they don't move without his permission. Enjoy these last few weeks with our son, because soon he'll be calling the next chick mama and you'll be a distant memory."

Sidebar: Ladies it is true what they say. God bless the child who's got his own! You really need to have your own. I don't care how much money your husband or Baby Daddy or boyfriend has. It doesn't make a damn difference. You need money to fight money. It's as simple as that. If you don't have money you can't fight to get any money. You know that saying, *innocent until proven broke?* If a man still has feelings for you, because there is such a thin line between love and hate and he still cares, he will do anything to make you miserable because he is miserable. Here I was dealing with a psycho who was chipped. There is nothing worse than that. If I had my own paper, I could tell him to go fuck himself and think nothing of it.

I tossed and turned the whole night replaying the revolting threats Brian made against me. I was staring into the eyes of evil when I listened to his bold faced intimidation tactics. It blew my mind that this was the same man I believed I was in love with. He was actually plotting how to take away my son; a baby that he didn't pay one medical expense for, or even attempt to support. All he tried to do for the last several months is bring me down emotionally and physically. He was cold and calculating not giving a damn about what was best for our son. The Brian I thought I knew was dead and a monster had emerged. As I watched Christian sleep, I found comfort in how peaceful and pure he was. He gave me strength to fight and realize that although Brian seemed to be winning the battles, the most important thing was to win the war.

Chapter Thirteen: The Battle Ends

(My Pink Fate)

*A*s I said before, we all must go through battles and obstacles in life that we sometimes feel we can't endure. But as the saying goes, "If it doesn't kill you, it will make you stronger." I believe that statement is true to life because when you are going through a war with someone, it's the battles that eat away at you little by little. You start off tall and sturdy and if you are not made of a strong and durable substance, then piece by piece, you will crumble and eventually totally break down. In most cases people want to give up because the likelihood of defeat is too great and the fear overrides their motivation to succeed. But when someone is kicking you hard, you have to reach deep down inside and uncover the strength we are all born with. I knew with every bullet Brian fired at me, that was one less shot I had to dodge. If I kept bobbing and weaving eventually he would run out of ammunition. That fact is what kept me pushing forward every time I wanted to give in.

As promised Brian came to court with his well prepared witness list, which included the ever so down ass chick Courtney, the ever so loyal partner Leon, some wannabe lead singer of his girl group Diva's and some two bit players which consisted of; industry groupies, label flunkies, and well paid Assistants. I was hoping that if it came down to it, the truth would speak for itself and the Judge wouldn't fall for the circus show that Brian and his attorney wanted to put on. I was ready for the next chapter of my life. My greatest concern was getting custody of Christian.

While Richard was going over all the paper work that Mr. Armstrong submitted, it was revealed that Brian had hired a private investigator to be all in my shit. What he conjured up was more lies that

Brian fed him. He claimed that he checked my phone records and through further investigation he discovered I was fucking a player from the Washington Wizards for money. The thought flashed in my mind that if I was, I wouldn't be in such dire straits financially.

"Although these are all lies, how damaging is this stuff?" I inquired to my attorney.

"Tyler it's not good. Brian has used all his financial resources to paint you as the harlot from hell. In all my many years of practice I've never seen a man go through so much trouble to depict a woman in such a foul manner. You would think you were seeking half of his past and future earnings, instead of what your son is entitled to which is child support."

"Richard take this," I stated sternly handing him an envelope.

"What's this?"

"Take a moment before you go in the Judge's chambers and open it."

"Tyler, I really don't have time. The Judge will be calling for us any minute."

"Make time. It's worth it."

Richard asked the court clerk for a few extra minutes and he excused himself to an undisclosed room. I was hoping things wouldn't come to this, but Brian was playing for keeps. He was determined to ruin my life and that of my son, by removing me from his life. His lies were relentless and behavior erratic. He left me no choice but to pull out all the stops and protect what was mine. Brian stood across from me in his seven thousand dollar *Valentino* suit speaking to his overpaid crooked attorney and making haughty smirks. He believed he had the case all sewn up and would eat me alive. That over-confident sonofabitch deserved to rot in hell.

"Why are you just now giving me this?" My attorney asked seeming somewhat irritated.

"Richard you startled me." I was so fixated on observing Brian and his obnoxious attorney that I didn't see him walking towards me.

"I'm sorry, but Tyler why would you sit on this type of information?"

"It was going to be my last resort. Do you really think I want to air all my dirty laundry in a courtroom in front of a bunch of strangers? But Brian is leaving me no choice. I have to protect my son because his father is a borderline Sociopath."

"You've been recording your conversations with Brian every since you were four months pregnant, and you have printed out documentation from emails and two-way messages he sent you. You have every promise he made and broke, and every threat he is playing out. Some of this stuff is criminal. If a Judge ever heard a word of this, he would be lucky to get supervised visitations. How in the world did you know back then that it would come to this, and you would need this sort of ammunition?"

"Being lied to and deceived one too many times. I was hoping that Brian would have a change of heart and do the right thing on his own, but he has shown me he has no conscious. I don't believe any woman truly wants to bring down the father of her child, but when your back is pushed against the wall, you have no choice," I shrugged.

"Well excuse me Tyler I have some negotiating to do," Richard said shaking my hand and heading towards Mr. Armstrong. As Richard asked to speak to Brian's attorney, Brian still had that same smirk that I wanted to smack off just a few minutes ago. Now I actually pitied him.

As a little girl my Father once said, "Beware of the fork in the road, sometimes the hunter gets captured by the game." Brian was caught and he didn't even know it yet. But in a few minutes, he would well aware of his fate.

After fifteen minutes both attorney's appeared and the grievous look on Mr. Armstrong's face said it all. From the short distance I saw the once condescending look on Brian's face turn to pure devastation. His normal glowing cinnamon complexion was now hollow and gray.

"Congratulations Tyler. You have conspicuously outsmarted us all. I gave Mr. Armstrong until Friday morning to present a creditable offer, or we would be more than happy to go before the Judge." he said delighted by his victory.

"Thank you Mr. Dunn."

"Tyler you should be ecstatic, you've won. I guarantee you'll be more than pleased with the settlement deal I will get for you. By the way, what's with this Mr. Dunn? Call me Richard."

"I haven't won anything. My son isn't a prize. He's actually the one that will suffer and get the short end of the stick. He will grow up with two parents who are torn apart and will forever be at odds. No one wins from a situation like that except for the attorneys. And by the way, I won't be calling you Richard. Mr. Dunn keeps it impersonal. Have a good day."

As I walked out the courthouse furious how attorneys only care about the bottom line; which is money, Brian grabbed my arm and said modestly, "I underestimated you. I can honestly say I never saw it coming. Is it true what they say? When a man is sleeping a woman is thinking?"

"I don't know Brian. I haven't given it much thought."

"Tyler is it too late to say sorry?"

I chuckled for a second before saying, "Brian the only reason you're sorry is because you didn't get what you wanted. You were willing to destroy the mother of your son because of an over inflated ego. But no matter what you have done this past year I'm not mad at you. What started off as your curse ended up being my salvation. I finally love me, and not because of the admiration from a man but for the admiration I have for myself. I'm truly every woman." I walked down the stairs not even bothering to read the expression on Brian's face. His ideas were meaningless and held no importance to my new found freedom. As the cold breeze hit my face, the self love inside warmed me up. This journey truly made me discover how to be So Pretty In Pink.

Chapter Fourteen: Freedom

(The Pink Bird Flies)

"Cheers," Chrissie said as we toasted to what they insisted was a victory. Cynthia White and Ella were also in attendance as we had a celebratory dinner at *Spice Market*; a hot restaurant in the Meat Packing District.

"I have something to say to the woman of the hour," Mrs. White said as she banged the spoon on her champagne glass. "You know you're like a daughter to me Tyler, and it broke my heart to see that man put you through hell. But with sheer determination you came out on top. I'm so proud of you. God has blessed you with a beautiful baby and I know whatever dreams you want to fulfill, no one will keep them out of your reach."

"Thank you. That means the world to me," I cooed as I gave Mrs. White a hug.

"My turn, my turn," Ella stood up and yelped. "You are my baby sister and I always felt that I had to protect you. But in the last year you've grown up overnight into a woman that I truly admire and respect. I know the decisions you've made weren't easy and the average woman would've broken down and folded, but not you Tyler. You fought for what you wanted and believed in, and that makes you a winner. I love you little sis, and I hope to grow up to be just like you...Oh before I forget, Mother sends her best and wishes she could be here, but she's out sealing the deal for husband number three." We all burst out laughing in chorus.

"Wait I have something to say," Chrissie said humbly. Growing up in Temecula, California, if someone would've told me my best friend was going to be a black girl from Atlanta, Georgia I'd laughed in their face. But not only are you my best friend, you're my sister Tyler. We've both gone through so much since as you like to put it, 'Just Got Off the Bus' but it has all been worth it because we have a bond that will last for the rest of our lives. We're family."

"Yes we are," I hugged Chrissie and said. "You all are my family. Not only are we bonded by love, we're bonded as women. Each of you has been a part of my support system, and if I didn't have your strength I couldn't have gotten through this. Every woman needs support and understanding from other women, because as a team we are so much more powerful than if we stand alone. The three of you are my team. I hope that other women are blessed enough to have the same All-Star lineup that I do."

"To that, we need another bottle of champagne. Waiter..." Chrissie screamed.

The bird does fly pink, because not only are all ladies pink but pink really is my favorite color. No matter how bad my life may seem, when I want to feel sky high I always turn to something pink. Whether it's pink lip gloss, pink panties, or a pink negligee, something pink always brings a smile to my face and a certain strut to my walk. I feel confident and free when wearing pink. And this is all about me being free. What actually defines freedom? Is freedom a state of mind or is freedom a total and complete happiness with oneself. Freedom in my eyes was to put the past behind me and concentrate on 'Doing Me.'

Months had passed and I was finally at peace with my life. Driving down River Road with the sunroof back and blasting Jay Z's the Black Album, track #14 on an unseasonably warm day, I felt alive. This was the first time in so long that I had no man to answer to about what Tyler wanted. I had the power to decide what I wanted to do and who I wanted to be with, if anybody. I like to think of myself as an optimistic person, but my disastrous encounters with men in the past tarnished my views on relationships. I no longer trusted the whole institution of loyalty and commitment. I'd seen too much and been through too much to think otherwise. But the pink in me hasn't given up all hope. I'm waiting for that special man to walk up to me with a sign on his head reading, "God sent me to you." But until then I decided to focus on my career, and felt it was time to now pursue my dreams and aspirations. The blueprint to my path was a little shaky, but I wanted to pursue my dream of becoming an actress-- not just an actress but a movie star. I wasn't eighteen years old anymore and just getting off the bus, but I felt that I had talent. And if you put your mind to anything and focus, no goal is out of reach.

I enrolled in an acting workshop and got my creative juices flowing. I had a fabulous teacher who immediately took to me. She told me that I had incredible natural talent and should continue to nurture it. Between giving all my love to Christian, studying monologues, and the history of Hollywood, I barely had anytime to realize that I hadn't been intimate with a man in over a year. It was very empowering though, because I knew if I wanted to, I could have a different man in my bed every night, but I chose not to. Mother used to always tell me that when you sleep with a man whatever is inside of him goes into you, and whatever is inside of you goes into him. In the past I had given my body to men that weren't worthy. I decided that I was holding on to all my positive energy. Any man that I slept with would have to be able to have positive energy to give me, because like they say, "Fair exchange isn't robbery."

One day at my acting workshop William Donovan a famous movie star turned director, was our special guest. He wanted to give the class pointers about how a movie came together. I was immediately drawn to the tall and unbelievably handsome middle aged man. He looked even better in person than on the movie screen. Although he was married, I always dreamed of sharing a passionate kiss with the gorgeous star. He had the perfect deep brown complexion and even though he was in his late 40's his body was solid. His eyes were dark and beautiful. You could stare into them and see an abundance of wisdom. I hung onto his every word because I knew this was the man that would change my life.

William Donovan would take me to the next chapter of my life and help me become a star. I sensed it through my whole body.

"I would like for two of the students to perform a monologue in front of the class. When finished I will critique your performance," Mr. Donovan stated as if he knew whoever performed would do poorly.

The teacher pointed to me and a male student named Michael. Instantly I started getting butterflies in my stomach. I didn't want to fall on my face in front of the man I knew was going to be my mentor. We did a scene by Frank D. Gilroy called, 'The Only Game in Town.' I stepped up to the front of the class and I killed it. Michael did excellent too, but something about my performance encompassed raw emotion that ignited the room. There was dead silence as everyone paused and stared at Mr. Donovan for his reaction. When he stood and applauded, the teacher and entire class joined in.

"That was excellent. I must say I'm shocked but pleasantly surprised. My only advice to both of you is to continue with the path that you're on. I see great things ahead," Mr. Donovan praised. When the class ended and I was on my way out, Mr. Donovan stopped me and formally introduced himself. "Hello. My name is William, and your performance was superb. You have a bright future as an actress. "

I was hoping that I wasn't blushing too hard, but I managed to say, "Thank you Mr. Donovan. That is an honor coming from you."

"No need to be formal, call me William," he said as he gently touched my shoulder. "Are you in a rush? Because there's a lounge across the street, and I would love to talk to you about your goals for the future."

"I'd like that too," I said sincerely. We stayed in the lounge and talked for hours. William was the most intelligent man I had ever met and I wanted him in my life. After that evening, I knew this was the beginning of a long and prosperous relationship.

A few days later he called and asked if I could meet him at his office in the city. Of course I agreed and decided to put on my pink

Diane von Furstenberg wrap dress. I was definitely feeling pink and I could sense that something amazing was about to happen for me. It was a beautiful day outside as I made my way through Jersey heading towards Manhattan. When I reached the Lincoln Tunnel and there was no traffic, a smile crossed my face because today was definitely a good day.

Upon reaching my final destination I stood outside the tall building in Midtown gaping through the glass doors wondering with delight about the possible news coming my way. I could no longer keep my destiny waiting and took the elevator to the top floor. As I was sitting in the reception area waiting for William, I was a little antsy. A million and one thoughts were flashing through my mind and all the pondering was driving me crazy. William finally emerged from his office wearing some jeans that fit his bow legs perfectly and he gave me a warm hug.

"You look beautiful Tyler," William said as he gently spun me around, admiring my Marilyn Monroe inspired wrap dress.

"Thank you," I said graciously.

"Come with me to my office. I want to introduce you to someone named Albert Moore." I marveled at who Albert Moore was, and why William wanted to introduce him to me. With a beaming smile spread across his face, William lovingly grabbed my hand and put up his arms as though introducing the new homecoming Queen and said, "Albert this is Angel." I speculated in my head who the hell was Angel and what did she have to do with me. I could tell the short pudgy white man was giving me the once over. He started at my silver *Manolo's*, and worked his way up my pink dress, to my glossy pink lips. After a small smirk appeared on his face, I instantly felt he liked what he saw, but I still wanted to know why I cared. Albert Moore finally spoke for the first time, and I realized my mouth was wide open dying of anticipation about whom this man was and why William obviously felt he was important.

"It seems you have found your Angel and a potential Superstar," the man said with a wide smile.

I couldn't contain my enthusiasm and blurted out, "Superstar, me?" William smiled and gave me a proud look as when a father is seeing his daughter graduate from an Ivy League University.

"Tyler this is Albert Moore, the head of Icon Pictures. He just gave the stamp of approval that I needed for my project." William finally explained that the character Angel was the star in the upcoming movie he was directing and wanted me to play her. One tear slowly began to roll down my cheek, and William wiped the tear away and said, "My beautiful Tyler, don't cry you're in good hands, I will make all your dreams come true." He didn't understand yet, but that was why the tear fell, because in my heart I knew he would do just that. I prayed to the sky and changed my stars. I finally changed the cards that had been dealt me. This was a new beginning.

After a few weeks of preparation I was on my way to Hollywood. Of course Brian tried to make a big hoopla about me taking Christian, but with a top attorney that William had gotten me, the Judge came up with a temporary new visitation schedule for Christian. Brian had to come to LA to see him. Of course that was just the beginning. I was positive that once again Brian would try to fight me tooth and nail to have Christian back in New Jersey. I couldn't let that worry me because too many extraordinary things were happening in my life. I was on my way to Hollywood to become a major movie star and there was no looking back.

When the stretch limo pulled up to the red carpet at the Ziefeld Theater, all you heard was the paparazzi screaming that Andre Jackson was in the car. Chantal lived to go to these events. All the cameras flashing and people screaming her name, it gave her a rush, because she was a celebrity too in her own right. People wanted to grab at Chantal and take her picture. Some pathetic idiots even wanted her autograph all because she was with Andre. Chantal was his woman, so now all she needed to do was become his wife.

As they stepped out the limo Chantal smiled and gave her standard beauty pageant wave to all the cameras and fans. She was just as beautiful as any other celebrity walking the red carpet. This was the East Coast premiere for Colin Farrell's new movie and everyone from Denzel Washington to Julia Roberts was in attendance. The Hollywood elite were so different than their normal music industry bunch. Everyone there looked refined. Where as the music industry set looked like 'brand new about to go broke money.'

This crowd here was right up Chantal's alley, as for the other crowd, she had been there and done that; literally. Chantal had basically fucked every music big wig and couldn't get any of them to sponsor her on a long term basis. She was their trophy piece for a minute and then after they had twisted her back out and partied with her every which way, they traded her in for the next hot chick. Thank goodness she met Andre when she did, because Chantal Morgan had come one step from being a has-been in this town.

As they made their way to their seats, Andre stopped to chat with Tom Hanks and Harvey Weinstein. While he was doing that Chantal checked out the competition in the room; Catherine Zeta Jones was looking gorgeous in a red, what looked to be a *Valentino* dress. The new up and coming 'It Girl' of Hollywood Tyler Blake had on an unbelievable white *Zac Posen* dress and of course the newly separated Jennifer Aniston had on her standard but beautiful black dress. Still in Chantal's mind none of them could hold a candle to her.

By the time the movie ended Chantal was ready to get the hell out of there. She never liked sitting through a long movie, especially one that was borderline boring, and all movies were boring to Chantal unless it was one she was making in the privacy of her home. When Andre finally located their limo she just sat back and poured herself a glass of champagne. She was beginning to relax when Andre caught her eye with his devilish grin. Chantal could always tell when he was horny because his eyes would start dancing and he would give her a lustful half smirk.

"Baby why don't you come over here and kiss Daddy's dick," Andre said. Why not, if Chantal didn't the next bitch would. She had no problem giving Andre head or whatever else he wanted anytime he pleased. She tried to fulfill every sexual fantasy he had and then some. The way these chicks were putting it out she had to stay on top of her game. Chantal gladly got down on her hands and knees in her new $10,000 dress and deep throated her man's penis to the point she had him cumming before they reached the third stop light.

Seeing how aroused Andre was got Chantal all worked up, she massaged his penis to get it back to a rock hard position. Since she never wore panties she simply lifted up her dress and began to straddle her man. Andre was grabbing at her dress trying to get a hold of her voluptuous breasts. Once he did he put his warm mouth around her erect nipples and squeezed the other breast continuing to go back and forth. Andre was moaning in pleasure and they continued to fuck until the driver told them they reached their destination. Even then they stayed in the limo for another fifteen minutes until both reached their climax.

Chantal had to throw it on Andre like that every so often so he wouldn't forget who had the best pussy out there. Everybody has a gift and seducing a man was Chantal's gift. She knew how to put it on her man like a professional. Sometimes she wondered if she was too good. Andre knew her past for the most part, but at the same time she thought it bothered him when she screwed his brains out. She assumed it made him skeptical as to think that every man got the complete mojo package like that and not just him. But what in the hell did Andre expect. Being the baddest bitch inside and outside of the bedroom used to be Chantal's livelihood. That's how she got Andre and that's how she planned on keeping him too.

COMING
SOON

HOOKER
TO
HOUSEWIFE

TYLER BLAKE'S SAGA CONTINUES
Introducing her archenemy
Chantal Morgan...Take a peek